RAVES FOR
JAMES PATTERSON

"BEHIND ALL THE NOISE AND NUMBERS, WE SHOULDN'T FORGET THAT NO ONE GETS THIS BIG WITHOUT NATURAL STORYTELLING TALENT—WHICH IS WHAT JAMES PATTERSON HAS, IN SPADES."
—Lee Child, #1 *New York Times* bestselling author
of the Jack Reacher series

"EVERY ONCE IN A WHILE, A WRITER COMES ALONG AND FUNDAMENTALLY CHANGES THE WAY PEOPLE READ...WITH HIS MISSION STILL UNFOLDING, JAMES PATTERSON IS THE GOLD STANDARD BY WHICH ALL OTHERS ARE JUDGED."
—Steve Berry, #1 bestselling author
of the Cotton Malone series

"JAMES PATTERSON IS THE BOSS. END OF."
—Ian Rankin, *New York Times* bestselling
author of the Inspector Rebus series

"PATTERSON BOILS A SCENE DOWN TO A SINGLE, TELLING DETAIL, THE ELEMENT THAT DEFINES A CHARACTER OR MOVES A PLOT ALONG. IT'S WHAT FIRES OFF THE MOVIE PROJECTOR IN THE READER'S MIND."
—Michael Connelly

"WHEN IT COMES TO CONSTRUCTING A

HARROWING PLOT, AUTHOR JAMES PATTERSON CAN TURN A SCREW ALL RIGHT."
—*New York Daily News*

"JAMES KNOWS HOW TO SELL THRILLS AND SUSPENSE IN CLEAR, UNWAVERING PROSE."
—*People*

"PATTERSON HAS MASTERED THE ART OF WRITING PAGE-TURNING BESTSELLERS."
—*Chicago Sun-Times*

"PATTERSON KNOWS WHERE OUR DEEPEST FEARS ARE BURIED…THERE'S NO STOPPING HIS IMAGINATION."
—*New York Times Book Review*

"JAMES PATTERSON WRITES HIS THRILLERS AS IF HE WERE BUILDING ROLLER COASTERS. He grounds the stories with a bare-bones plot, then builds them over the top and tries to throw readers for a loop a few times along the way."
—Associated Press

"A MUST-READ AUTHOR…A MASTER OF THE CRAFT."
—*Providence Sunday Journal*

"THE PAGE-TURNINGEST AUTHOR IN THE GAME RIGHT NOW."
—*San Francisco Chronicle*

"JAMES PATTERSON ALWAYS DELIVERS A FASCINATING, ACTION-PACKED THRILLER."
—*Midwest Book Review*

"PATTERSON IS A MASTER."
—*Toronto Globe and Mail*

THE CORNWALLS VANISH

For a complete list of books,
visit JamesPatterson.com.

THE CORNWALLS VANISH

(previously published as *The Cornwalls Are Gone*)

JAMES PATTERSON
AND BRENDAN DuBOIS

GRAND CENTRAL
PUBLISHING

New York Boston

Copyright © 2019 by James Patterson

Hachette Book Group supports the right to free expression and the value of copyright. The purpose of copyright is to encourage writers and artists to produce the creative works that enrich our culture.

The scanning, uploading, and distribution of this book without permission is a theft of the author's intellectual property. If you would like permission to use material from the book (other than for review purposes), please contact permissions@hbgusa.com. Thank you for your support of the author's rights.

Grand Central Publishing
Hachette Book Group
1290 Avenue of the Americas, New York, NY 10104
grandcentralpublishing.com
twitter.com/grandcentralpub

Originally published in hardcover and ebook as *The Cornwalls Are Gone* by Little, Brown & Company in March 2019
First oversize mass market edition: July 2020

Grand Central Publishing is a division of Hachette Book Group, Inc. The Grand Central Publishing name and logo is a trademark of Hachette Book Group, Inc.

The publisher is not responsible for websites (or their content) that are not owned by the publisher.

The Hachette Speakers Bureau provides a wide range of authors for speaking events. To find out more, go to hachettespeakersbureau.com or call (866) 376-6591.

ISBNs: 978-1-5387-3161-1 (oversize mass market), 978-0-316-42260-4 (ebook)

Printed in the United States of America

OPM

10 9 8 7 6 5 4 3 2 1

From Brendan: For my wife, Mona.

From Jim: For Sue. Of course, of course.

THE CORNWALLS VANISH

CHAPTER 1

I KNOW within thirty-three seconds of entering the front door that my home is empty and my husband and daughter are missing.

As a US Army captain, assigned to the Military Intelligence Command, I have years of training and battlefield experience in Iraq and Afghanistan in evaluating patterns, scraps of information, and bits of communication.

This experience comes in handy when I enter our nice little suburban home in Kingstowne, Virginia, about eight miles from my current duty station at Fort Belvoir. Our light-blue Honda CR-V is parked in the driveway, school has been out for hours, and when I take my first two steps into our house, there's no television on, no smell of dinner cooking—which my husband, Tom, said would be ready when I got home, since I am late once again—and, most puzzling, no ambient noise or presence from our ten-year-old, Denise, who is usually singing, chatting on her phone, or tap-dancing in the front hallway. Hard to explain, but the moment after I open the door, I know the place is empty and my loved ones are in trouble.

I gently put my black leather purse and soft leather briefcase on the floor. I don't bother calling out. Instead I go to the near wall, where there's a framed photo of a Maine lighthouse, and I tug the photo free, revealing a small metal safe built into the wall and a combination keypad next to a handle. I punch in 9999 (in an emergency like this, trying to remember a complex code is a one-way ticket to disaster), tug the handle free, and reach in and pull out a loaded stainless-steel Ruger .357 hammerless revolver.

It's always loaded. Always. When we first moved in here three years ago, Tom teased me about my paranoia, but he stopped teasing when one of my fellow intelligence officers died in a home invasion gone bad in California: nothing was stolen during this supposed home invasion, and my colleague was nailed to the wall of his bedroom with eight-inch steel spikes.

I kick off my black shoes, move down the short hallway. Kitchen is empty. Tom's cluttered office is also empty. Since leaving his reporting job last year, Tom has spent many hours in this office writing a book—about what, I don't know—and I remember he's supposed to leave to interview a source for said book in two days.

I move on to the also empty dining room, which has an oval-shaped table, six dining room chairs, and a glass-enclosed hutch holding our best china. A single rose stands in a slim glass vase in the center of the table. A gift from Tom last night.

Living room, with reclining chair, two couches, bookcases, flat-screen television with Denise's collection of DVDs shelved beneath.

Also empty.

I open the door to the basement, sidle down, and then quickly switch on the lights.

Furnace, stored boxes, Denise's old bicycle, some odds and ends, broken toys and hand tools, Bowflex machine Tom claims he'll get to one of these days, next to a dusty treadmill I also promise to get to one of these days.

Clear.

Now I'm on the stairs leading to the second floor, creeping up, keeping myself close to the wall so my quiet footfalls won't cause nails or wood to creak.

I've been through basic, extended basic, two infantry tours in Iraq, and was one of the first women to make it through US Army Ranger training. In the past few years, I've gone face-to-face with some of the most dangerous people in the world, interviewing Al-Qaeda, ISIS, and Taliban men (always men!) who looked at me with such hate from their black and brown eyes that it has caused terrible dreams at night and paranoia during the day; I am always looking over my shoulder.

But nothing so far has scared me as much as walking up these fourteen typical steps in a typical American house in a typical Virginia suburb. Among the many skills an intelligence officer needs is an active and extensive imagination, and I'm imagining—

Tom, facedown on our marital bed, the back of his head a bloody mush from being shot.

Denise, in the corner of her bedroom, holding a stuffed Mickey Mouse toy in her dead arms, her throat slit, blood staining her *Frozen* T-shirt purchased on a Disney vacation last year.

Tom and Denise, their butchered bodies dumped in the bathtub, a mocking message smeared on the bathroom mirror, written in their blood.

My family, my loves, my life, all dead because of where I've gone, whom I've fought, and the sins I've committed over the years in service to my country.

I've never been a particularly religious woman, but as I reach the top of the stairs, my prayers to whatever god is "up there" have deteriorated from "Please, God, let my family be safe," to "Please, God," and now, as I step onto the second floor, just to whispers of "Please, please, please."

My mom instinct kicks in, and I go into Denise's room.

Messy, but clear.

Our bedroom, across the way.

Much neater, but also clear.

The bathroom.

The door is closed.

I take a deep breath, bat my eyelids to blink out the tears. I spin the doorknob and fling the door open.

The floor mat is tumbled, like it's been disturbed.

Clothes from Denise—her practice soccer uniform—are in a pile on the floor.

My girl's room may be messy, but she knows enough to pop her soiled clothes in the nearby hamper.

Wrong, it's all wrong.

With a hard, deep breath, I rip the shower curtain open.

Clear.

But still oh so wrong.

And now I'm on the ground floor, revolver still in both hands, still looking, hunting, evaluating, and there's a smell I hadn't noted before.

A scent of fear, of sweat, of terror.

I pass by the dining room and there's something there I missed earlier, partially hidden by the vase holding the single rose.

I go into the room, pushing back the happy memories made at this very table—of family dinners, helping Denise with her math homework, Christmas mornings and Thanksgiving afternoons, meals with my fellow officers and civvies from Fort Belvoir—all sorts of pleasant thoughts that are now gone.

There's a sheet of paper on the table.

Next to the paper is a cell phone I don't recognize. Mine is in my purse, and both Tom and Denise have iPhones.

This cell phone is square, with a small screen and a keypad underneath.

I step closer to the paper.

Look down.

Standard eight-and-a-half-by-eleven sheet of white paper, with the words centered, the black letters looking like they came off an inkjet printer.

Typical and usual, except the words underneath are neither typical nor usual.

WE HAVE YOUR HUSBAND AND DAUGHTER. NO FBI, STATE POLICE, CID, MILITARY POLICE. YOU AND YOU ALONE. FOLLOW OUR INSTRUCTIONS TO THE LETTER AND COMPLETE YOUR TASK IN 48 HOURS, OR THEY BOTH DIE.

I read and re-read the message, clear and to the point, and I'm in the middle of reading it for the third time when the strange phone rings, jolting me so hard that I nearly drop my weapon.

CHAPTER 2

I KEEP the revolver in my right hand and pick up the unfamiliar phone with my left, push the Answer button, and say, "Cornwall."

There's a male voice on the other end. No hint of static, or crackling, or anything else. This is a burner phone, but it's a high-end burner phone.

"We have your husband and your daughter," he starts, in a low but straightforward voice with just a hint of an accent that I can't place. "They are perfectly fine for now. Within the next forty-eight hours, you are to proceed to Three Rivers, Texas, to a secure location under the control of your intelligence services and free a man very important to us. Forty-eight hours. Once this man is free, we will perform the exchange for the safe return of your husband and daughter."

I close my eyes, forcing myself to memorize the man's voice, the inflections, the slight accent, and I do my best to tamp down the emotions roaring through me, from fear to terror to pure hate.

"All right," I say.

He says, "I know there are instructions for you, left on your dining room table. Those instructions are not a joke. If we get any indication that you have contacted any law enforcement agency, either civilian or military, then you will never hear back from us, and you will never see your husband or daughter again."

"Who is the prisoner?" I ask.

The man says, "Let's just say one man's terrorist is another man's freedom fighter, and leave it at that."

"Where is this man?" I go on, eyes still closed, still working the problem. "Where in Three Rivers?"

"Do you agree to this task?"

The black hate in me that's been stirred up by this man wants me to scream, *What choice do you think I have, asshole?*

But I keep it professional.

Trying to keep my voice calmer than my mind, I say, "I need assurances that my husband and daughter are safe."

The man says, "That sounds reasonable. Hold on."

I put the Ruger on the table, push a finger into my other ear, try to see if I can hear anything going on, anything that will help me later.

Nothing.

Another male voice comes on the phone, and this voice nearly buckles my knees. It's clear but filled with emotion.

"Amy," my husband says, his voice strained but tired. "Denise and I are just fine."

I dig my finger deeper into my ear, focusing hard on listening for any sounds in the background that might provide a clue to where Tom is calling from.

But I don't hear anything useful.

I ask, "Tom, what's the day today?"

He sounds puzzled. "It's Tuesday."

A murmur and the other man comes back on the line. "What was that all about?"

I open my eyes, and the safe and happy dining room seems to mock me.

"I needed to know that my husband's voice wasn't

a recording," I say. "I have the assurance. I'll perform your task. What's the address?"

"Linden Street, Three Rivers, Texas. Number forty-six."

"What's the prisoner's name?"

The caller pauses, just for the briefest of seconds. *Why?*

He goes on. "His name can change from month to month. It makes no difference to you successfully doing your job. You'll know him when you see him. He'll be the one without a weapon."

"Why is he being held? What has he done?"

The man says, "Captain, please. Will that make any difference to you? If he made car bombs in Afghanistan, or shot up a school in Pakistan, or dropped an airliner over the Sudan, will you still not free him to retrieve your family?"

I keep my mouth shut. I'm ashamed that he knows exactly what I'm thinking.

He clears his throat. "There's a pre-programmed number in the phone. That will be your only means of contacting me, but I only expect two more phone calls from you via that number: one telling me that you've retrieved the prisoner, and one when you have arrived at the exchange site. Phone calls begging for more time, for more flexibility, for another chance to speak to your husband or daughter—those will be ignored. Is that clear?"

"Quite clear," I say.

"All right."

Another quick pause, and then he chuckles, again with the slight accent I can't place. "Isn't this the point where you warn me that you'll kill me if anything happens to your husband and daughter?"

"No," I say.

"Really?"

I say sharply, "Yeah. Really. You want to know why?"

"Of course," he says.

"Because I don't have the goddamn time to waste."

And I hang up on him.

CHAPTER 3

AFTER DISCONNECTING the call, I check the burner's screen and memorize the ten-digit phone number.

I look away to the far wall, jam-packed with photos of me in full battle rattle in Afghanistan and Iraq, Tom in his reporter's gear somewhere in Venezuela, our wedding photo from Bar Harbor, photos of the two of us with an increasingly taller and older Denise, and I repeat the number under my breath three times, look back at the burner phone.

Exact match.

I'll never forget that number—not now, not ever.

I pick up the Ruger, drop the burner phone in my jacket pocket, and get to work.

Upstairs first, to our bedroom, where I fling open the closet door and retrieve a black zippered duffel bag with two carrying straps from a locked trunk. My go bag, filled with spare clothes, water, rations, cash, a SIG Sauer P320, and other items. Tom's go bag is in there as well, and when we first moved in three years back, I was surprised he didn't give me any pushback about having a go bag prepared.

"Amy," he said, while we were washing dishes together, "I've been grabbing an airplane, boat, or train to get to a story for years. Don't worry about me. I know the drill."

But one of us didn't know the drill, and I often hoped she would never learn it. Nestled behind Tom's duffel bag is a pink-and-white Minnie Mouse knapsack, which I've never told Denise about and which I've always maintained. My ten-year-old daughter's go bag, to quickly go with Mom and Dad in case of disaster, natural or man-made. Denise's mom, determined to protect her daughter, no matter what.

And Denise's mom, a failure.

For a moment I grab one of Tom's shirts, bring it to my face. Tom doesn't smoke and doesn't wear cologne, but his scent is here, and I rub a sleeve against my face—so many memories rushing in, from first kisses to the birth of Denise and our many moves across the country.

Then I slam the closet door shut before I break down and lose my focus. I can't lose my focus.

I just can't.

I race downstairs and damn it all to hell, a phone rings and it's mine, stashed in my soft leather briefcase, and I'm tempted to ignore it while I prep to get the hell going, but suppose—just suppose—it's good news?

Tom was a tough reporter and is now a tough writer, working on a nonfiction book. I know he wouldn't sit back and be a nice, cooperative prisoner. He would fight back. He would look for means and ways of escape. He would—

I drop my iPhone on the floor, think, *Tom, Tom, Tom,* as I grab it and pick it up.

CHAPTER 4

WITH MY iPhone finally firmly in my hand, I see the name on the screen.

BRUNO WENNER

Damn, of all times.

Bruno is a major assigned to my unit, the executive officer to my boss, Lieutenant Colonel Hugh Denton.

The phone keeps on ringing.

I should let it go to voice mail, but Bruno's a good guy who's backed me up and helped me along in navigating the increasingly bureaucratic world of an eighteenth-century organization adjusting to one very challenging and strange twenty-first century.

I slide my finger across the screen, bring the phone up to my ear.

"Cornwall."

"Oh, Amy, glad I caught you," Bruno says. "You at home?"

"Yes, sir."

"Tom and Denise okay?"

I clench my jaw and say, "They're fine, sir."

"Of course they are...I just sent you an email, and just to reconfirm, your meeting is on for oh-eight hundred tomorrow."

"The meeting..."

Right now about 90 percent of my body and being—the other 10 percent focusing on breathing, heart beating, so on—is wrapped up in one thing, and one thing only.

Bruno sounds concerned. "You know, the meeting with Warrant Officer Vasquez? From the CID? To interview you about…well, what happened in Afghanistan two months back. The incident with the prisoner."

Afghanistan.

Like a stone-and-dirt avalanche, the memory of the "incident" pours over me. The grueling hours interviewing a captured Taliban member who shouldn't have been in the government-controlled territory we were supporting. The grin, the joking from the prisoner…his utter assurance that nothing would happen to him, especially with me—a woman!—in charge of his questioning. The heat, the sand, the dust that got into everything, the messages from on high demanding to know why the Taliban member was there, what I was going to do about it, what I was going to learn. *Come on, Captain Cornwall, we've got lives depending on your skills. Get to it!*

Yeah. Right up to the point where I went to pick him up in his cell for another go-around and found him huddled in the corner, blood and foam around his nose, lips, and beard.

Dead.

On my watch, under my control.

"You sure, sir, oh-eight hundred?"

"That's right, Amy." His voice lowers. "Just so you know, the colonel is increasingly going apeshit over this matter. So far it's been kept out of the news, but the more people know about it, the better the chances it'll get leaked. He really wants you to…cooperate with the CID officer as much as possible tomorrow. To nip everything in the bud."

And relieve *my* superior officer of any troubles from *his* superior officers, I think.

"Okay, Major, message received," I say. "I'm on it, sir."

"Good," Bruno replies, almost in relief. "Amy... this could be a career-ender. Or worse, if your meeting tomorrow doesn't go well."

Yeah, I think. Worse means exchanging my usual uniform for a brown, heavily starched outfit at Leavenworth, joining other prisoners who are in there for rape, murder, drug trafficking, and, at last count, two for treason.

"Thanks for the reminder, Major. May I go, sir?"

"Very well, Captain."

I disconnect the call, shove my iPhone back into my leather bag along with the Ruger and burner phone, grab that and my purse, and toss my duffel bag over my shoulder.

In the movies, this would be where the frightened yet determined heroine would stand mournfully in the hallway outside of the door, recall and flash back to all those happy times in here with her strong and smart husband and her precious and also smart young daughter, ready to start those fearful steps from childhood to growing into a young woman.

To hell with that.

I don't have time, so I open the front door and get the hell out of this place that used to be a safe home.

CHAPTER 5

AND THEN this brave heroine, off on a quest to save her family, comes within inches of bowling over an elderly woman standing on the concrete steps.

I do a half dance and jig, and then land with both feet on the lawn. Shirley Gaetz, our next-door neighbor, utters a mixed laugh and cry of surprise as she steps away.

"Oh, Amy, I'm sorry. I didn't mean to startle you."

"It's okay, Mrs. Gaetz, honest," I say, rearranging my duffel bag, which nearly fell off my left shoulder. "What can I do for you?"

"Well, it's this, my younger son, Timmy, ever since his father passed on years back," she begins, and she starts a long and winding tale of how her son had agreed to help take care of the house after Shirley's husband, Roger, had passed on after serving more than thirty years in this man's army, and on and on and on...

Mrs. Gaetz is the oldest resident in the development. She's watched over Denise when Tom and I were out on our respective jobs, and she looks adorable in black stretch slacks and a floral top that could camouflage a dirt mound into a flower bed.

I look longingly at my black Jeep Wrangler, and I interrupt her and say, "Mrs. Gaetz, I'm terribly sorry, but my office called. I need to get back to the base, straightaway. How can I help you?"

"Oh, I'm sorry," she says, reaching up to adjust her white-rimmed eyeglasses, secured by a thin gold chain around her fleshy neck. "It's just that I'm curious if you and Tom were pleased with your carpet-cleaning service, the one that stopped by a few hours ago."

I stand there like the proverbial dopey wife who doesn't know what's going on with her family. With our weird work schedules and occasional separate trips, organizing our lives and that of our daughter's sometimes feels akin to planning the invasion of Normandy. Lots of moving parts, lots of time-sensitive schedules. I'm ashamed to say it, but twice poor Denise has been left abandoned at soccer practice because Tom and I each thought the other had it covered.

But a carpet-cleaning service?

"Ah...well, I haven't talked to Tom yet, so I really don't know," I say.

"Oh," she says with disappointment. "I was hoping you could give me a recommendation."

Then it clicks, just like that. "You know, I didn't really notice. I'll have to ask Tom when I see him."

"Oh," she says, glancing at the CR-V. "He's not here?"

"Ah...he's out with Denise."

"I see."

"Tell me, did you get the name of the company?"

She shakes her head. "No, I'm sorry. It was a bright-red van, and I saw letters on the side, advertising some carpet-cleaning place. Funny thing, I saw it drive in, and then turn around and back in, right up to the garage door."

I thought, *Driver makes a mistake, heads in with the front, then turns around so whatever they're doing can be blocked from view from most neighbors.*

"Was there one guy, or two?"

"Two," she says. "Wearing those gray...what do you call them, jumpsuits." A pause. "Amy, is everything all right?"

Good God, what a goddamn question.

"Things are fine," I say. "Did they stay long?"

"Now, funny you should say that. No, they didn't stay that long at all. I just saw them come out with two of your Oriental carpets and put them in the back of the van."

It feels like there's a giant hand in the center of my chest, squeezing, and squeezing hard.

Tom and I don't own any Oriental rugs.

"Well, I hope they do a good job," I say. "I bet they wrapped them up nice and secure."

Mrs. Gaetz smiles and nods. "That's what struck me, when they left. They opened the garage door and came out with the rolled-up rugs between them, and they put them in the van, real careful like, one by one. Like those two rugs were very precious."

I manage to say, "You have no idea," before hustling by her and getting into my Jeep.

CHAPTER 6

I STOP at the intersection, waiting for the light to change. Our house is on a cul-de-sac, meaning there's only one way in and one way out.

One way out.

Before me is the busy traffic of Kingstowne Boulevard, which eventually leads into the extremely busy traffic of I-95 if you make a left-hand turn. If you were kidnapping a dad and young child from this neighborhood, heading to I-95 would be your best bet. Get buried in traffic, lots of options north and south to make your escape...

Escape where?

Just across the street is a Sunoco service station and minimart.

The light changes.

I hit the accelerator.

Drive across the street and behind the service station.

I take a deep breath, step out.

Inside the service station there's a coffee setup, a pastry cabinet, and the usual narrow aisles filled with overpriced junk food, from chips to cupcakes—and I shouldn't be a wiseass, because there have been a number of times when I've stopped here with Denise to pick up something to drink or munch on while going on an errand or a school trip.

At the left is a counter with two register stations with piles of cigarettes in shelves on the rear wall, and there are lines of three people each in front of the registers.

Busy day.

I'm wearing my class B service uniform with a short zippered dark-blue jacket, and that has the benefit of not displaying my name tag. Good enough.

But the lines aren't moving.

Any other time, any other day, I'd be patient.

By God, this sure as hell isn't any other time or day.

I push my way forward, saying, "Excuse me," in a low but brisk voice, and I pull out my military ID—making sure my thumb is covering my name—and I come up against a cashier named Sarah, plump with brown hair and a silver nose ring.

I flash my ID at her. "Ma'am, I need to see the manager. Right now."

"Ah." Her eyes widen. "That's Tommy…he's on break."

"Then who's in charge?"

She looks over to another woman, older, with long pink fingernails and bright blond hair. Her name is Tina, and she shrugs and says, "It's you, hon. You've been here longer than me."

Sarah nods, takes her new responsibility well, puts up a sign saying USE NEXT REGISTER PLEASE with a little arrow pointing to Tina's station, and leads me around to the side office as the three good Americans in line quietly join the other one.

I don't waste time. "Sarah, I'm investigating a matter of national security. Can I look at your surveillance camera system, please?"

"Sure," she says, pointing to a wall that has a bank of six small monitors, with a larger monitor nearby, and a computer and keyboard. The wall is cluttered with tacked-up greeting cards, notices from the Virginia Department of Labor and Industry, and sloppy photocopies of memos from the home office, warning workers about the latest phone scams.

There's a counter below the keyboard and two chairs, and I take one and Sarah takes the other, and I look at the six monitors and oh my God, *yes, yes, yes,* monitor number 4 shows the entrance to the Sunoco station, Kingstowne Boulevard, and the very beginning of our street, Jackson Street.

"Sarah, I know you have lots of questions, but I'm sorry, I can't answer them," I say. "But I need for you to go back and review the footage for monitor number four."

She scoots the chair closer, starts working on the keyboard. "How far back do you want to go?"

I check my watch. It's six p.m. Mrs. Gaetz said the supposed carpet guys were at our house "a few hours ago." Call it four hours, just to be safe.

"Starting at two p.m.," I say.

"All right."

She works with a wireless mouse, and on the large monitor, a menu appears. After a series of clicks, we're watching the video feed from monitor number 4, and the time stamp is for two p.m.

"Great, Sarah, that's just great," I say. "Now…can you fast-forward it for me, please?"

"Sure," she says, and soon enough, the images of the cars and trucks are moving along—*flick flick flick*—like a silent film from the 1920s speeded up, and at the 2:46 p.m. mark I see our CR-V turn into Jackson Avenue, and I just nod and think, *Okay, Tom's home,* and the *flick flick flick* goes on until—

A school bus stops, extends the Stop sign from the

driver's side, and when the bus moves away, there are four little shapes racing out of view, one with a pixie blond haircut, wearing a soccer uniform, and I must have gasped or made some sort of noise, because Sarah says, "Oh, do you want me to stop there?"

"No," I say firmly. "Keep on going."

And, thank God, I don't have long to wait.

A red van shows up at the traffic light and I say, "There, right there."

Sarah works the keyboard again. The view goes into normal time. In the movies you get to see the keyboard operator freeze the film, zoom in so you can see the license plate of the suspect vehicle, and sometimes you can even see the driver's lips move and decipher what he's saying.

This little Sunoco station is definitely not Hollywood. On the screen the van makes a left-hand turn onto Jackson Street and I catch some of the letters on the side: ABLE CARPET. It looks like it has Virginia license plates, but the numbers and letters are too fuzzy. I check the time.

Wait.

Per the video feed, the van comes back sixteen minutes later. There are two men in the front. Can't tell if they're Caucasian, Asian, African American, or any mixture thereof. I chew on my right thumbnail. My two loved ones are in the rear of this van. I'm positive.

The van makes a left and then disappears. I know the geography. The exit to I-95 is only about five minutes away.

That's that.

I push the chair back and say, "Sarah, thank you so very much."

She nods, looking quite serious. "Glad I could help. And I promise, I won't tell anyone."

"Thanks," I say. "One more favor? I need to use a restroom."

Sarah says, "I'm not supposed to let customers use it…but this is important, right? Follow me."

Six minutes later, at the rear of the service station, I've changed into civilian clothes—blue jeans, black turtleneck, short black leather jacket. I quickly walk to my Wrangler, lots of thoughts and plans bouncing around in my head.

I suddenly remember being with Tom on a warm night in McLean, walking off a fine restaurant meal, and as we went past a corner Walgreens, a man leaning against the wall, smoking a cigarette, smiled at us both and said something I didn't understand.

Tom said, "Excuse me," and walked back to the man, said something. The man said something back and went after Tom, and in a quick movement Tom made a boxing stance, and in one hard punch, the man was on the ground.

Tom later said, "He called you a whore in Farsi. I told him he shouldn't have said that. You saw what happened."

"I didn't know you knew boxing."

"For a while, I did."

"Why did you stop?" I said.

"Every time I got hit in the face, I cried," he said.

So I knew Tom would do his best to keep Denise and himself alive.

But it was up to me to get them safely free.

Near the Wrangler is a pump island for diesel, and four tractor-trailer trucks are lined up, refueling. I tug out the burner phone. This is my connection to the kidnappers, the ones who have upended my life, have stolen my husband and child, and who've put them in danger.

I go to a nearby tractor-trailer truck, belonging to Walmart. I shove the phone in a crack under the doors and go back to my Wrangler.

Earlier the kidnapper thought he had sent me on a mission.

He has.

Mine.

Not his.

CHAPTER 7

IN HIS years as a journalist, Tom Cornwall has been in some tight places: under artillery bombardment in a Kurdish *peshmerga* outpost in Syria, accidentally separated from a Filipino army patrol while they were hunting Abu Sayyaf terrorists in the jungles of Jolo Island, and in an armored-up Humvee convoy in Afghanistan when the lead vehicle did a flaming backflip after it ran over an IED.

In all of these close calls, Tom had one sustaining mantra: *his circus, his monkey*. He was in danger because that was his choice, his life, and if things went to shit, well, he'd be the only one bloodied out.

Sitting on the edge of a cot in a concrete cube somewhere, he sighs, rubs his head. Now he is in danger again, but now it is so terribly different.

He lifts his head. His daughter, Denise, is curled up on an identical cot, on the other side of the room. She's barefoot, wearing black tights and an oversized sweatshirt from Epcot. She's clutching a stuffed Tigger in her arms, and it's been ten minutes since she last let out a sob.

Progress, of a sort.

She looks up and says, "What about Mister Banjo?"

Tom gets up and examines their quarters. A square room, made of light-green cinder blocks. Concrete ceiling with a small air vent. Concrete floor with a drain in the center. One metal door, leading out. No handle or doorknob on this side. Four lightbulbs dangling from black cords. A dial that can lower the lights but not turn them off. In the corner of the room, a metal sink and metal toilet.

That's it.

"Daddy, what about Mister Banjo?"

He walks back and forth, back and forth, working out the kinks in his legs and arms. The events of the past hours keep on running back and forth in his mind, like a defective DVD that skips and repeats the same scene.

A regular day at home. Denise in the kitchen, running the blender, making a fruit smoothie, having just changed and dumped her soccer clothes in the bathroom, with a promise that she'll pick them up, real-soon-now. He in his office, supposedly doing research on his book, but going down a YouTube rabbit hole showing black-and-white science-fiction movie clips from the 1950s. Looking out the window, seeing a red van make a turn in a driveway two homes down.

Back to YouTube, seeing old footage of a V-2 rocket launching from White Sands, pretending to be a moon rocket. Hearing a vehicle come into the driveway, leave, and then return.

Doorbell rings. He gets up, goes to the door.

Whirring sound of the blender.

Open the door to two smiling yet nervous men wearing gray jumpsuits, one of them holding a clipboard, and the one on the left, in an accented voice, says, "Sir? We're here for the carpet cleaning?"

Situational awareness.

It all comes right to him at that moment.

The men are nervous, jittery, their dark-skinned faces sweaty.

He and Amy haven't ordered a carpet-cleaning service.

This is wrong.

He smiles at the two men, starts closing the door, knowing the gun safe is right at his shoulder, and says, "Sorry, there must be some mistake."

No more smiles, no more nervousness.

The larger of the two men snaps out something in a foreign language, and they break in, and now it's like a bad dream that's only getting worse, and he shouts, "Denise! Run!"

Then on the floor, gasping, legs and arms trembling, as some sort of Taser-like device is being pushed into his ribs. He's thrown on his stomach, hands and feet are being bound, and in a high-pitched voice that will haunt him to his deathbed, he hears Denise screaming.

He fades in and out. He's rolled into something. It goes dark. He's lifted up. Dropped. Movement. Engine sounds. Stops and starts, stops and starts. More lifting. Engine sounds.

Lifting up and down, up and down.

Then…

Unwrapped in this room by the same two men, plastic ties cut away, Denise sobbing next to him, long hours trying to calm her down…

Knowing they are trapped, knowing he is in the greatest danger of his life, and also knowing he has put his ten-year-old girl in a depth of jeopardy he dares not even consider.

CHAPTER 8

NOW, IN their concrete prison, trying not to obsess over his mistakes that got them here.

Right now, trying not to panic in front of the little girl who's depending on him to make it all right.

"Daddy! Mister Banjo!"

Her scream cuts through his thinking, his memories, and another chunk of guilt has just been added to the monument piling up in his gut.

"Sorry, hon," he says.

He goes over, sits down on the cot next to Denise. He strokes her back, looks around at their surroundings. Where are they? He's not sure. He was so out of sorts for such a long time that he has no idea if it's been three or six or nine hours since their kidnapping.

He tried talking, reasoning, and even begging the two men who deposited them here, taking the unrolled carpets with them.

He tries to remember the word the larger man said back at the house. Middle Eastern, of course, but he didn't understand it.

And his wife, Amy, a captain in military intelligence.

Lots of puzzle pieces out there.

"I'm sorry, hon, who's Mister Banjo?"

Her voice is filled with accusation. "I already told you!"

Tom grits his teeth, tries to keep it together. "I'm sorry, hon. Could you tell me again?"

Tears come back to her eyes. "Mister Banjo. In Mrs. Millett's class. He's our pet hamster. I was going to bring him home tomorrow and keep him a week, like the other kids. This week it's my turn…and I won't be there tomorrow!"

She starts sobbing again, and Tom brings his hand up higher, to Denise's head and soft blond hair. He strokes her hair and she sniffs and rubs a hand across her runny nose. She's ten and normally wouldn't be hugging a stuffed Tigger like this, but nothing here is normal. Still, despite the anger and fear and anguish, there's pride in his little girl. She's not your typical ten-year-old, especially since she has parents who sometimes depart for weeks or months, spending quality time on Skype or FaceTime.

He says, "I'm sure Mrs. Millett will understand. Mom…Mom will probably tell her when she can. And then we can fix the schedule so you can get Mister Banjo later."

Denise nods and Tom wonders at what point his little girl will no longer be convinced that her dad can solve any problem in the world.

"Daddy?" she finally asks.

"Yes, love?"

"I'm scared."

"I know," he says.

"Are you scared?"

"I'm…okay. I'm concerned. This will be figured out. I'm sure."

He strokes her fine hair, a part of him still wondering how he—with brown hair, and Amy, with black hair—managed to come up with this little blond princess. Not an angel, good Lord, no, not with her temper and her insane curiosity and daring—like the time she saw a Bugs Bunny cartoon and climbed up on the garage roof, black umbrella in hand, convinced she could come down like an eight-year-old parachutist.

In his daughter's profile, Tom sees the outline of Amy's face, first time they met. It was at an afternoon college lecture series in Maine—where, full of himself and a year into his first journalism job at the *Boston Globe,* he pontificated on the state of the world and the military—and at a following reception, she came up to him in her Army uniform, a sergeant.

"Nice lecture," she said. "Too bad fifty percent of it was bullshit."

Stunned but instantly attracted to her smile and bright eyes, he said, "Which fifty percent?"

"Take me out to dinner, and I'll tell you," she said.

And he did just that, and for years afterward.

Denise stares up at him, still looking like a much younger version of her mother.

"Why did they take us, Daddy?"

"Because…they want something. And we're going to be traded, like when you trade those Magic trading cards."

"What do they want?"

"I don't know."

Denise rolls over and now he's stroking her forehead. "Who are they, Dad? I mean…they're so scary. And it hurt. It really hurt when they zapped me."

"I don't know who they are, either. I'm sorry."

He takes his hand away from her smooth forehead, and she scrunches her face, like she's trying not to cry.

"Dad?" she asks.

"Yes, hon?"

"Will Mom and her friends rescue us?"

Tom says, "I'm sure."

"The Army. I bet those bad guys kidnapped us because of Mom and her job."

"Maybe," Tom says. "In the meantime, let's see if we can't rescue ourselves."

"Huh?"

He rubs the side of her face. "We're smart. We're tough. Maybe we can figure out a way of escaping. What do you think?"

She nods, barely smiling. "That sounds good. I'll start thinking, okay? And when we get out, maybe you can call Mrs. Millett. About Mister Banjo."

He now rubs her belly. "Sure. That sounds great."

Now she's smiling and he turns away, because he's afraid he's going to choke up in front of his daughter, who is relying on Daddy to save her. And who believes—and makes a good case—that this kidnapping is due to Amy's work in the Army.

But Tom knows better, and the guilt is threatening to consume him.

For he has secrets, secrets he's been keeping from Amy.

And he's terrified they will end up killing him and Denise.

CHAPTER 9

IN THE kidnap note that I've left behind at the house, I was warned not to contact any military or law enforcement personnel.

But they didn't say anything about public libraries.

I'm at a computer terminal in the corner of the Kingstowne Library, which on the outside looks like an outlet mall—no doubt because it was built in the Landsdowne Centre shopping complex—and on the inside has lots of bright colors and white ceilings and open shelves. I grew up in a small town in Maine, and our library was one of those places donated by Andrew Carnegie, a dark, Victorian-style building with lots of brick and turrets. Sometimes, when the librarian dozed, I'd play hide-and-go-seek with my gal pals.

Back then, there were no computers, but this library has a nice little section for public use, and I'm hard at work, believe it or not. A few years ago the president and the secretary of defense made a big deal of transferring millions of dollars from our DoD budget to help upgrade computer systems in libraries across the country. *Yay,* everyone said. But there might have been a few nays if folks realized that in all this upgrading a back door was installed in the software for the use of nosy intelligence officers like myself who were stuck somewhere in flyover country or on the run.

Call it defense in depth, or increasing the stability

of vital DoD intelligence services, or another few bricks in the wall-to-wall surveillance of everything we do in the States, but all I know is that it works, and I need it.

I go to an obscure federal government website about protecting rare flowers and click on a tiny gray box in the lower right-hand corner, which brings up a log-in box. I gain access by using my name, Army service number, and password.

There's a host of options available to me but first on my list is getting a readout of all surveillance cameras in and around Kingstowne, including those at service stations (like our friendly Sunoco from down the way), ATMs, drugstores, malls, banks, private homes, private businesses, and anywhere else with a view of the busy streets of Fairfax County. That program is called TANGO TRAPPER.

Once I "caught" the carpet-cleaning van going down our street, I saved the blurry photo, then repeated the process when it exited. And then I caught it one more time, just as it was heading onto exit 169A north on I-95.

Three catches.

Enough.

I go to another program, feed in the three blurry photos. Wait.

Wait some more.

Deep in some heavily guarded and secure server farm out there somewhere, things are hard at work.

Do I know exactly what is going on?

Nope.

But I'm not worried.

I take a moment and look around the pretty and safe library. A number of kids sitting at the tables, or gliding past the crowded shelves. Seeing a blond girl working at a round table stabs at me so hard that I have to turn around and look elsewhere.

Once upon a time, places like these that contained books and knowledge were stored in heavily fortified monasteries in Europe, to protect them from the barbarians.

Now the barbarians are no longer at the gates. Thanks to the wonders of this century, the barbarians could reach across half the globe and give you a deadly tap on the shoulder with a digital finger. Viruses, malware, phishing…

I go back to the screen, using the program called BORAX.

There's my target van, sharpened up, clean, and looking fine.

ABLE CAREPT CLEANERS, ALEXANDRIA.

With a local phone number painted below.

The van looks legit.

Stolen?

Probably.

I'll look into that later.

With the sharpened photo of the van in my digital grasp, I send it along to another complicated tracking program that uses algorithms, predictive software, traffic analysis programs, and other cool stuff to watch vehicle traffic on the nation's roads, from highways to dirt paths, as long as there is a surveillance camera in the area. This one is called CYCLOPS. I imagine some bored bureaucrat somewhere in Crystal City, whose job it is, all day long, to assign code names to various programs.

Do I know the intricacies of the CYCLOPS program?

No.

Just like the sweet kids wandering around out in

the safe confines of this library don't know how their handheld devices work.

Just a tool.

That's all.

I go back to the screen.

The spinning little doohickey, spinning away.

Look away once more.

Ah, damn it!

Out in the general area of the library is Sue Judson, an assistant librarian who's taken a shine to Denise, helping her find books about whatever obsession my daughter is exploring that month: astronomy, genealogy, the history of Victorian fashion…my smart, tough, and sweet little girl.

Now Sue is looking this way, and I turn, hoping I'm not spotted.

She's lovely, about my age, desperately trying to have a child with her handsome husband, Luke, an E-6 in the Army and stationed in my building, and any other day, I'd love to talk to her.

But not now.

Not today.

I go back to the screen.

The doohickey is still spinning, spinning…stops.

A map of Fairfax County pops up, every street, avenue, and highway lit up in pink. Little symbols of steering wheels are blinking at me.

I click one.

There's the van, heading north on I-95.

I click on the next one.

Two miles farther north on I-95.

And with this magic hunting system, I track the van as it goes up the highway…then to an exit…and then to a state road, and then another state road. The van moves along in a specific direction, no doubt about it, and I try very, very hard not to think of Tom and Denise, wrapped up and terrified, bouncing in the back of that stolen van, which has left Fairfax County and is going into Fauquier County.

Then there's no more blinking steering wheels.

Damn!

The van containing my life and loves is gone.

CHAPTER 10

I TAKE a deep breath, trying not to panic, trying not to lose faith.

I check the last viewing of the van, passing by a private home that has a camera overlooking its driveway gate. Then...

It's gone.

Somewhere in this area, the van has disappeared. But where?

"Hey, Lucianne, how goes it?"

Sue Judson is coming this way, having just greeted someone named Lucianne. I scrunch up my shoulders, desperately trying to avoid Sue's notice.

I examine the map again.

A rural area near the small town of Atoka.

I don't know anything about it.

I do a bit more research.

Not much to know.

There are single-family homes, a lot of farms, and—

A private airport.

Morgan Airport.

More digging and dumping through the miracle of the Internet.

It belongs to a medical device company with its main offices in Alexandria. It has a five-thousand-foot paved runway. Nice. No manned control tower, no real facilities except for those who have a reason to land or take off there.

And no Internet-linked surveillance cameras at the two small buildings.

Damn, damn, damn.

CYCLOPS is now down for the count.

What now?

What other resources are out there for an Army intelligence officer on the run?

If there was a security camera overhead right now, it would see me tapping away furiously at the keyboard, like the cliché scenes from movies and TV shows about dedicated hackers who can solve a knotty plot problem in five minutes by slapping a keyboard around and getting someone's third-grade report card.

The thing about clichés, of course, is that they're always based on something real.

Tapping away, I find something called GILLNET, which lists all sorts of external visual and audio devices away from highways or roads that can be accessed by a curious Uncle Sam and his minions, and after I plug in the GPS coordinates for Morgan Airport, I get a—

A hit.

I get a hit.

And then I get a hand on my shoulder.

"Amy, what a surprise!"

CHAPTER 11

PELAYO ABBOUD is standing outside the thick metal door when his trusted lieutenant, Casper Khourery, arrives holding an ice-cold sixteen-ounce bottle of Coca-Cola, a white straw sticking out of the top. Pelayo nods in gratitude and gestures to the door, and Casper—a bulky man in his early thirties with perfect white teeth, light-brown skin, close-cropped curly black hair, and a carefully trimmed mustache—unlocks the door, stepping back. Casper is wearing a fine gray suit, a Savile Row knockoff, with a crisp white shirt, blue necktie, and red kerchief sticking out of the jacket pocket, which Pelayo thinks is a bit too much, but he's a gracious boss and will allow Casper that one fashion statement.

The door swings open and Pelayo walks in. The young girl is hunched up against the wall on her bed, coloring something in a book, and her father is drying his hands at the corner sink. Pelayo is pleased that the girl is using the coloring book, which he earlier supplied. Something to keep the little brat occupied so her father can focus on the trouble they are in. The father turns, and Pelayo sees the man is struggling to keep his emotions under guard, but Pelayo is no fool. The man before him wants to kill him and would try in this very instant, save that the little girl is here and Casper is standing in the doorway.

Pelayo nods to the other bed. "May I sit?"

"Do I have a choice?" comes the reply.

"No," Pelayo says, sitting down on the edge. "Still, I always try to keep as much courtesy in the air as I can." He takes a sip of the cold Coke, relishes the sharp, sugary bite. He holds the bottle up and says, "My apologies. Would you and Denise like one?"

"No," the man says.

"You didn't ask her."

"I didn't have to."

Pelayo shrugs. "Your loss. This bottle comes from Coca-Cola FEMSA, which produces it in Mexico. There, they use the traditional cane sugar, unlike the corn fructose sugar used in the States. The experts say there is no difference in taste, but the experts, once again, are wrong."

He takes another taste and says, "And I must apologize for something else."

"The kidnapping?" the man asks. He's tall, with muscular shoulders and arms that show he likes to work out, but with a pudgy middle and sides that show he spends a lot of time sitting in front of a desk. He has on blue jeans, no shoes, black socks, and a wrinkled pink polo shirt. Pelayo thinks of himself as a global man with global tastes, but really, a man wearing pink?

"That's a harsh word, a harsh phrase," Pelayo says. "Let's just call it an unfortunate turn of events, a matter of business, that's all. Hopefully, in two days or so, all will be settled and you will be rejoined with your wife, Captain Amy Travis Cornwall, 297th Military Intelligence Battalion, Military Intelligence Corps, Fort Belvoir, Virginia, recently home after an eight-month deployment to Afghanistan."

The man's face colors but he stands still. The little girl is staring at Pelayo, and he offers her a slight smile. She returns to her coloring book. The hand holding a colored pencil is shaking.

Pelayo says, "In the meantime, is there anything else I can provide to you and your daughter?"

"How about our freedom?"

He smiles. "I wish, but, ah, my hands are tied at the moment. I've dispatched your wife on a very, very important mission. To have that mission succeed, unfortunately, I need to have you and your daughter in our possession."

"Fuck you," the man says. His daughter doesn't say a word.

Pelayo stands up. "I won't take that as an insult. You're a father, a husband, under serious stress. That insult…I will let it slide. But remember this in the hours ahead: be very, very happy and prayerful that you're not in the presence of my cousin Miguel. If you were…well, let's just say at this point, you would be begging for the sweet relief of being killed."

He takes another satisfying sip of the Coca-Cola—really, how could anyone not tell the difference?—and as he turns, the man calls out, his voice pleading, "Wait, please. Just a moment? Please?"

Pelayo sees the man is no longer angry, no longer ready to curse him again. Instead, well, the man's shoulders are slumped. He is showing he is defeated.

But Pelayo sees that as just a temporary success. Many times, a defeated and humiliated man will come back with a surprising vengeance and fury at the most inopportune time.

"Go ahead."

The man says, nearly looking down, "We've eaten just once. It was quite the nice meal. I…I thank you. But could we have some snacks and other drinks, just in case we get hungry? And my daughter…she loves chewing gum. Could we get that for her as well?"

He smiles. This is going better than he expected. "You will have it all within the hour."

Pelayo now is beyond the door, and Casper is ready to close it, when the man says one last thing:

"Why? Why did you do this to us?"

Pelayo shrugs again. "You know very well why. And soon so will your wife."

He steps back, and the plain gray metal door closes shut on the American father and his daughter.

CHAPTER 12

I RESTRAIN myself from jumping up and slapping Sue Judson on her pretty face, but I manage to minimize the screen for GILLNET so she doesn't know what I'm up to.

But even then, she knows I'm up to something, which is just as bad.

Her expression is a mix of curiosity and concern, and she says, "Is everything okay at home, Amy?"

Instantly I'm on guard, and I say, "Of course everything's okay. Why do you ask?" And I'm thinking, *All right, what does she know, has her husband, Luke, said something about me and work and that appointment tomorrow with the CID officer*—another problem the size of the moon I'm trying to ignore—and then I try to dial it back and add, "Are you all right?"

"Me? Oh, yes, fine, it's just that…well, I've seen you here plenty of times with Denise, and I've never seen you at one of these terminals. Is your computer at home broken?"

"Well, it's been giving me some hiccups, and I was running some errands and—"

She puts her hand on my right shoulder and says, "I hate to interrupt you, but your daughter was asking me about getting a book for her from the interlibrary system, and darn it, I can't remember the title. Do you know it?"

"No, I don't," I say, conscious that with every passing second, every passing minute, Tom and Denise are farther away from me. If they are still in the back of the van, each sixty seconds of blather with Sue is taking them a mile farther.

She gives my shoulder a reassuring squeeze. "Well, I'm sure Denise is home right now. If you want to give her a text, I'll wait here."

"I'm not really sure…" and I was about to say, *where she is,* but I can't say those words out loud—no, I refuse to say those words out loud.

"Oh," Sue says, smiling widely. "It'll only take a second. I can wait. Then I can take care of her."

"Sue," I say, also conscious that with every passing minute, my presence on this parallel classified computer system is being recorded, "I really don't have the time."

"Amy, just a quick text, that's all."

"Sue…"

"Amy, just a quick text, and we can take care of it right here," she says, and she quiets her voice—I suppose so the other computer users around us don't hear. "I'm sure Denise will be happy to see how thoughtful you are."

Thoughtful. Sure. How thoughtful. I should have left the Army after having her and gone into private industry, and she and Tom would be safe at home, with better clothes, better gadgets, fatter savings accounts, and above all, safe.

Safe from her mom's sins.

"Sue?"

"Yes?"

I crook my finger at her, so she leans down, still smiling.

I lift myself up so I can whisper in her ear without anyone else overhearing.

"Sue," I say, choosing my words carefully, using my best parade-ground command voice. "Leave me the hell alone or I'll hurt you."

CHAPTER 13

WITHIN TWO seconds I'm back at the screen, face warm, back tingly, knowing I've just tossed a hand grenade into the comfortable civilian life of one Sue Judson, and right now, not particularly giving a crap.

I double-click on the icon for GILLNET and go to the hit, indicating some sort of audio or visual surveillance system at or near Morgan Airport, and a lit acronym comes up.

USFWS.

In this man and woman's Army, I've come across and memorized scores of acronyms, but this one is a puzzle until I click on it and come up with...

US Fish and Wildlife Service.

Well.

Not really part of what one would call the nation's intelligence agencies, but I navigate GILLNET and find a video system piggybacked on a cell phone tower, used to film certain patterns of bird migration. How fascinating.

But it also overlooks part of Morgan Airport.

With apologies to naturalists everywhere, I manage to seize control of the surveillance system and rewind back to the time when I last saw the van — I wait.

And wait.

The video feed comes back to life, and I get a shot of the airport, its strip, and the two outbuildings.

Nothing else.

I fast-forward, but not too fast, because I don't want to miss anything.

Some minutes flicker before me. I hear harsh whispers. I look up, and Sue Judson is having a serious talk with two other librarian staffers at a center workstation.

I make the informed guess that I'm the subject of the irritated chatter and go back to the screen.

The camera captures something flying by.

A bird?

No.

I hunch forward, peering at the screen.

Oh, yeah, it's a bird all right, but a man-made bird.

A jet aircraft, lining up for a landing. It gets closer and closer, and then it makes the landing and slows itself, and I recognize it as a twin-engine Learjet 60, one of the most popular business-sized jets in the world.

I rub my fingers together.

All right.

Not a big deal. This airport belongs to a medical device company, and maybe they're here to drop off or pick up someone.

The jet taxis to the end of the runway, slowly circles around, the view now being blocked by the two buildings. I can make out the nose of the fuselage and nothing else.

Strike that.

I can make out that no one's walking in or walking out.

The jet seems to be waiting for somebody.

"Oh, God, yes," I whisper. At the very limits of the camera, one can make out a dirt access road leading to the small airport.

Bouncing along this dirt road is a red van.

I get three seconds of view, but it's enough.

I reach to the screen, give the van a quick touch as it, too, disappears from view.

All I can see now is the fuselage of the Learjet.

It stays still.

I know why the earlier system, CYCLOPS, didn't pick up on the van. It was too far away, fuzzy, indistinct.

But now I've seen it.

And I know who is in it.

I touch the screen again.

The Learjet starts to taxi out and—

There!

I freeze the view and I catch the registration numbers, painted on the near engine nacelle. The letters and numbers aren't sharp, but they're sharp enough.

I quickly write them down.

NS-28312.

I let the video play again, and the jet gains speed, goes down the runway, and lifts off, and within seconds, it's gone from view.

"Fly safe, you bastards," I whisper. "You've got my family in there."

Then I clear everything, shut down, log off, and push my chair back.

I need to get moving, but I also need to do something else. On my way out I catch a red-faced Sue Judson's attention and put a reassuring hand over hers.

"Sue, I'm so sorry I snapped at you back there. Work...I'm under a lot of pressure, and there are things going on at home. I'm sorry you had to take the brunt of it."

She smiles wanly. "I understand. We all have problems like that, here and there." Sue's face brightens up. "Someday, I'm sure you'll look back on this and have a good laugh, am I right?"

I head to the doors.

"No, Sue, you're very wrong."

CHAPTER 14

PELAYO ABBOUD makes a slurping sound with the straw and the last of the Coca-Cola, and passes the empty bottle over to Casper Khourery, who cocks his head a couple of millimeters, a gesture just large enough so Pelayo knows what's next.

"Ah, yes," he says. "One more errand to undertake. Are they ready?"

Casper nods and takes the lead, still holding the empty glass Coke bottle with the straw sticking out as they maneuver their way across the filthy basement, cluttered with construction materials, pallets of packaged food and drinks, and boxes of open tiles and polished wood. The air is hot and muggy, pierced with the sound of hammering, power tools buzzing, and shouts of construction workers.

They head down a wide corridor, freshly installed Sheetrock on either side, little metal screw heads still visible. There's a pallet with empty Coke bottles in open wooden crates, and Casper withdraws the straw, puts the bottle in with a little *clink,* then drops the used straw on the dirty floor. A few more meters and there's an open door to the right, which they both enter.

The two men who successfully kidnapped the two Americans are sitting on a large black folding table, both wearing gray jumpsuits. When Pelayo comes in, the two men stand up, looking intently at him and Casper. Pelayo nods, gives them a slight smile. No need to overdo it, for these two men have grown up in blasted and destroyed areas of the Middle East that Pelayo doesn't even want to think about.

"Gentlemen…Amir, Hakim, you've done exactly as you were hired to do," Pelayo says. "My thanks once more."

The older, harder one—Amir—says in an accented voice, "We would like to depart now. After we are settled."

"But of course. Casper?"

Casper leaves and then quickly returns with two gym bags, each marked by the blue-and-yellow insignia of the El Tigre football club. Amir steps forward and there's a small knife in his hand. Not bad. A good man with a good knife can close in on any armed man and slit his throat before a trigger is pulled. Amir is prepared and suspicious, a good man to hire.

"You…open them up. Show me what's in them."

Casper looks to Pelayo, and he nods. Both bags are unzipped, displayed, showing mounds of banded American one-hundred-dollar bills inside. Amir says something sharp, and Hakim comes over, takes the bags, examines a few sample bands, smiles and laughs.

Amir takes one of the bags, and Hakim takes the other.

"We are finished here," Amir says. "Show us where to go."

Pelayo extends an arm, Casper backs out, and the two men slowly walk out into the wide hallway. Casper takes the lead, and Pelayo walks beside the two men. He says, "Outside there will be a van, with a change of clothing, and it will take you to your friends at the airport. From there, *vaya con dios*."

The two men say nothing as they approach a wide ramp leading outside to the even hotter, muggier air.

The younger of the men says something, and as Amir replies, Pelayo steps back. The two men are now walking across a heavy green plastic tarp. Pelayo takes a 10mm Glock out of an open cardboard box to his right marked GOYA and shoots both men in the back of the head.

A minute later, after walking away from the two dead men and back into the basement, Pelayo and Casper enter a wide construction-scale elevator. As it grumbles its way up, Casper—with both bags of cash slung over his shoulders—takes the Glock from Pelayo's right hand and gives him a moist cloth, which he uses to wipe the gun oil and powder residue off his hands.

"Ungrateful, weren't they?" he says to Casper. "I wished them well on their journey, with God at their side, and they didn't even say thank you."

Casper says, "Too greedy, too eager to leave."

"Lessons learned, eh?"

"Well, perhaps they suspected there was no one waiting for them at the airport."

Pelayo emits a loud sigh. "Suspicious lot, weren't they?"

The elevator door opens up to another hallway cluttered with construction equipment, and Pelayo walks to the corridor's end. Casper opens one door, closes it behind them as they enter a very short hallway, and then opens another. From there, it's like going from a slum to a rich man's estate in less than two meters.

Pelayo feels the tingle of appreciation and gratitude as he enters the top-floor suite, with its curtained floor-to-ceiling windows, balconies overlooking the rest of the complex and the nearby Gulf of Mexico, luxurious furniture and big-screen televisions, as well as cool, air-conditioned air, so unlike the hot and humid basement. Two of his men are sitting at a low table, heads bowed, cleaning two American-made M4 automatic rifles. The table is covered with a work cloth. Good boys.

He looks around, sees two of his other boys sitting on a leather couch, reading magazines. They are magazines about guns and cars, which is fine. No porn lying around, no adult DVDs, no young women lounging about with thong bikinis, laughing and touching too much. Those are distractions he will not allow.

It is through very hard and dangerous work, pure focus and discipline, that Pelayo has gotten here, and he will never, ever forget those lessons, including never, ever sampling the merchandise, whether it's smuggled cocaine, opium, marijuana, Fresca soda, or frightened teenage girls from Eastern Europe filled with lying promises about a new life in the New World.

He goes down a short, wood-paneled corridor and then to the left. This room is his own little communications hub, stuffy, the windows taped with thick cardboard against the glass. There are banks of communications gear, keyboards, and computers. One man looks up and Casper goes to him, leaning over, the two of them softly talking.

Casper stands up, a troubled look on his face.

Pelayo says, "Yes?"

"The Cornwall woman has departed. But the phone we left for her...it's going in the wrong direction. It's now in New Jersey. She's going in the wrong direction."

Pelayo smiles. "No, she's sending us a sweet message. A nasty one, but a sweet one. She is telling us that she will do the job, but that she is a force to be reckoned with."

He steps forward, gives Casper a comforting pat on the shoulder, noting a few flecks of blood on the back of his hand.

"But so are we," Pelayo says.

CHAPTER 15

AS FAR as waiting rooms go, this one in Fort Belvoir is all right. Special Agent Rosaria Vasquez of the Army's Criminal Investigation Command has been in some real rat holes in her years of dedication to the service that she loves. Beat-up mobile homes with rusting sides and leaking ceilings. Apartment buildings built near railroad tracks, meaning she would have to pause her interrogation each time a freight train rattled through. Army-issued tents, the sides flapping, wind whistling by, sand getting into everything, the constant drumming roar of diesel generators and passing vehicles threatening her concentration as she diligently asked questions and waited for answers.

In all of those locations, she was doing her job: interrogating various Army enlisted men and women, NCOs and officers, chasing down crimes that are as old as humankind—rape, theft, homicide—as well as those only pertinent to her Army, from mishandling of classified documents to espionage.

Today's interrogation is one of those belonging to the Army, the death of a prisoner in a foreign land, in the custody of an occupying force, said force being the Army of the United States. A CID unit in Afghanistan is up to its ears re-investigating that end of the case and Rosaria is here on the other end, conducting the first domestic interview with the supervising officer who ended up with a dead Taliban fighter in her custody.

This waiting area is small, with two chairs, a coffee table with today's *Washington Post* and *USA Today,* and framed photos of Army personnel deployed across the world, from Afghanistan to Sudan. A door leads out into a hallway and another leads to the office of the commanding officer of her scheduled interviewee.

Both doors are closed.

Rosaria checks her watch.

It is 0840. Her appointment with Captain Amy Cornwall was supposed to have taken place forty minutes ago. Rosaria thinks a five- or ten-minute delay is reasonable, fifteen or more is insulting, and more than a half hour is a gut punch of insubordination.

Still, she waits. Patience and persistence are two of the many things she has learned in the CID.

Rosaria is a warrant officer in the Army, assigned to the 701st Military Group (CID) at Marine Corps Base, Quantico, Virginia, but is wearing civilian clothing— black slacks with a crisp plain white blouse and black jacket. CID investigators always wear civilian clothing, save for ceremonial duties or if they are in a combat zone.

There will be conflict aplenty during her visit here today at Fort Belvoir, but at least it's not an official combat zone. Still, in a hip holster is her Army-issued SIG Sauer 9mm P228 pistol, and in her inside jacket pocket is her government ID and gold-and-blue CID badge.

Her black leather courier bag is on the carpeted floor, next to her chair.

She waits.

The door before her opens up and an apologetic Army major pokes his head out, his name tag saying

WENNER, wearing the camouflage Army combat uniform.

"Special Agent Vasquez, Lieutenant Colonel Denton will see you now."

"Outstanding," she says, grabbing her dispatch case and following the slim, young-looking major into the lieutenant colonel's office.

The office is twice as large as the waiting area, with the same type of framed photos as wall decorations. There's a small black leather couch on the left that Major Bruno Wenner takes, and one wall is covered by filing cabinets. Three unlocked drawers have bright-red cardboard signs saying OPEN slid in just above the handles. There are two brown leather chairs in front of Lieutenant Colonel Hugh Denton's desk. He doesn't get up, just gives her a crisp nod.

She takes one of the chairs, and says, "Sir."

"A moment," he says, looking down through a pair of reading glasses at an open file folder, a telephone system before him, a computer terminal at his elbow. Denton has broad shoulders and a barrel chest, wiry gray hair, and a frowning weathered face. He seems to be about forty-five.

Rosaria waits. She knows the lieutenant colonel hates having her here, hates having her presence known on Fort Belvoir, quietly spreading the news that some sort of blemish has been placed on his unit.

He finally looks up. "Captain Cornwall isn't here."

"Yes, sir," she says. "Will she be in at all today?"

Major Wenner speaks up from the other side of the room. "She's…ah…she called in sick."

Rosaria doesn't turn her head to the major. She keeps looking at Lieutenant Colonel Denton. "Sir…I've come up here today from Quantico, expecting to meet with Captain Cornwall about an incident that occurred while she was on deployment in Afghanistan. This interview is vital to my investigation, sir. Is it my understanding that she could not make this appointment because she is ill? Sir?"

Lieutenant Colonel Denton's eyes narrow. His eyebrows are the same gray color as his hair.

Major Wenner speaks up. "She is ill."

Rosaria says, "Is she in a hospital? At some medical facility? Major?"

Some quiet seconds pass. Rosaria hears a jet overhead, probably heading to DC.

Major Wenner says, "I believe she's at home, Special Agent Vasquez. And not at a medical facility."

Rosaria can tell the lieutenant colonel's executive officer is very good at his job, being the quiet intermediary, the one who calms the lieutenant colonel, who supplies information, excuses, and anything to make the office run smoothly and cleanly. Like the good mom, trying to smooth things over among squabbling siblings, although Rosaria has never known a real mom or dad in her life. Although she's only just met the executive officer, she's sure he's popular among the personnel at this intelligence battalion.

"Colonel Denton…is that true?"

"If Major Wenner says it, then it must be true."

"I see, sir."

"You should consider yourself lucky that you've just wasted a morning drive," he says sourly. "Three years ago, we were at Fort Gordon, in Georgia. It was a nice posting, until some bureaucrats and a congressman moved us here to Virginia in some high-class shuffle."

Rosaria says, "I'll certainly keep that in mind, sir."

He abruptly closes the manila folder. "I suggest you come back tomorrow."

Rosaria slowly picks up her leather bag. "At oh-eight hundred, sir?"

Lieutenant Colonel Denton stares at her. "My XO will advise you later today."

"Very well, sir."

She stands up and Denton says, "Call me old-fashioned and cranky, Special Agent Vasquez, but I don't like seeing on-duty Army personnel wearing civilian clothes on my post."

Rosaria says, "Then I won't do it, sir."

"What?"

She starts out of the office. "I won't call you old-fashioned or cranky. Sir."

CHAPTER 16

LESS THAN twenty minutes later, Rosaria Vasquez is parked in the driveway of Captain Cornwall's home in Kingstowne, Virginia. She steps out of her government-issued white GMC sedan, notes a light-blue Honda CR-V with Virginia license plates in the driveway. She checks paperwork in her folder. Registered to Captain Cornwall and her husband, Tom, a former reporter for the AP, the *New York Times,* and other news outlets. They have a young girl, named Denise. Ten years old. They've been together for eleven years, got married when they were in their early twenties. Lots of moving around in the States due to their respective careers, and Rosaria wonders how somebody could be so much in love with someone else to put up with so many disruptions.

She finds she's envious of Tom and Amy Cornwall, despite the trouble Amy is in. Rosaria is sure that however this is resolved, Amy's husband will be right at her side, backing her up no matter what.

To be so fortunate.

She goes back to the paperwork. There's a Jeep Wrangler, also registered in Captain Cornwall's name, that's not in the driveway. She walks up to the garage, peers in.

Empty.

She digs out her Galaxy cell phone, dials the numbers for Captain Cornwall. Home and mobile.

Both go to voice mail, the home voice belonging to her husband, the cell belonging to the captain. Her voice is clear, clean, with a hint of a New England accent.

She backs away from the garage, goes to the front door, rings the doorbell three times, and then hammers on the door with her fist.

"Hello? Anybody home? Hello?"

No answer.

So much for Major Wenner's excuse that she called in sick from home this morning.

She walks around the house. Very nice. In-ground pool out back, barbecue, deck, and lawn chairs. Smooth grass lawn. Wood stockade fence at the far end of the yard. A couple of soccer balls, a tangled mess of a croquet set, and a volleyball and its net dumped in a big plastic bin.

The house looks just as fine from the backyard as the front.

Something cold settles along her hands and feet. There's an ache here, looking at this fine home in a safe neighborhood, the quiet residences marking not only wealth but security. Not the kind of security where you live with bars on the first-floor windows and doors—which she's experienced—but the security of knowing you can sleep without a rat crawling over your bed, that you can wake up with the lights working, and that the refrigerator will never be empty.

And additional security that you don't have to learn and relearn and relearn yet again the name of the foster family that has taken you in that month, supposedly out of the goodness of their hearts, but almost always because of the government stipend they get for keeping you alive and breathing.

"Hello?" a woman's voice calls out. "Hello?"

"Yes, right here," Rosaria answers.

An older woman joins her in the backyard, smiling with guarded friendliness and welcome. She's wearing sensible white slacks, white sneakers, and a floral top that seems to billow around her as she approaches. White-rimmed eyeglasses dangle from a chain around her fleshy neck.

The woman says, "I'm sorry, I'm a neighbor of the Cornwalls. Can I help you?"

Rosaria smiles. "I'm looking for Captain Cornwall."

"Are you a friend?" Her voice is still friendly but there's a hint of suspicion in those syllables, and an old feeling comes to Rosaria. Is this older woman asking the questions because Rosaria is a trespasser, or because Rosaria is Hispanic? Once again, Rosaria has to struggle to keep a smile on her face while enduring the challenges of having the wrong skin color in the wrong neighborhood.

"No, ma'am, I'm in the Army as well."

"Really?" she asks, her voice rising up a notch. "But you're not in uniform."

Rosaria steps forward, quickly shows the neighbor her Army identification, not bothering with the shield, which sometimes intimidates civilians, cops being cops everywhere to some. "Not all of us have to work in uniform."

"Oh, okay then," the older woman says. "My dear husband, he spent decades in the Army…I've never seen a soldier like you."

"Not many have, if they're lucky," Rosaria says. "Do you know where Captain Cornwall might be?"

"Ah, well, I think she's at her base. That's what she told me."

Those few words have snapped Rosaria into full investigative mode. "And when did she tell you that, ma'am?"

"Yesterday evening."

"About what time?"

"Oh…near six p.m., I think."

"And she told you she was going back to work?"

"Yes," the woman says, now opening up freely, and Rosaria gets the feeling this woman is lonely and loves to be the focus of attention. "But it was…odd."

"Odd in what way?"

The woman utters a strained laugh. "It was just odd. She came out carrying a…you know, a big bag. With two handles."

"A duffel bag?"

"That's right," the woman says. "I was asking her questions about the carpet-cleaning firm that came by earlier yesterday, and she seemed to be in quite the hurry. Even apologized for it."

"And she said she was returning to work?"

The woman nodded. "That's right."

Rosaria walks around to the front of the house, seeing the parked CR-V. The woman tags along, like she still wants to be in the spotlight, still wants to be here to answer Rosaria's questions.

Rosaria doesn't disappoint her. "Her husband. Do you know where he is?"

"Well…he should be home. I mean, that's his car. And for the past several months he's been working at home, on a book. Sometimes he flies out on research trips. Amy drives her Jeep. So…he should be home."

Rosaria gives the house a good stare. The quiet and empty windows seem to be mocking her. The woman's voice lowers. "Is…something wrong?"

"They have a daughter. Have you seen her today?"

"No…but she should be at school. I mean…she should."

Rosaria nods. Captain Amy Cornwall is now in some serious trouble. She's not sick. She's not back at Fort Belvoir, despite what she told her neighbor yesterday. Captain Cornwall is gone, with a stuffed duffel bag over her shoulder, leaving in a hurry. And husband and daughter…gone as well. Husband's CR-V is still in the yard, but there are stores and such within easy walking distance.

How would it work?

Captain Cornwall wants to bug out. The Afghanistan investigation…it must mean something much bigger than just a dead Taliban prisoner in her custody. Captain Cornwall makes arrangements, husband and daughter walk off to a nearby restaurant or service station, leaving the CR-V behind, and mom and wife rolls by, picks them up, and off they go.

Very serious indeed.

"Is everything all right?" the neighbor asks. "Is everything okay?"

Rosaria snaps to. "Yes, everything's fine. Just routine."

She digs into her jacket and takes out the leather wallet holding her badge, slips out a business card with her Quantico number and cell phone number, passes it over. The woman holds the card in both hands.

"That's my name and phone number," Rosaria explains. "If you think of anything else about Captain Cornwall, or if she comes back or contacts you, will you call me? Right away?"

"I…I guess so," she says, reluctantly.

"May I ask your name, ma'am?"

"Gaetz. Shirley Gaetz."

Rosaria extends her hand, and the woman takes it with a soft handshake. She says, "Thanks for your co-operation. I greatly appreciate it."

Mrs. Gaetz nods. "Can you tell me what's going on?"

Rosaria smiles. "You have a nice day now."

CHAPTER 17

ROSARIA GETS back into her sedan, reaches out to her team leader in Quantico, and thinks, *Well, that's it*. Captain Cornwall is gone with her family, and if she doesn't report back within thirty days, then she's officially AWOL and will be placed in the NCIC system so that even a random traffic stop anywhere in the States will pick her up.

By then, Captain Cornwall's location and what she may be doing will no longer be any of Rosaria's business, or that of the CID. It's really not broadcast that much, but the Army pretty much ignores deserters. It's a small percentage to begin with, and the Army has better things to do with its CID officers. Rosaria has about a half dozen open case files piled on her desk back at Quantico, and she's happy that she can put Captain Amy Cornwall's file in the inactive pile. She'll let the CID crew in Afghanistan do their part.

Rosaria is content for about a minute, and then she holds the phone tighter to her ear and says, "Sir, I'm sorry? Can you repeat that?"

From Quantico, the rough voice of Senior Warrant Officer Fred McCarthy comes through loud and clear. "You heard me, Vasquez. The Amy Cornwall matter has escalated. You're to find her, as soon as possible. Use any resources and travel as you see fit."

"Boss…I'm sorry, I don't understand. She's not even officially AWOL yet."

Her boss sounds irritated. "No matter. Go after her, right now. Go through her personnel file, see what might be driving her, talk to her coworkers, run her to the ground. This is now your priority."

Rosaria doesn't like for one moment what she's hearing. Something odd is going on with some higher-ups, probably in DC, and chances are, when you're dumped into something odd, you don't emerge later with handshakes all around and a promotion. Usually you get transferred to Omaha, or end up testifying in front of a panel of hard-faced JAG judges.

"All right boss. I'll begin right away."

"Good. Anything else?"

"Sir…do you know why it's been escalated?"

Her boss says, "Vasquez, you're a good investigator, one of our best. Locate her and get back to me soonest."

"Sir, I—"

Senior Warrant Officer McCarthy interrupts. "Figure it out."

McCarthy disconnects the phone call from his end. There was one more sentence Rosaria was sure her boss was going to add, but decided not to.

Figure it out.

Or else.

CHAPTER 18

I'M PARKED across the street from the regional library near Newport, Tennessee, after having driven for most of the night, save for a several-hour nap at a truck stop on I-81 near someplace in Virginia called Max Meadows. Using the atlases and maps stored in my go bag—and without going online or leaving ghostly traces from any GPS unit—I know that it takes around twenty-five hours to go from Alexandria to my final destination of Three Rivers, Texas.

This gives me plenty of time, but I'm not going to race down there at a high rate of balls-to-the-walls speed. I want to arrive in reasonably good shape, and with a hell of a lot more information than I have at the moment. Years back there was a story about a woman astronaut who supposedly made a high-speed run from Houston to Orlando while carrying adult diapers with her, so she wouldn't lose time by taking bathroom breaks on her way to murder a romantic rival, but that's too extreme, even for me.

I check my watch. It's 9:07 a.m. The squat one-story library with the rough stone exterior over there should have opened seven minutes ago, but no one's shown up yet. And it's a Wednesday, so there's no holiday that should be observed.

Extreme, I think. Maybe I should break a window, sneak in, find where their computers are located.

Yeah. Extreme.

I take out a burner phone that I keep powered up in my go bag, look through my contact list on a sheet of paper contained in the leather case, hesitate. The woman I want to call is currently stationed at Fort Lewis, near Tacoma, Washington. I'd probably end up waking her, but still...

I touch the keypad, wait and wait as it rings.

A click.

"Huh?"

"Freddy, it's me, Amy."

"Amy...Jesus Christ, do you know what time it is?"

"I sure do. Hey, how's your eyesight?"

"What?"

"You know. Under four eyes. Glasses. That sort of thing."

She's no longer sleepy. "I get it. Give me about... fifteen minutes."

"You're a dear."

"And you're a nut."

"No argument there."

She disconnects.

A light-red Honda Civic comes into the library lot, moving slowly, very slowly. It parks near a sign that says STAFF ONLY.

An older woman steps out, carefully closes and locks the door. I look around. There are a couple of houses near some tree groves, but that's about it. This is a secondary road, not even near a highway.

The woman moves to the entrance of the library. I put my hand on the door handle of my Wrangler.

She pauses.

Opens her purse.

Roots around inside.

Pulls out a key, goes to the door.

The key apparently doesn't work.

Back into the purse.

"Ma'am," I whisper, "you get that door open or I'm coming right over there with a tire iron to help you out."

I'm not sure if there's a Patron Saint of Librarians, but if there is, he or she has just helped the elderly librarian. The door opens up at the same time mine does.

CHAPTER 19

TEN MINUTES later I'm at a computer terminal, having just smiled at the nice librarian and walked by like I'm a local taxpayer, checking things out. Once more I enter the classified computer system, and after poking around in the Fairfax County Police Department, I quickly confirm what I suspect: the Able Carpet van was stolen yesterday out of a parking lot.

The theft report is a basic document, with no witnesses, no information on who might have stolen it.

A slight chance, but I had to check it out, in case there was some information as to where the two thieves—and eventual kidnappers of my loved ones—had come from, but there's no joy.

I won't waste my time going back there.

I call up a site linked to the FAA, and quickly punch in the tail number for yesterday's Learjet videotape—NS-28312—and wait for its identity to be revealed. This is my best lead, to find out who owns the jet and who's operating it. There aren't that many organizations that can own a $1.5 million aircraft or that can rent one for four or five thousand dollars an hour. And I was guessing that it was the owner or owner's representatives who were flying that jet. An aircraft rental to help along a double kidnapping would raise lots of awkward questions.

And the FAA comes through for me.

But not in the way I want.

NUMBER NOT ASSIGNED.

I try again, a thick feeling in my stomach getting thicker, from this bit of bad news combined with the fast-food breakfast sandwich I ate an hour ago.

I carefully look at my notes, carefully punch in the number, and just as carefully, the answer comes back.

NUMBER NOT ASSIGNED.

Damn it!

I log off, clear the cache, and walk away, staring straight ahead. The nice older woman at the curved library counter looks up at me and says, "Did you find what you were looking for, hon?"

I attempt a smile in her direction. "What a beautiful library you have."

I move my Jeep Wrangler out, find a small strip mall, and park underneath an oak tree to give me shade. What does NUMBER NOT ASSIGNED mean?

It means the Learjet 60, as white as it appeared to me yesterday, is black. It belongs to one of the seventeen official domestic or overseas intelligence agencies that supposedly exist here in the United States—trust me, the number is much higher—or to some off-the-books well-financed group that does freelance work for intelligence groups, so in case something goes sour or appears on the front page of the *Washington Post,* there's the ever plausible deniability for the White House.

Or it might mean that some corporation or billionaire on the boundary between legal and illegal has the money and pull to keep a registration number on that Learjet in the shadows.

However you want to slice it or dice it, my family—my Tom and my Denise!—were dragged into my world yesterday.

Damn it once more.

My burner phone rings, and I'm happy it doesn't make me jump. It means I'm still focused on the job at hand.

"Amy," I answer.

"It's Freddy," she says. Most people in the Army know her as Major Fredericka West, but one drunken night—after we both successfully passed the grueling hell-on-jungle that is Ranger training—she told me her real family name was von Westphal, and her great-grandfather had been a prominent general in World War II, fighting on the wrong side.

At some roadhouse in Georgia, both of us in muddy fatigues, hair cut crewcut short to keep it clean, she muttered, "He was a good general, but he stuck around too long. Then he joined the other generals to blow up the little crazy Nazi bastard, and he ended up getting garroted by piano wire for his troubles."

Now she says, "Under four eyes, huh?"

"The most four eyes you've ever seen."

Over the years Freddy has researched and admired her great-grandfather's military skills—even if they were used in the service of evil—and one German phrase she taught me was *unter vier Augen,* meaning to talk to someone under four eyes, meaning in strictest privacy.

"What's up?"

"Two questions, one easier than the other."

"Which one's easier?"

I say, "You'll have to decide."

A dry laugh. "Okay. Go."

"There's an airplane registration number that doesn't appear in the public records. It's been scrubbed. I need to know who owns the aircraft."

"You can't find it through your usual channels?"

"Freddy, I'm calling you at home early in the

morning using a burner phone. Does that tell you I'm doing anything usual?"

She yawns. "Good point. What's the tail number?"

I read off the letters and numbers to her, and she reads them back to me.

"All right," Freddy says. "Question one. What's number two?"

"I need to know what installations we might have in a small town in Texas called Three Rivers."

"How small?"

"Last I checked, less than two thousand people."

Freddy whistles. "Pretty hard to hide a base or depot there."

"That's not what I'm looking for," I say. "I'm looking for a safe house, a bunker, a dry-cleaning business that might be a front for something."

"A black site?"

"Yes."

"You know those are illegal, even in countries that used to welcome them. Like Poland or Estonia."

"Sure, that's what we're officially told, but this is still very unofficial," I say. "I need a deep and thorough search. Property ownership that doesn't make sense. Utility bills paid by a law firm in Maryland. Parking tickets for vehicles belonging to the Agriculture Department's regional office in Boise. Anything that gives a hint of a place that might be used to hide a high-value target."

Freddy says slowly, "That's a pretty big shopping list, Amy."

"Yeah, well, I remember a pretty big whining session a few years back from someone who was going to give it up and go find a Motel 6 to take a hot shower."

"Jesus, Amy, how many times do you want me to pay you back for that?"

I bite my lip. Damn it, why are my eyes welling up?

"Last time, I promise," and my voice shudders, and Freddy, a major and executive officer for the Second Ranger Battalion, 75th Ranger Regiment, picks up on it instantly.

"Amy," she says sharply.

"Yes."

"What's going on?"

I keep quiet.

Freddy says, "Amy…is this professional? Or personal?"

I talk through the tears. "As personal as it gets."

CHAPTER 20

IN THE plain but comfortable office at Fort Belvoir with a sign on the door that says LT. COL. DENTON COMMANDING/297TH MILITARY INTELLIGENCE BATTALION, he sits at the wide and clean desk, slowly rubbing his hands against the polished surface, knowing that if a subordinate were to walk in, right at this moment, he or she would give him an odd look, but he doesn't care.

A clean desk to call your own is one of the perks of getting this high up the ladder, this high up the pecking order, that slippery pyramid of command and responsibility.

Oh, yes, responsibility indeed.

Lots of burdens of command, both professional and personal, and while the professional burdens are widely known, evaluated, discussed, and probed, the personal are never examined. It is like a big crack in a home's foundation that is never talked about, for fear it will bring something rotten into the open. Like the dreams, the memories of sharp explosions, the taste of someone else's blood on your lips, and the trembling that sometimes happens so fast and so hard you retreat to the nearest latrine so no one can see you.

Best to ignore it, and hope no one else sees it.

Transferring this unit from Fort Gordon three years back was a logistical and personnel nightmare, but one does what one has to do, especially when the dim higher-ups dragged them here from Georgia to make some assistant secretary of defense or congressman happy.

So he did what had to be done. Which is always a good way to manage one's life in the Army.

The phone in the plain and powerful office rings.

He picks up the receiver.

"Yes?"

"What's going on? It looks like it's falling apart."

He knows his caller is thousands of miles away, and he's amazed once again at how clear and crisp the voice is.

"It is falling apart," he replies.

"What are you doing about it?"

He says, "I'm fixing it."

"You better."

The caller hangs up.

No matter.

He moves his hands across the desk again.

So smooth and powerful.

CHAPTER 21

CAPTAIN ROSARIA Vasquez is sitting in her government-issued GMC sedan, balancing a cup of Cumberland Farms coffee in one hand while flipping through the service file of Captain Amy Cornwall, reading and reflecting, looking for those little bits of information that will stand out, make her take notice, that little thread she hopes she can pull that will lead to a string out there somewhere, and not just a bit of nothing.

But so far, nothing is what she's finding.

Born in Maine, joined the Army after high school, finished college in Maine, had a variety of schools and assignments, assigned to an infantry unit, one tour in Iraq, went through the sixty-two-day Ranger school—one of only a few women who managed to pass—and then ended up in military intelligence.

Two tours in Afghanistan—including the last one that resulted in the death of a Taliban prisoner—but otherwise reasonably routine.

Rosaria goes through the file, again and again.

Different schools—one thing about the Army is that if you want to learn, they are ready to offer it to you, one of the reasons she loves her service so—and it all seems routine. Scratch that, Captain Cornwall is a fine officer, with a bright future ahead of her.

So why did she bail out with her husband and kid?

Over the Afghanistan investigation?

Doesn't make sense.

Nothing she saw of Cornwall in this folder stands out, all her time is accounted for—the different dates, the different schools and assignments. Everything—

Hold on.

She flips through the pages again.

Odd.

Just before her last deployment to Afghanistan, she went on an exchange mission, to Fort Campbell in Kentucky, one of the largest Army bases in CONUS—continental United States.

What kind of mission?

Hard to tell.

Lots of abbreviations and acronyms.

It looks like it was a unit assigned to work with an Air National Guard section that had deployed from Nellis Air Force Base in Nevada.

What was Captain Cornwall doing in Kentucky?

And the biggest question…she was assigned there for six months.

Left after four.

Ahead of schedule.

But why?

She smiles when she sees a familiar name attached to another form.

CAPT. A. MITCHUM.

She closes the folder.

That's what civvies never, ever understand about military service. You can have friends across the world at various stations and bases, like an archipelago of relationships and friendships. It is odd to be transferred somewhere without having an acquaintance there to welcome you. In a usual time and place, to talk to Captain Aaron Mitchum would take phone calls, emails, appointments, and official paperwork.

But this isn't a usual time.

She checks her watch, takes out her Galaxy phone, starts flipping through various map and travel apps, sees it would take about twelve hours to drive to Fort Campbell in Kentucky. Too long.

Then air travel it will be, using her government-issued Visa credit card, although the travel vouchers and paperwork will eventually be a pain in the ass before she got reimbursed. But to get from Ronald Reagan National Airport to Nashville…about two hours. Add three hours for additional travel to and from the airports.

Yeah.

She looks again at the smeared photocopy and the name Mitchum. Two years ago they dated briefly while they were both taking a course on logistics, and there was one thing that bonded them, even though he was as white as Wonder bread and straight as a ruler.

Both were orphans who had found a family in the Army, and who would do anything to protect their family.

CHAPTER 22

I'M NOW driving on Interstate 75, heading southwest through Tennessee, about an hour south of Knoxville. The highway is two lanes west and two lanes east, with a wide, grassy median in between and lots of open farmland and wooded hills in the distance. Kentucky is north of me and I'm trying not to think about the last disastrous time I was in the Bluegrass State.

Instead, I'm driving fast and sweet, keeping my speed about five miles above the speed limit, waiting for my burner phone to ring from Washington State and my old friend Freddy. I try not to be impatient. I try not to think of bad things—Freddy having second thoughts, Freddy being in a car accident, Freddy having a sudden aneurysm and keeling over just as she gets the information I need—and keep on driving.

I also try very, very hard not to think of anything bad that might be going on with my beloveds, my Tom, my Denise. A cold, hard kernel inside of me demands attention, demands me to acknowledge that in most kidnappings, the victim or victims are dead after the initial demand, but I'm trying hard to convince myself that it won't happen here, because my mysterious caller wants to make an exchange, and he knows that I will demand to see Tom and Denise in good shape before presenting him with…with whoever the hell he wants.

That mystery man in remote Texas.

Another bad thought pops into my mind, and I check the burner phone.

Okay.

It's still on.

I had a bad feeling I had accidentally switched it off or the battery was dead, but no, it's fine. It's operating. It's keeping my presence in the telecommunications world unknown at the present time.

I pass a Walmart truck, think of where the other burner phone has ended up. No matter. And still, I know I'm violating lots of tradecraft by taking this major highway to my destination in Texas. Here I'm vulnerable, I can be tracked—hell, maybe I'm being tracked at this very moment via drones, surveillance cameras, passing vans and trucks that secretly belong to the DoD and are part of the grand, unknown domestic surveillance system.

It's a trade-off. To keep from view and surveillance, I should be taking secondary roads and state roads all the way to Texas, avoid being out in the open on the interstate.

But that would triple my travel time, and that's what I don't have.

Time.

My burner phone rings. I switch on the directional and slowly pull over to the side of the road, and then go into the grassy area running parallel to the pavement. No use being parked close to the side of the highway and having some distracted trucker pancake me and my Jeep into steel, blood, and rubber. There's a thick grove of trees off to the right.

"Cornwall," I say.

"Amy…ah crap, hold on for a minute, will you?"

It's Freddy and I'm eager to learn what she's discovered—if anything—and what I'll do about it.

A voice from past training comes to me: *Intelligence is intelligence.* It's neither good nor bad. It's information to be used. That is all. Stop trying to weld feelings on something that is inherently neutral.

Intelligence.

I take a breath. All right, then.

"Amy," comes Freddy's voice. "Another minute."

"Sure."

I need something to distract me from the roaring traffic going by me and the view of the nearby woods and wide fields. My iPhone is in my hand now. I flick through various prompts and screens, and come to a favorite: Last summer on Virginia Beach. Tom in his black swimming trunks, strongly striding his way back in from the water, standing in front of me, his body an okay body—he can't get rid of those soft handles around those hips—but it's his damn smile and eyes that still warm me and tug at me.

The sound's off so I can't hear the sound of the waves or any other ambient noise, but that's just fine. In the corner of the screen is Denise in a bright-orange swimsuit—she had asked me earlier, "Why such a bright suit, Mom?" and I never told her the truth, *So I can always see you, no matter how far you go*   digging at something with a yellow plastic shovel.

Then she dumps out the wet sand in her pail, scoops up a couple of quarts of cold Atlantic water, and starts racing toward her father. She's giggling and the water is spilling out of the bucket, and something in my voice or attitude must have betrayed me, because Tom looks and sees her approaching, and he stands still.

He doesn't tell her to stop.

He doesn't try to run away.

He doesn't try to spoil her fun.

Tom stands there and takes it, and grimaces as the cold water strikes his lower back, and Denise nearly collapses she's laughing so hard.

My Tom, my little girl.

CHAPTER 23

THE VOICE of my friend jolts me back to my grim reality.

"Amy?"

"Still here," I say.

"First things first," she says. "If there's a black site in Three Rivers, Texas, it doesn't belong to Uncle Sam or anyone connected to Uncle Sam, including any third-party contractors doing dirty work."

I'm about to ask if she's sure, and bite my lip. I don't want to insult Freddy. She's with the Second Battalion, 75th Rangers, some of the best Special Forces soldiers in the world, and highly connected to the intelligence community.

"That's interesting," I say.

"You want to tell me why you want to know this?"

"No," I say.

"Okay. Now. The second request you gave me is where it goes a bit off the rails."

"Why's that?"

Freddy says, "The airplane registration number you sent me. Any chance it's wrong?"

"Not a chance."

"You sure?"

"Freddy..."

"All right," she says briskly. "I needed to check. Amy, on the surface, the aircraft is leased to a condominium developer in the Cayman Islands. Bright Sun Lives Limited. But that's just the surface."

"What's in the mud and muck, then?"

"Your Learjet belongs to First Republic Global Bank, NA, based in Guadalajara, and with branches and sub-branches all over the world."

Tom likes to tease me that my memory is like a computer chip, but it's really like an old-fashioned card catalog dumped on the floor, with lots of bits and pieces of information lying around.

"I know that name."

"You should," Freddy says. "Back in the eighties, there was a bank called BCCI, up to its neck in laundering money for terrorists and narco-terrorist gangs. This First Republic Global is its bastard offspring."

"Shit," I say.

There's a pause in the conversation, and Freddy says, "You're not doing anything with money launderers, are you?"

I look at the frozen picture on my iPhone of my Denise and my Tom. My husband, my man. My girl, my princess.

"No, I'm not," I say.

"Amy…"

I keep quiet.

"You okay?"

"Not really," I say.

"You need anything else?" she asks.

"You told me this was going to be the last favor you'll ever do me."

"When are you going to stop believing me?" Freddy says. "And…well, I've always wanted to tell you this. What happened at Fort Campbell wasn't your fault."

"It didn't happen at Fort Campbell," I say. "It happened a half a world away."

"And the other things," Freddy goes on. "I know what horrible shit you have to see, day after day. Even most in the military don't know that—they think all you do is file paper. But I know better, know how it haunts you. You should talk to someone, Amy."

I sit up straighter in my Jeep Wrangler, get ready to return to my quest.

"I'm talking to you, aren't I?" I ask.

Freddy sighs. "This information…I hope it turns out to be useful."

"You have no idea."

"You'll let me know?"

"Sure," I say. "At our mutual retirement ceremonies, if we live that long."

She laughs. "Okay…you know what you're fighting for, right?"

I look at the freeze-frame of my Tom and my Denise, on Virginia Beach.

"I sure as hell do," I say.

She hangs up and so do I, and I'm about to return to traffic when I look in the rearview mirror and see the flashing blue lights of a Tennessee Highway Patrol cruiser pulling up behind me.

CHAPTER 24

LESS THAN a year ago an orphaned Hamid Aziz left his nearly destroyed village in Afghanistan to fight for his tribe, for his leader, for his God, and to send money home to his remaining family, and he left with dreams of being a powerful lion, a man who would be feared in the West, and what is he now?

A waiter for a soft American and his little brat.

Hamid is at the door leading into the cell that holds the two Americans, carrying a metal food tray, with two dishes that are covered by round white plastic tops. Another man is with him, named Tonton, and Tonton is the muscle, wearing a short-sleeved white shirt and tight blue jeans, with a pistol hanging off a shoulder holster about his wide arms. He wears sunglasses all the time, and has a thin strip of a beard that crosses his bulky chin.

From his pants pocket Tonton pulls out a simple key, and inserts it into the lock—Hamid senses something is off. There are muffled, loud voices coming from inside the room, but if Tonton is nervous, he doesn't show it. He unlocks the door, keeps a good hold on the handle. As he opens the door, the yelling gets louder.

The father is yelling at his daughter, and the daughter's stamping her feet, screaming at the father, and Hamid thinks nothing like this would be allowed in his village, and Tonton yells, "Hey! Shut up!"

The girl is still screaming and turns and says, "I want my mommy!" and she starts running to the door.

Hamid juggles the tray—the chef, a bulky Mexican man with a thick scar on his face and one eye missing, always says, *If you drop it, I'll cut you*—and tries to block the little girl from running, and Tonton moves by, bumping Hamid so he's practically dancing in place, trying not to drop the two meals.

The girl manages to push by, and Tonton grabs her hair, twists it, and she screams louder and higher. The father finally does what a father should do—protect his daughter—and he comes at them both. Tonton's pistol is in his hand, and he shouts at the father to step back, and the father yells and holds up his hands, and the little girl is grabbing onto the open door frame with both hands.

Hamid gets into the room, puts the tray down, and he and Tonton give the girl's legs a good pull, and she lets go of the door frame. Hamid drops her on the other bed, crying now, no longer screaming.

Tonton still has his pistol out. Hamid backs away, wishes he had a weapon as well, and is glad that no one from his village is here to see this humiliation.

Tonton says, "Stay still until I close the door. No more moves. Or I will tell Mister Pelayo."

Hamid steps out first and Tonton follows, slamming the door shut. Tonton replaces the pistol in his holster and says something in his poor English to Hamid, and then laughs.

He has no idea what the other man is laughing about, but Hamid decides to play it safe and laughs as well.

CHAPTER 25

TOM CORNWALL waits a few minutes, standing still, just in case the two men come back in.

They don't.

The older one, who had the gun and spoke to them, seems Hispanic. The other one, younger, thinner, and with a thick, long beard, isn't Hispanic. Middle Eastern, Asian, Tom's not sure.

But they both worked fast to prevent Denise from escaping, and Tom begins to calm down some when it appears that his girl isn't hurt.

He sits down and she rolls over, eyes still moist from the screaming and crying, but with a sly smile on her face.

"I did good, Dad, didn't I?"

"The very best."

"Do you think they noticed?"

"No," Tom says. "The bigger guy was too busy keeping you from running out, and that other guy, he was too busy trying not to drop the tray."

She sits up and wipes her eyes with the hem of her T-shirt, and says, "Dad...I really, really hate chewing gum."

"I know. But you did good."

Tom gets up and says, "Stay on the bed, all right?" and Denise being Denise, she ignores him and follows him over to the door.

He presses his ear against the metal.

Nothing.

Just the slow hum of machinery being used somewhere, deep in this building.

And where is this building? he thinks, as he draws his head back and goes to the other side of the door, repeats the process.

Someplace tropical, he thinks. Maybe an island in the Caribbean, or off the coast of Mexico. The weather seems warm enough, and he's noted fine beach sand has trickled into their little cell.

More humming of machinery.

He's certain they're in this building's basement, based on what he's seen those few times when the door has been open. There are pallets of plastic-wrapped boxes and piles of lumber and pipes, and wires and conduits up above in the open ceiling.

Denise is next to him. "Daddy...did it work? Did I do good?"

"Hold on."

Tom leans against the door one more time, not listening this time, but thinking.

Was this the time? Should he wait?

Waiting awhile longer had its advantages, as the day went on, but still...

Pelayo could come by at any time.

Whatever negotiations were happening out there could have gone wrong.

That armed guy with the thin strip of beard could come back in, and with two quick shots, end it all, and his and Denise's bodies could be rolled up in the blankets and sheets and taken away.

No.

This was the time.

"Stand back," he says, and this time, Denise pays

attention. She steps back and Tom utters a quick and silent prayer, and pushes on the door.

Nothing moves.

He digs in with his bare feet and pushes again, and maybe it's his imagination, but he feels something deep in the door vibrate, or shake, or move, and then the door pops open.

Tom curses and grabs the door edge, so it doesn't fly all the way open. Denise squeals in excitement, and he turns and whispers, "Shhh," but her eyes are wide with joy.

"I did it, didn't I, Daddy?" she whispers. "I did a good job."

Tom glances down at the lock recess, which a few minutes ago Denise had plugged with a wad of chewing gum. In the excitement and in their eagerness to leave them alone, the two men had shoved the door closed.

But the door didn't lock.

Tom hugs his smart and tough little girl.

"You did a very good job," he says.

He opens the door and peers out.

Nobody.

Just a wide basement and piles of boxes and construction equipment.

He reaches down and takes her soft hand.

"Let's get out of here," Tom says.

CHAPTER 26

FORT CAMPBELL is one of the largest Army bases in CONUS and Rosaria Vasquez feels like her section at Quantico could be dropped into the surrounding woods and not be missed at all. Here at Fort Campbell are the many elite spears in America's arsenal, including the 101st Airborne, 160th Special Operations Aviation Regiment, 5th Special Forces Group, and 52nd Ordnance Group.

She's with Captain Aaron Mitchum, and she hasn't seen him—either clothed or unclothed—in more than two years. He looks pretty much the same. Light-blond hair, cut high and tight, some freckles on his cheeks and pug nose, and very dark-blue eyes. He's been smiling at her ever since she was ushered into his office, and the smile stays there as he sits down. His desk is cluttered high on both sides with envelopes, forms, and file folders, and the office is cluttered as well, with two sets of filing cabinets, one designed to hold classified information, the bright-red cardboard sign saying OPEN attached to its drawers. Unlike Rosaria, he's wearing ACUs, the camouflage uniform of the day at Fort Campbell.

"Rosaria…boy, you look great," he says. "How long has it been?"

"Two years," she says, smiling as well at the fond memories of sneaking out after school for little get-togethers or trysts at motels in the area.

"You doing well?"

"Good," Rosaria says, "and you and Molly?"

He gestures to a framed photo teetering on the edge of his desk, showing a plump redhead holding an infant in her arms. "She's doing fine, as well as our boy, Paul."

Aaron pulls the framed photo two inches toward him and says quietly, "This isn't a social visit, is it."

"Nope."

"What do you need?"

She goes to the personnel file. "I'm investigating a Captain Amy Cornwall, assigned to the 297th Military Intelligence Battalion. The captain spent four months here at Fort Campbell last summer."

Aaron says, "Lots of folks come through here."

As if it were a sign from above, there's a roaring sound as a number of Black Hawk helicopters fly overhead. The framed photo of Aaron's wife and son vibrates back to the edge of his desk.

Rosaria says, "She was assigned here for six months." She makes a point of looking down at the open file folder. "Something called JOINT CLAW. I can't find anything else about JOINT CLAW, but there's a memo here about her going back to her original duty station two months ahead of schedule. Fort Belvoir. And your name was cc'ed on the memo, in your position here. In the 502nd Military Police Battalion."

Rosaria closes the folder. Aaron sighs, rubs at the top of his head.

"This off-the-record?"

"I'm looking into her," Rosaria says. "I don't care what black stuff she might have been involved in, or what it entails. I want to know why she left two months early. There's no explanation in her personnel file."

"Because she was involved in a foul-up."

"What kind of foul-up? And why was she connected with an Air National Guard unit from Nellis?"

"You know a lot."

"Not enough."

He gets up and says, "Let's go for a walk."

"Sure," she says.

CHAPTER 27

FIFTEEN MINUTES later they approach an isolated cement cube of a building, festooned with satellite dishes and antennas. Rosaria tries not to show it, but she feels overwhelmed at the soldiers and vehicles, armored and flying, that she sees during the brief walk. It's times like these when the tiny discouraging voice inside of her says, *Babe, this is the real Army. You're nothing but a cop in a pretty uniform.*

Aaron says, "Last month I finally got Molly to meet my foster parents, at a family reunion in South Dakota. It went better than I thought."

"Good for you," she says.

"You ever meet up with any of yours?"

"I had six sets of foster parents," she says.

"Is that a no, then?"

"You're pretty smart today, Aaron."

At a plain gray metal door there's a key-card lock. Aaron slides an identification card through the side, and the door clicks open. Inside is a glass-enclosed booth, and both have to show their identification to a female military police staff sergeant dressed in ACUs and wearing a holstered sidearm. There's another loud buzz, and a door to the right is unlocked.

Aaron hesitates. "Remember four years back, that senator from Nevada was complaining about all the drones being controlled in her home state? How the state of Nevada and its citizens were complicit in extrajudicial killings overseas?"

Rosaria says, "Was it in the news?"

"All over the news."

"I try to avoid the news," she says.

Aaron just shakes his head. "Some days, Rosie, you need to look around and not just at your feet."

"Aaron?"

"Yes?" he replies, hand still on the door.

"You called me Rosie two years ago. Don't do it again."

He pauses, and says, "The senator put pressure on the secretary of defense, the DoD put pressure on the Army, and as you know, crap rolls downhill. We couldn't expand our drone ops at Nellis. The honorable senator was making too much fuss. And like the Marines, the Army overcame and adapted. Come on in."

He opens the door and she follows him in, and they're both standing on a narrow but wide terrace with handrailings, looking down at what seems to be a curved auditorium. There are rows of comfortable-looking chairs and overhead video screens, and Rosaria breathes in deeply as she takes it all in.

This is a control center for drone attacks, and in the video feeds coming in, Rosaria knows that she's gaining overhead views of Pakistan, Afghanistan, Iraq, and so many other troubled places.

Aaron whispers, "So here we are."

The rows of chairs are all filled with men and women, wearing headsets, holding joysticks. Some have bottled water at their elbows. A number of signs hang from the padded, dark ceiling. The near one says, YOU CAN RUN, BUT YOU'LL ONLY DIE TIRED.

Rosaria whispers back, "What was Captain Cornwall doing here?"

"One of those touchy-feely programs that some idiot at the Pentagon comes up with when he or she is bored," Aaron quietly explains. "Bringing in intelligence officers in an exchange program so they can see what their work can lead to in the field."

"And Captain Cornwall was here?"

"She was."

"What happened, then? What was the foul-up?"

Aaron seems to grip the railing tighter. "We still off-the-record, Rosaria?"

"At the moment."

He shuffles over like he doesn't want to be overheard by anyone in the pit below. "I didn't see it, but I heard about it later...When the intelligence officers came in, they were paired with an experienced drone driver. Eventually, they would take over the flying if they had the feel for it, which Captain Cornwall did. Then, one day, she and her partner, they were tracking a target in southern Afghanistan."

"What kind of target?"

Aaron lowers his voice even more, so Rosaria has to lean in to make out the words. "A white SUV, on some desert road north of Khost, with six Taliban soldiers inside, supposedly on their way to attack a camp operated by Doctors Without Borders. So it was a high-value, very significant target. Captain Cornwall and her Air National Guard partner were tracking it with a Predator drone. The word came down from above. Smoke it."

Then it came to Rosaria, looking down into this cool, comfortable building, with malls and Burger Kings and Walmarts nearby, that the men and women in here were killing targets thousands of miles away, all the while sitting in a comfortable chair with a cold drink at their side.

"Was it smoked, then?"

"Yes," Aaron says. "But that's not what went wrong. In the last few minutes, her Nellis partner, he was fighting the flu, and he had to leave to hit the latrine, otherwise he would have shit his drawers. That meant Captain Cornwall was in charge. And she followed the orders. She pulled the trigger and destroyed the SUV."

Rosaria says, "A foul-up then, was it?"

Aaron sighs. "Yeah. Bad intelligence. It seems there was a family in that SUV…going to a wedding. And there was some old feud between the father of that family and another tribe, and they used us…used us to do a contract killing. That's what happened."

"Crap," Rosaria says.

"But that wasn't the worst part."

Rosaria says, "There was a worse part?"

Aaron turns, his skin looking pale in the artificial lights. "Oh, yeah. A couple of days later, it came out what really happened. Although there was never an official report, Captain Cornwall lost it, lost it bad."

"How?"

Aaron says softly, "She said, 'Damn you all, I killed an innocent family out there, and now they'll be looking for revenge, and they'll be coming after my family for it.'"

"Crap," Rosaria says again.

"Yes," Aaron says. "And she finished it up by saying, 'And if they come after my family, I'll be coming after all of you.'"

CHAPTER 28

TOM CORNWALL'S heart is pounding harder than it ever has in his life. In those tight times doing stories overseas, with explosions, with the *thud-thud-thud* of automatic rifle fire, and seeing black-clad armed figures come toward him, he has always kept a steady calm, doing his job.

Not today, not here.

His hand is on Denise's shoulder as he peers again through the open door. He squats down and holds her thin shoulders tight. "Now," he whispers. "Listen, and listen to me good, Denise. This isn't a joke. This isn't a game. This is serious. Do you understand?"

She nods her head, biting her lower lip, her eyes red-rimmed. But Denise seems to be listening.

"We're going out now, all right? We're going out together...but if something happens, if the bad men come, you run. All right? Run hard, run fast, and get out of here. Find a grown-up, a woman, and tell her what happened. Tell her to call the police and take you someplace safe."

"Daddy, I'm so scared..." The tears are trickling down her cheeks.

"Me, too," he admits. "But I'm counting on you, honey. You were brave, putting the gum in the lock. But you have to be brave again. And if I tell you to run, run!"

He stands up, takes her hand, and they're out the door.

Tom takes two steps, looks to the left and the right. Where now?

Move, he thinks. *Don't be frozen by indecision.*

Move.

He takes his daughter's hand, starts walking quickly. They're both in bare feet, and if they're someplace warm, he needs to get them both outside. If this is somewhere in the tropics, being outside in bare feet will fit in. But not in a building's basement.

More pallets, more construction equipment. There's a corridor to the right and he takes Denise down the corridor and—

It ends in a jumble of piles of Sheetrock and metal frames.

Damn it!

He backs out and there are voices, and he picks her up and pulls her behind a pallet of shoulder-high cardboard boxes, wrapped in light-green plastic.

"Shhh," Tom says, "stay quiet."

It seems like two men walk by, arguing in a foreign language, and Tom can't believe it, but he recognizes a couple of the words the men are using.

Pashto.

The language of people in Afghanistan and Pakistan.

What the hell?

The voices fade away.

"Come on," he whispers, and he holds her hand, and when Denise shrieks, it hits him like a blow to the back of his head.

CHAPTER 29

GOOD GOD, that shriek…Tom thinks it'll be a miracle if no one within a mile has noticed it.

"Shhh, what's wrong, what's wrong?" he says, and Denise goes, "Ow, ow, ow…I stepped on something!"

She lifts her right leg and there's blood on the bottom of her foot, and he sees a discarded piece of scrap metal his girl has stepped on.

"It hurts, it hurts, it hurts," and he has a flash of memory from two years back, in northern Syria, after a mortar attack, a poor wounded Kurdish fighter saying the same thing, *It hurts, it hurts,* and Tom had the brutal realization back then, *Well, better you than me, pal,* as he ran to a trench for safety.

There is no running here, no safety.

This is his little girl. He can't run away, can't leave her.

"Shhh," he whispers. "Please, be quiet. Let me see."

He gently puts her down, examines her right foot, notes a widening splotch of blood. He presses his handkerchief against it, removes it, tries to wipe away more of the blood, as Denise moans and tightens her tear-filled eyes.

"Daddy…"

"C'mon," he says, "we're still leaving. I'll carry you."

He picks up Denise and she squeezes him tight, burrows her head into his shoulder, and he starts walking fast, knowing it's only up to him now, that if things go bad, he can't rely on Denise running to safety with that cut on her foot.

He has to make it.

He has to.

Tom catches a smell of salt air, maneuvers past piles of long plastic pipe, sees light up ahead.

Move, move, move.

The light is coming from an open roll-up door.

Open to the outside.

His bare feet slap on the concrete as he kicks up his speed. Denise is as light as a feather. He has no real plan, just the base, raw emotion of getting his girl out of here, into the daylight, and finding someplace safe, any place.

"Yes," he whispers, and now they're outside.

A parking lot.

Dump trucks.

Two white vans with tools and construction equipment inside. He quickly thinks of checking to see if the vans have their keys inside, but both vans are occupied, one by a guy drinking a cup of coffee, the other by an older guy checking his cell phone.

He keeps on moving, slowing down. Running attracts attention. Can't do that.

Denise lifts her head. "Daddy?" and her voice is stronger.

"Almost there, hon, almost there."

He gets them out of the parking lot, and now they're in a set of little green parks, walkways, other parking lots. Palm trees. Spiky bushes. Men and women and children walking around, almost all in beach gear. His heart is thumping so hard he's sure that Denise can feel the vibration in her chest.

Where now?

The beachgoers are looking at them with open curiosity, and it's easy to see why, for they're not dressed for rest and relaxation, haven't bathed in a while, and the panic on both of their faces is probably as clear as a siren cutting through the night.

"Almost there," he whispers. "Almost…"

But where the hell is "there"?

There are four- or five-story resort-type buildings, with brass numbers on the doorways, but if they are in some foreign land, can he waste the time to try to talk to whoever's on duty, to find a phone, to find someone in authority?

Now they are on a smooth paved road, curving to the right, that leads to a metal gate and a high stone wall, but the gate is open iron and there is a crowded street out there, with lots of pedestrians and traffic, and yes, that's where they are going. Get lost in the crowd. Find out where the hell they are, find a phone, or a cell phone, or a goddamn telegraph station.

Next to the large gate is a smaller opening allowing pedestrians in and out, and at the gate is a black SUV with dark windows, and the gate starts rattling to the right.

Fine, he thinks, *fine.*

We walk past the SUV, get through the pedestrian gate, and we're out, we're free.

Tom kisses the top of Denise's head.

"Just a few seconds, hon, just a few seconds more."

"Daddy…my foot really, really hurts…"

"I know, I know," he says, and now the weight of his ten-year-old girl has suddenly materialized, and he realizes how damn bone-tired he is, but seeing the open street out there and the lines of people…

Make it, he thinks. *We're going to make it.*

Just a few yards more.

He can hear the people out there talking as they walk by, the rumble of the traffic, a few horns.

Just a couple of yards more.

He squeezes Denise's waist, hunches her up more so her legs are wrapped around his waist, and then —

The rear passenger door to the SUV suddenly opens up.

He dodges to the left, and a man is blocking his way, smiling.

Pelayo Abboud is blocking his way, wearing a light-blue linen suit, crisp white shirt, a wide smile on his face, holding a glass Coca-Cola bottle in his beefy hand, a straw jutting out.

He lifts up the bottle in a salute.

"Are you sure I can't offer you both a drink?" he asks. "You two look very, very thirsty."

CHAPTER 30

TROOPER CLAY Hancock from District Two, Troop C, of the Tennessee Highway Patrol spots a black Jeep Wrangler with Virginia license plates pulled over on the side of southbound I-75 and slows down his white Chevrolet Caprice. He switches on the overhead light bar and pulls in right behind the Wrangler, lifts up his Motorola radio handset, and calls in the traffic stop.

He waits for just a second, to see if anyone's in the area. Nope, the near grassy strip is clear, which means the driver hasn't let a passenger out for an unofficial rest stop. There also doesn't seem to be anyone lurking in a nearby grove of trees. The driver has both hands on the steering wheel and is looking back at him via the Jeep's rearview mirror.

All right, he thinks. *Let's see what's what.*

He picks up his round campaign hat, steps outside, and tugs it on. It looks routine—maybe the driver needed a break, or to check the GPS, or heard something funny from the engine—but Hancock knows no traffic stop is ever routine. Last year he pulled over an RV with Kentucky plates that was weaving back and forth on this same stretch of highway, and the little old lady said she was just tired and needed a cup of coffee.

Maybe she was tired, but a quick search revealed about a hundred pounds of plastic-wrapped weed hidden in the RV's rear storage unit.

He approaches the Wrangler and presses four fingers on the Jeep's rear, leaving his fingerprints behind. If something untoward were to happen in the next few minutes, at least his fellow troopers would have forensic proof that he had stopped this Jeep.

Not being paranoid, he thought. *Just being careful.*

Careful highway patrolmen live to go home at end of shift.

A Tennessee highway patrolman is pulling his cruiser right up behind my Jeep Wrangler, and thoughts and options are rattling through my mind like an avalanche of rocks and stones.

Relax, I think, *just relax.* Keep the hands on the steering wheel. Act calm and courteous. These guys are professionals, and they have a sixth sense if anything appears odd or unusual.

My goal now is to get a ticket for whatever Tennessee state law I may be violating and get going, but above all, don't let him search the Jeep. I'm not sure what the law here is concerning driving with two concealed firearms, but I'm sure it's not a laugh and a lollipop and being sent on one's way.

I lower the window and put my hands back up on my steering wheel.

The highway patrolman comes up and stands at a distance from the door, so I have to crane my neck to look at him. He's a male, early thirties, and his lean face is impassive. He has on dark-green trousers and a light-tan shirt with dark-green pocket flaps. With his round campaign hat firmly on his big head, he looks like he could be an Army drill instructor in his spare time.

"Afternoon, ma'am," he says. "Are you all right? Is there a problem?"

"No, sir, no problem," I say, giving him a sweet smile. "I've been driving for a while and just needed a moment to stretch my legs. Sorry if I shouldn't have parked here."

He peers in, sees my duffel bag in the rear, maps in the seat next to me.

"Are you traveling by yourself, ma'am?"

"Yes, sir, I am."

He steps back, and I think, *All right, that seems to be it,* and then he leans back in.

"Could I see your license and registration, please?"

Hancock sees the woman is in her midthirties, dark hair, tanned skin, and she's smiling and being cooperative, but something just doesn't seem right to him. He can't put his finger on it, but something just seems…off.

He had been ready to send her on her way, but now he wants to dig a bit.

"License and registration?" she repeats. "Certainly. My registration is in my glove box, my license is in my purse."

"Very well, ma'am," he says, stepping back and putting his hand on his holstered .357 Glock Model 31 with fifteen rounds. "Take your time."

Which is a very polite way of saying no fast movements, keep your hands visible, and if this Jeep had been filled with skinny tattooed meth heads, that's exactly what he would have said.

So why is he talking this way to this single woman?

Because his gut tells him to do it.

He keeps a close eye on her hands as she opens a large black leather carrying bag, and she takes out a small purse, snaps it open, and passes over her Virginia driver's license and an Armed Forces identification card.

He puts them aside and watches very, very carefully as she opens the glove box—always being ready in case something comes out besides a slip of paper—and yes, out comes a little green plastic folder, and from that, she pulls out the Jeep's registration.

Now it makes sense, as he examines the two IDs and the registration, all in the name of Amy Cornwall. There have been lots of vehicle stops where Hancock had to wait while the driver dug and dug through a pile of papers, napkins, and ketchup containers, looking for his or her registration, like some impatient and deranged archaeologist.

At least this gal has her act together.

He holds up the paperwork and says, "Just give me a couple of minutes, ma'am, check things out, and then I'll get you on your way."

From my side-view mirror I watch him amble back into his cruiser, and right now, lots of options, plans, and arguments are bouncing around my increasingly overwhelmed mind.

The biggest problem facing me is if I'm listed in the National Crime Information Center system as an Army deserter. That only happens after I've been AWOL for thirty days or more, but with that damn Afghanistan investigation hanging over my head like a hundred-pound sack of cement, that might have changed. I've also blown off a meeting with a CID investigator and pissed off my CO—Lieutenant Colonel Denton—so who knows if I'm in the system or not. Having angered the official Army police and my commanding officer might just have put me in the NCIC system last night.

And if I am…that hunk of a highway patrolman is going to come back and arrest me after he runs my identification.

I will not allow that to happen.

CHAPTER 31

I KEEP on staring back at the man who unwittingly now has my future and that of my kidnapped family in his hands.

All right, I keep thinking, *suppose I'm not in the NCIC system, but he's a suspicious sort, and he may want me to consent to a search of the Jeep. If he does that—and unless I tell him first—he's going to find my Ruger .357 revolver and my 9mm SIG Sauer pistol.*

That will certainly get his attention, and not in a good way.

I keep my hands on the steering wheel.

I didn't have to give him my Armed Forces identification, but I wanted to appeal to his patriotic nature. Sometimes it works, and I've heard stories of off-duty guys and gals using their uniforms and ID to get free upgrades at hotels and airline counters. Considering what we get paid and how we're treated, that's a perk I can't argue with.

But it doesn't look like I'm getting any perks today.

I keep staring at the rearview mirror. It looks like the bulky highway patrolman is talking into a cell phone. Looking for guidance from a supervisor? Did a BOLO come up on me in the NCIC system already?

A cold chunk of lead has just formed in my chest.

I will not be detained today.

I will not be arrested today.

I will not be delayed.

I keep my left hand on the steering wheel and slide my right hand into my open dispatch case, put my hand around the smooth metal of the Ruger revolver.

A hateful decision, but one I've just made.

I don't know this cop, but I do know he won't keep me from my mission.

Hancock is running Amy Cornwall's driver's license through the NCIC system via the cruiser's computer, and she comes up clean. No outstanding warrants or summonses.

Fine.

His personal cell phone rings, and he glances at the number, recognizes his home number.

"Hey, hon," he answers, "what's up?"

His wife, Lucille—whom everyone calls LuLu—says, "God, Clay, I'm sorry to bother you, but the pharmacy just called. The cough syrup for Kimmy's ready to be picked up. You think you can swing by when your shift's over?"

"Sure, Lu, I can do that," he says, keeping an eye on the black Wrangler and the driver.

Something is wrong.

He keeps his eyes on the Jeep and says, "How's her cough?"

"Pretty rough," his wife says. "For a six-year-old, I can't believe how loud she is. Maybe the three of us can get some sleep tonight if that syrup works."

"That'd be great, Lu," he says. "Look, I'm in the middle of something and ⸺"

"I know, I know," she says, laughing. "And tell you what, if our little patient gets to sleep early tonight, I'll give you a nice big reward later on."

He smiles, feels something stir within him.

"Thanks, babe. You're gonna make the rest of my shift fly right by."

His wife whispers, "Be safe, come home, okay?"

"Okay."

He picks up the driver's license, registration, and Armed Forces ID from the seat, and just waits one more second.

What's bothering him?

The Wrangler is parked, the engine is off, the driver is sitting there with both hands up on the steering wheel—

That's it.

She's sitting there, hands up on the steering wheel, like she's guilty of something, like she's done something wrong and she doesn't want to raise any suspicions.

Huh, he thinks, opening the cruiser door. *Sorry, driver, you've just done the opposite.*

Hancock slowly walks to the Wrangler, one hand holding the paperwork, his other on the butt of his pistol, ready to pull it free in a second's notice.

CHAPTER 32

I LOOK again at the highway patrolman coming at me via my Jeep's side-view mirror, and his face is still flat, impassive, and I don't like it. He seems to be trying to look cool and collected, and it's having the opposite effect on me.

My right hand is still curved around the Ruger revolver.

I start to tear up.

This cop doesn't know it, but whatever decision he's going to make in the next sixty seconds or so is going to determine whether he gets shot on the side of this empty Tennessee highway.

Hancock positions himself again safely behind the open window, and passes in the paperwork to the driver, who seems very relieved to get it back, and then he lowers his head and says, "Everything looks fine, miss."

"Thank you, sir."

"You in the Army?"

"I am."

"What's your rank, if you don't mind me asking?"

"Captain."

"Wow, that's impressive," he says, looking again in the rear seat, seeing the stuffed duffel bag, and then back to the passenger's seat, with open maps and atlases on top of the black leather bag.

Where her hand is resting, inside.

All right, then.

He pulls his pistol free but does so quietly and without moving much, so the driver won't notice. "Mind telling me where you're going, ma'am?"

A slight hesitation. "Chattanooga."

"Really? I didn't know there was an Army base in Chattanooga."

"There isn't," she says. "I'm taking a few days' leave, meeting up with an old girlfriend of mine from school. Going to spend a few days relaxing and pampering ourselves at a hotel."

"Uh-huh," he says, the pistol calmly in his hand.

The duffel bag.

He imagines his wife, LuLu, spending a few days with a girlfriend. Would she just dump a bunch of clothes into some ratty duffel bag? Or pack up nice and neat?

Enough.

Hancock steps back, brings up his pistol, and says in a clear and loud voice, "Ma'am, show me your hands. And then exit the vehicle."

No reply.

"Ma'am?"

Then the damnedest thing happens. From the driver's side-view mirror he can make out her face, and she's starting to cry.

"For God's sake," she says, "don't do this."

CHAPTER 33

SPECIAL AGENT Rosaria Vasquez is sitting on a hard plastic chair in the main terminal at Nashville Airport when she makes the call. The terminal is wide and airy, looking like the set of a fifty-year-old science-fiction movie promising a sweet and peaceful future with lots of white plastic and exposed concrete. Surprise of surprises, her call goes right through, and a brisk voice says, "Major Wenner speaking."

"Major, this is Special Agent Vasquez calling. How are you, sir?"

His voice goes down a notch. "All right, I suppose, Agent Vasquez."

"Outstanding, sir," she says. "I'm conducting a bit of a follow-up from yesterday, sir."

"Yes?"

She shifts her weight on the hard plastic. "Well, sir, I'm just checking on something I thought Colonel Denton said yesterday. About Captain Cornwall. If you may recall. Sir."

"And what's that?"

"Well, if I recall correctly," she says, while thinking, *Got you, you squirrelly bastard,* "just before I left yesterday afternoon, your colonel told me that you'd be giving me an update today on Captain Cornwall's health. Am I correct, sir?"

The guy's good, for he quickly says, "Yes, you're absolutely correct, Special Agent, and I'm sorry I've not gotten back to you today. We had a visit from the SecDef to the base this morning, and I've just been buried."

"Sir, do you consider yourself unburied now?"

A cold pause. "I don't think I appreciate that question, Special Agent."

"Sorry, sir, I meant no disrespect." *As if,* she thinks. "Right now I'm in the beginning stages of a very important investigation involving the death of a civilian in Army custody in Afghanistan, under the command of Captain Cornwall. Is she still ill?"

"I...believe so."

"Sir?"

The cold voice changes its tone. "Special Agent, she's not reported to work, and it appears she's not at home."

"Do you know where she is, sir?"

"No, I don't."

Out in the terminal lobby two soldiers in ACUs stride by, coming from one of the four concourses, carrying knapsacks and wearing tan boots, and Rosaria feels a stir, looking at the strong young men. Her brothers. Her family. She doesn't know their names but doesn't have to. They are still family.

"Sir," she says. "Right now, with Captain Cornwall's absence, I don't have much to go on. Can you think of any officer at your base who might be able to give me insight into her and her service in Afghanistan?"

"Well, I, uh, I did serve with the captain for a while in the 'stan."

"Major, no disrespect, but I'm looking for someone of her rank or lower. Sir."

Another pause. "No names readily come to mind."

Rosaria watches the two soldiers walk up to a

group of civilians, who start applauding and cheering as they approach. The civilians are holding balloons and handmade signs with bright markings.

She says, "Major, as previously noted, this investigation is in its preliminary stages here in the states, but I have no doubt how this case goes will get lots of attention, both within the Army and without, as we proceed. Do you understand what I'm saying, sir?"

"I think so," comes the cautious reply.

"So far, the section of my report concerning the co-operation I'm receiving from senior officers is blank. How and when I fill out this section, and what I will say about you and Colonel Denton, well, that remains to be seen."

The major doesn't reply.

The two soldiers are being surrounded by their family members, their loved ones.

Rosaria says, "Are you sure you can't come up with a name?"

"Lieutenant Baker," he says. "Lieutenant Preston Baker. He was with her during her entire deployment in Afghanistan. If you give me your email address, I'll send you his contact information within the hour."

She gives him her email address and says, "Thank you so much, Major, for your cooperation."

He hangs up without another word.

So what? she thinks. She's got another lead.

Rosaria should feel good, should feel triumphant, but she doesn't.

The sight of those two soldiers over there being welcomed back by their families is gnawing at her. Ever since she enlisted in the Army, she has always considered the Army her family, the ones who would back her up, who would befriend her, and who would even love her.

Now those thoughts are like old dust in her mouth.

Over there, in that happy little crowd, that is a true family.

Her Army?

Her phone chimes and she brings up the device. Her boss, Senior Warrant Officer Fred McCarthy, is calling her.

She brings the phone up and checks the departure board. Her flight leaves in under an hour. Time to get through the checkpoints and to her gate.

"Special Agent Vasquez," she says. "What's up, sir?"

"Where are you?"

"At the Nashville Airport."

"What the hell are you doing in Nashville?"

"Looking for Graceland."

"That's in Memphis," he says.

"I was misinformed, boss," she says. "What do you think I'm doing? I'm working on the Amy Cornwall case."

"What's your current plan?"

"Heading back to Reagan National, on the way to return to Fort Belvoir."

"You've got a lead?"

"I do, boss."

"At Fort Belvoir?"

"Yes."

"Too bad," he says. "You're not going back there."

CHAPTER 34

I'M WIRED and ready for whatever comes my way, but I'm also trying not to get sick to my stomach. The polite and impressive-looking state trooper has come back to my parked Wrangler, has passed over my paperwork, engaged in a bit of idle chitchat, and I'm hoping that he's about to send me along. Each minute delayed here means another mile lost in my travel to Texas.

Then the trooper starts asking me questions.

"Mind telling me where you're going, ma'am?"

Excellent question, and recalling a highway sign I had seen ten minutes back, I say, "Chattanooga."

"Really? I didn't know there was an Army base in Chattanooga."

"There isn't," I say, trying to sound calm and relaxed. "I'm taking a few days' leave, meeting up with an old girlfriend of mine from school. Going to spend a few days relaxing and pampering ourselves at a hotel."

"Uh-huh," he says, and I think, *Great, just say so long and we'll both be on our way.*

Then it goes straight to hell.

The trooper steps back, brings up his service pistol from his holster, and says, "Ma'am, show me your hands. And then exit the vehicle."

Ah, shit, I think.

"Ma'am?"

No, no, no, I think, my eyes tearing up again.

"For God's sake," I say, "don't do this."

"What?" the trooper asks. "Hands up. Get out of your vehicle. Now!"

My hand is near the butt of the .357 Ruger. If I bring it up and try to shoot him through the open Jeep window, that'll give him plenty of time to cut me down before I can even pull the trigger.

Which leaves the side of the Jeep. It's a thin-skinned vehicle, and if I bring the Ruger back around my lap and shoot to the side and the rear, then the rounds will go through the thin metal and hit him.

Hit the police officer. A representative of the State of Tennessee, a defender of law and order, and I'm about to put a bullet in him.

My stomach is roiling, my mouth is dry.

I have no choice.

I think one more time.

I reach out and grab what I need.

Trooper Clay Hancock takes one more step back, because this situation is going to the shits real quick now, and then, thankfully and to his surprise, the driver does just what he asked, sticking out both hands through the open window. One hand is holding her driver's license and registration.

All right, he thinks, *progress.*

"Driver, lower your left hand, open your door from the outside. Now."

The woman's left hand moves down, fumbles some with the outside door handle, and she pulls it open.

"Now, slowly step out, and face toward the front of your vehicle."

The door swings open and she steps out, and then steps back, both arms up in the air, and he's confident now that he's onto something, because she's lifted her arms without being ordered to do so.

Which means she's hiding something.

"Driver, slowly step—"

She starts coming back and then her driver's license and registration drop from her right hand, and she says, "Oh, let me get that."

The driver bends down to pick up the two slips of identification, and then—

It happens in so few seconds.

The woman is on her hands, and then she lifts up both legs, and propels herself back with her arms, and her legs open up in a V shape, and Hancock tries to step back, lifts up his pistol, but the woman is too damn fast!

Her strong legs wrap around his own lower legs, she twists her legs and he falls, hitting his head on the pavement, and his pistol is out of his hand, and he's trying to fight back, but the woman tugs at his utility belt and he yelps as he's struck in his eyes with his own pepper spray.

CHAPTER 35

IN AFGHANISTAN, I learned how to take down a gunman or a disguised cop at a government checkpoint, to ensure my not getting kidnapped by the Taliban, and I'm stunned that it actually works. The trooper falls heavy on his head and side, I grab his pistol and toss it into the grass, and I find his pepper spray canister and give him a good jolt in his eyes. He cries out and I move as quickly as I can because all I need now is a Tennessee driver who's an NRA member slowing down and seeing me handcuffing this trooper.

The highway is clear.

I handcuff him, haul him up, and he's talking to me, and I'm ignoring his words and pleas, and I manage to shove him into the rear seat of his cruiser. I slam the door and go to the driver's seat. Luckily the engine is still running and the trooper is still trying to talk to me, and I'm ignoring him.

Where to?

There.

That grove of trees.

I glance up at the side-view mirror.

White van coming right down at us.

I duck down.

Wait.

Wait.

I say, "Just be quiet back there, all right? I'm not going to hurt you…I need…I just need time."

I hear the van roar by, feel the cruiser shake a bit from its passing, and when I think enough seconds have passed, I sit up, check the mirror one more time.

Clear.

I shift the cruiser into drive, swing the steering wheel, and we go down the uneven, grassy ground, until I find a place to pull in among the trees. The right side of the cruiser gets scraped by a pine trunk and I say, "Sorry about that."

I lower the windows some, switch off the engine. I take the keys. I go around and open the rear door, and the guy tries to kick me.

I dodge it easily and pat his lower shins.

"Trooper, I'm sorry...you have no idea how sorry I am. I'll call the state police in a while, let them know where they can find you."

His eyes are swollen, red, and weepy. "You... you're going to jail for this, bitch, I can guarantee it. I will hurt you. No matter how long it takes."

I recall that rear police doors can't be opened from the inside. With him being handcuffed, it's going to take a lot of time and effort for him to break free.

"You're going to hurt me?" I ask. "Take a number."

I slam the rear door shut and start running back up to the highway.

CHAPTER 36

HANCOCK SWEARS and tries to hammer at the door with his booted feet. No joy. Damn it all to hell! He knew something odd was going on with this Army woman, and now, here he is, humiliated, eyes hurting like hell, handcuffed in the rear of his own cruiser. He has no doubt that once he gets free, his brothers and sisters in law enforcement will do their best to track down this crazy bitch, but still...

Besides coming home safe, cops also have another steadfast rule.

Don't screw up in public.

Being disarmed, pepper-sprayed with his own canister, and then cuffed and tossed into the rear of your cruiser, like some damn sack of potatoes...after a dignified amount of time, his fellow troopers in his section are going to tease him without mercy in the years to come, unless he busts a couple of heads along the way and threatens his job.

He might even have to put in for a transfer, or go find another law enforcement job somewhere, try to start new and live this down.

A ringing noise interrupts his fast-moving thoughts, and he realizes it's his cell phone, and he can't get to it, and crap, maybe it's Lu calling, to check in on him, to remind him to pick up that prescription.

Damn. Screwing up on the job and in his personal life. What a day this has turned out to be.

He shimmies forward, and then lifts both feet and slams them against the rear door window. The glass trembles and his feet bounce right back.

What did that Army captain say? Something about needing time.

He tries again with his feet.

The window stays in place.

Hancock thinks that the Cornwall woman could be looking for enough time to save the planet, and he rightly doesn't give a crap.

When he gets free, there's going to be a law enforcement pursuit that will make that Army captain regret ever going after Clay Hancock, by God.

He tries again with his feet.

I'm going up near my Wrangler and a red Ford pickup truck is slowing down, like it wants to check me out or maybe offer some help, and I make an exaggerated motion at the front of my slacks, to look like I am zipping things up after taking a bathroom break.

The truck speeds up, there's a honk and some shouts from the two guys inside, and instead of doing what I want to do—give them a one-finger salute   I give them a big smile and wave and get back into my Jeep, after having picked up my license and registration from the ground.

Inside the Jeep I should gently place the .357 Ruger back into my leather carrying case, get out into traffic, and resume my mission to Three Rivers, Texas, and fast.

I should.

Instead I just bow my head against the steering wheel, shudder, and start sobbing.

I take a deep breath.

It's a hell of a thing, coming that close to shooting an innocent state trooper.

A hell of a thing.

Then I start up my Jeep and get the hell out of there.

CHAPTER 37

TOM CORNWALL is exhausted and discouraged, sitting on the end of the bunk bed, back in his cubical prison. His right arm is stretched out, gently holding Denise's hand. She's wide-eyed but keeping calm, sitting up against a pile of pillows. A dark-skinned woman wearing a black scarf around her head is smiling and whispering at Denise as she works on her cut foot.

"There's a good girl…"

"Be brave now…"

"Just a bit more…"

Denise's right leg and foot are extended into the woman's skirted lap, and there's an open leather case on the other bed. The woman doctor has gently washed and wiped Denise's foot, and now she tapes on a small bandage.

"There you go, princess," she says in a soft, accented voice. "The wound isn't that bad. It just looked bad, lots of blood. Try to stay off it as much as you can during the next few days. All right?"

Denise nods.

"Does it feel better now?"

"Uh-huh."

"Good girl."

The woman gathers up her medical gear and supplies, zips the case shut, and then stands up. She says a phrase in Pashto that Tom recognizes—"Good-bye, little girl"—and turns to leave.

Tom catches her eye. He hopes there's sympathy, or worry, or friendship in that doctor's face, but no.

There's just contempt.

That's all.

Tom knows why. It's the contempt of a woman seeing a man who can't take care of his little girl.

The doctor leaves and Pelayo Abboud steps in, with two other men, one older, one younger. The two men who had earlier dropped off their breakfast.

Tom squeezes Denise's hand.

Pelayo steps forward with Tonton and the young Afghan man, named Hamid. That's right. The American writer is tired, his face is sagging, and Pelayo knows he's been broken. To be within a few meters of freedom and escape, carrying his little girl in his arms, his writer's mind already composing the successful end of their escape…and Pelayo stepped in, destroying the story, destroying his hopes.

Tom Cornwall says, "Yes?"

Pelayo gently sits down on the opposite bunk, holding a crisp small brown paper bag in his hand. He says, "I'm sorry, perhaps I didn't make myself clear the last time we spoke. I'm in the middle of a delicate negotiation involving very high stakes, and your wife is a vital part of that dealing, which includes you and your daughter. You did understand that, did you not?"

A heavy breath. "I did."

"I also told you that having you here is a…guarantee of this transaction successfully taking place. I also told you that if my cousin Miguel were here…the situation wouldn't be so civilized. Even though he pretends to be a religious man."

"Look, I did what any dad would do, I was scared—"

Pelayo opens the top of the paper bag. "I also offered you some additional refreshments. One of the items you requested was chewing gum. It was a moistened piece of chewing gum, placed in that door behind me, that allowed you and your lovely little girl to escape. Correct?"

Tom just nods.

"So my gracious response to your request was a betrayal, then, wasn't it? A piece of gum that I thought would go to you and your daughter, to perhaps provide a means of relaxation and calm, was used to help your escape."

Tom's voice is quiet and dull. "I understand what you say, but what kind of father would just sit here without trying to escape?"

Pelayo reaches into the paper bag, takes something out. "The kind of father who would be smart would sit tight, wouldn't do anything to put himself or his daughter into jeopardy. That kind of father…and, Mister Cornwall, in the meanwhile, you've also embarrassed me in front of my staff. I can't let that stand, now, can I?"

Tom stares hard at the small metal object in Pelayo's right hand. He whispers, "No."

Pelayo says, "Oh, I'm so sorry. 'No' is not an option today."

CHAPTER 38

AT THE Nashville Airport, Special Agent Rosaria Vasquez says, "Boss, what do you mean, I'm not going back to Fort Belvoir?"

"I need a fire to be put out," Senior Warrant Officer Fred McCarthy says. "A fire that you caused earlier today. Did you tell me you were going to Fort Campbell?"

"No, I didn't," she says.

"Why?"

"I was conducting my investigation, sir—you know how it is. You've never asked me before to be briefed on what I do, hour by hour, even day by day."

"Well, now I've changed my mind."

"Sir?"

Before her the two happy soldiers are being escorted out of the terminal by members of their family, their *real* family, not a fake one.

He says, "Did you check in with anyone at the 502nd MP Battalion?"

"I did not," she says.

"Even though they're the CID group responsible for Fort Campbell and its personnel?"

She says, "I wasn't investigating their personnel. I was investigating Captain Cornwall and her temporary assignment there."

"Well, that's still a problem," he says. "Lieutenant Colonel Macrae, he runs the 502nd and he's one pissed-off CO. Military courtesy and all that. He's raising a fuss and he's getting some attention, attention we don't need, and I don't need. So you need to get back to Fort Campbell and make nice with him. Apologize. Now."

Rosaria says, "But that's more than an hour's drive away. I'll miss my flight."

"Then you should get started, and get that job done."

"But…don't you want to know what I've found out so far?"

"Special Agent, is your investigation complete? Do you know where Captain Amy Cornwall is at this moment?"

"No, I don't."

"Then I don't have to know a thing."

"Boss…" That old feeling of being kept in the dark, of being helpless and confused. *Rosaria, pack your bags, you're going back to Child Services. Rosaria, stay home tonight, we're taking our children out for our wedding anniversary. Rosaria, sorry, that's the way it is, you're going to another family, and we're sorry you'll miss your friends at school.*

"Yes? Make it snappy."

"What's going on? Who's gotten to you?"

"Special Agent, get ahold of Colonel Macrae and make nice."

He disconnects the call.

Rosaria sits there, feeling light-headed, wondering what is going on with this Cornwall investigation.

There's a *bing* coming from her phone, telling her she's just received an email.

It's from Major Wenner, at Fort Belvoir, giving her the contact information for Lieutenant Preston Baker, the officer who was with Captain Amy Cornwall during her last tour of Afghanistan.

She saves the information, toggles through her phone, fingers angrily sweeping across the screen and typing in names, until she finds what she's looking for.

The phone number for Lieutenant Colonel Angus Macrae, commanding officer for the 502nd MP Battalion at Fort Campbell.

She waits.

Hesitates.

Then punches in the numbers.

Gets the secretary for Lieutenant Colonel Macrae, and then gets Macrae's executive officer, Major Brian Coyne.

"Major Coyne? This is Special Agent Rosaria Vasquez, of the 701st Military Group at Marine Corps Base, Quantico."

"Yes?"

"Is Lieutenant Colonel Macrae available?"

"For what reason?"

She thinks, *To have me bow and scrape before him, and make him feel all right.*

"I believe the colonel knows why," Rosaria says.

"Well, he's in a conference right now. And I can't see him being available at all today. Tomorrow at eleven a.m. would be the soonest I could squeeze you in…if you could tell me what this is all about."

"At the moment, I'm afraid I can't," Rosaria says. "But may I leave a message with you, sir?"

A slight grunt. "All right. Go ahead."

"Tell him I'm sorry."

"What?"

Rosaria says, "Tell him I'm sorry. No, tell him this: I'm really, really sorry."

"Vasquez, is this some sort of joke?"

"No, sir, it isn't. Will you deliver the message?"

"I will, but I don't—"

"Thank you, Major, you have a good day now."

Rosaria disconnects the call, checks the time.

If she hustles, she can make her flight back to Reagan National, and within a few hours, find out what Lieutenant Preston Baker knows about the missing Captain Amy Cornwall.

Rosaria gets up, starts briskly walking to the TSA checkpoint, glances over at the other side of the terminal, sees that the two soldiers and their happy families are gone.

CHAPTER 39

THE LITTLE metal object in his right hand is light but so devilishly simple and effective. Pelayo says, "Before, you thought you had a choice. Staying here or trying to leave. You chose wrong. Now you have a second choice before you."

Tom says, "Please..."

Pelayo gestures to Hamid. "This young man is from a battered and poor province in Afghanistan. I know you're aware of Afghanistan and its history of clans, tribes, and warfare. Hamid is orphaned. His family and village have been nearly destroyed. He's here, working for me, and barely speaks English. Correct, Hamid?"

The young Pashto male—hearing his name—smiles nervously and nods his head. Pelayo says, "Now. What would you think would happen if I were to leave him alone in this room with your daughter, and before I closed the door, I told him your family had his family incinerated last year?"

Tom feels like the concrete cube has closed about him, squeezing his shoulders and torso. No escape. He tries not to stare at the small and familiar metal object in the man's right hand.

"What do you mean...my family?" he asks.

Pelayo gives a slight shrug. "You and your Army wife, don't you think you have blood on your clean and soft hands? Your wife…she's in the Army, but I don't have to say any more. But you, Tom Cornwall, you have killed with your words, your stories."

"Impossible," Tom whispers, knowing with a hard kernel inside of him that this tough yet soft-spoken man before him is even more dangerous than he can imagine.

"Oh, no, quite possible," his captor says. "You think you can rest comfortably in what's known as the Western world, write your stories, your opinion pieces, using unnamed sources or receiving leaks, not caring who or what might be feeding you information. Information that once is in print, under your name, can be used as a weapon and used to threaten, bribe, or kill others in far distant lands."

Tom keeps on staring at the metal object. "Please don't hurt Denise. Please. She's only ten."

Pelayo's voice gets sharp. "And you think your wife's actions and your crafted words haven't killed ten-year-old girls over the years? Really?"

"Please…"

"Enough, then. I will leave you with this choice, here and now. We depart this room and leave Hamid with your daughter, after I tell him what your family has done to his family. I tell him not to cause permanent damage…but we return thirty minutes later. Or…"

Pelayo holds up the small metal contraption. Tom sees it and remembers a dinner party last year, the husband of a prominent DC journalist was in attendance and insisted on preparing his own homemade desserts for all the guests…

"Not Hamid," Tom says.

"A good father, then. Are you left-handed or right?"

"Right."

"Then extend your left hand and roll up your sleeve."

Denise sees what's going on and says, "Daddy? Daddy?"

Tom tries to keep his voice even for his daughter's sake. "Can you take her out for a moment? I don't want her to see this."

Pelayo goes *tsk-tsk*. "That is not possible, my friend. Even at her age, she must suffer the actions of her family."

Tom's mouth is dry and his legs are shaking. The thick man named Tonton comes around and grabs his left arm by the elbow and wrist, holding it stretched out and still.

Tom tries to be brave. "That's not necessary."

Pelayo says, "Trust me, I know from experience. It is necessary."

Tom yells out, "Denise! Don't look!"

With that, Pelayo switches on the small crème brûlée torch, and gently runs the 2,700-degree flame up the length of Tom's exposed arm. The sizzling noise and smell of burnt hair and skin makes him yell until his throat is hoarse.

CHAPTER 40

I DON'T slow down until I cross the Georgia border into eastern Alabama, and then I get a good case of the shakes once again when I'm on US Highway 59, heading southwest. I'm still not sure why that Tennessee state trooper was interested in me, because I really doubt that my boss, Lieutenant Colonel Denton, would have listed me as AWOL after less than twenty-four hours, and then put my name and vehicle ID into the NCIC.

Unless he got pressure from someone to do so.

Who?

The people behind the kidnapping of Tom and Denise? Why? They would want me to get to Three Rivers. Why throw up a roadblock by listing me in the NCIC?

I squeeze my hands on the Wrangler's steering wheel. *Look at the evidence,* I think. *Look at the data points. The trooper didn't pull me over in traffic.* No, he made a routine traffic stop when he saw a Jeep with Virginia license plates pulled over to the side.

Routine, then.

All right.

If I wasn't in the NCIC, then what triggered him? Was it something I said? Something that he spotted that got his suspicious-cop mind working? I understand cops and their "gut feelings." Once you've performed hundreds of traffic stops, your subconscious and muscle memory work together to warn you when something doesn't feel right.

I take a deep breath, check the time.

I need something to eat.

I'm not hungry, but I need fuel to keep me going all the way to Texas.

I spot a sign for a truck stop called Love's, up ahead off exit 174. This interstate is really a narrow two-lane blacktop, with woods and flat farmland extending on each side, and a wide and grassy tree-covered median separating me from the northbound lanes. Back home in Virginia, serious commuters would laugh at calling this an interstate.

I come to the exit, make a right, and then turn left at the bottom, going a hundred or so yards on Steele Station Road. This Love's Travel Stop is part of a large, national chain, and it almost gives me a bit of comfort as I drive into the fuel pump area, step out, and start gassing up my Wrangler. With the pump running, I quickly walk to a Subway to the left of the truck stop, which is a wide, one-story building with a brick facade. It looks cute and homey.

A few minutes later I emerge with a steak-and-cheese sub, a bag of Lay's chips, and a Diet Coke, and after putting the nozzle back in the pump, I drive to the side of the parking lot, step out, and decide to have a quick little picnic on the hood of my Wrangler. I take out my maps and road atlases, start gauging distances and times, run some rough figures, check my watch.

I lost some additional time due to road work, but according to my figures, it will take me about fourteen hours to get to Three Rivers, Texas. I have plenty of time to stop for the night and arrive on time and fully rested.

The steak-and-cheese sandwich is probably tasty as hell, but I can't really taste it. I just chew, swallow, chew, swallow. It's an overcast day, with low clouds.

An Alabama state police cruiser slowly glides into the parking lot, parks in front of the brick building. I give the cruiser a quick glance, go back to my meal. A female trooper emerges, goes into the store. I finish up my sandwich, devour the chips, and take another good, long acid swallow of the Diet Coke.

Once I get to Three Rivers, I can scope out the address and then...well, come up with a perfect plan to seize somebody I don't know and toss him into my Jeep, to exchange later for my loved ones.

And where will the exchange take place? And how can I guarantee the safety of Tom and Denise?

Later, I think. *Later. Focus on the job in front of you. Drive to Texas with no delays, no problems.*

The trooper goes back to the cruiser, and I spot something I hadn't noticed before. The Love's Travel Stop has a logo consisting of three overlapping hearts, colored red, peach, and yellow.

Three symbols of love.

Tom, Denise, and me.

I try to take another swallow of the Diet Coke and I just can't. I burst into tears and sob, and bring up a paper napkin just as the Alabama State Police cruiser makes a wide turn and stops beside me.

The window rolls down. A young trooper, with her light-blond hair pulled tight in a bun at the back of her head, calls out, "Everything all right, ma'am?"

I know better than to bullshit her, because my last bullshit attempt with a member of law enforcement didn't go well. I wipe at my eyes and say, "My husband...and my daughter. I'm worried about them, that's all."

"They okay?"

I shake my head. "No, they're not…they were in an accident yesterday, and I'm driving as fast as I can to see them."

She purses her lips, gives a slight shake of her head. "Oh, ma'am, I'm sorry. Are you all right to drive? Is there anything I can do for you?"

I blow my nose. "Ma'am, you've been helpful. Honest. I just need to get going, that's all. I appreciate you checking in on me. That's very thoughtful of you."

She says, "Well, I know you're probably in a hurry, so travel safe. I'll say a prayer for you and your family. Nothing more important than family, am I right?"

"You're one hundred percent right," I say, wiping my fingers clean, and she gives me a wave, drives off, and it just hits me.

Denise and Tom.

That evil voice inside of me, once more.

You know what always happens to most kidnap victims…they may already be dead.

"Shut up," I whisper, and I clean the trash off my Wrangler's hood and get back to my mission.

CHAPTER 41

TOM CORNWALL'S catalog and memory of pain is pretty thin, ranging from a broken collarbone while playing high school football to having a jerk of a medical intern putting in two stitches without benefit of anesthesia to fix a cut finger to a piece of shrapnel that nicked him in the ribs in Syria two years back.

So he sees with horror the steady, hot flame of the hand-held torch that Pelayo Abboud is confidently holding in his right hand, and he thinks, *It'll be over soon, it'll be over soon,* knowing the pain that is coming his way will be the worst he's ever felt in his life, and with the terror coursing through him as the strong man holds his wrist steady, another voice inside of him says: *Be strong for Denise. Be strong for Denise. Don't traumatize her any more. Be strong for Denise.*

Then Pelayo lowers his clenched hand with the torch down and—

A lick of flame from the surface of the sun reaches out and laps his arm.

He screams in absolute and bone-crushing pain.

He's on the floor, sobbing, crying, holding his left arm, shaking all over, his arm shaking the worst, like an exposed tree limb being hit by a strong breeze. He hears another scream and it's his daughter, and in a sluggish way he thinks, *Little girl, what are you screaming about? I'm the one who's just been burnt.*

There's an acrid smell in the room, of burnt hair and flesh, and he grits his teeth, howling, still holding his wrist up, and then rolls over and vomits up his last meal, whatever the hell that was. Through a fog he hears voices and he's being moved around and checked and probed, and his little girl is still screaming, and in the thickness of it all, he wants to shout out, *Go away! All of you, go away!*

He's picked up and dropped on the other bed. His vision is gray, and his mouth tastes like old nickels, and his arm, his arm, oh my God, his arm, and a man grabs his hair and tugs him back, and Pelayo says slowly and carefully, "You've learned a lesson, my friend. Don't try to escape again. Don't try to fight me. Don't try to resist. Don't make me repeat this lesson, for if I do, your little girl will be the one receiving it."

Voices, then he hears the distant click of a door being opened, and then the sound of metal hitting metal as the door is slammed shut. He grits his teeth again as the pain continues to throb along his wrist and forearm and right to the base of his brain, one big throb at a time, like a slow wave of hot lava, moving like it's controlled by the tides.

"Daddy, Daddy," Denise says, sobbing, and now the guilt collapses over him and he takes a deep breath, and another, and he rolls over, trying to hide his wrist from his little girl, and in a shaky voice says, "You just stay there, all right? Don't come over here. Just stay there."

She sobs again. "Daddy, what can I do? What can I do?"

He closes his eyes. His girl is still one brave cookie, bless her.

The pain grows and grows along his forearm, and he lets out a low, heavy moan.

Tom grits his teeth. "Stay brave, hon. Stay brave. Do that for me...and your mother. All right?"

She sobs for another moment, and says, "Daddy?"

"Yes, hon?" God, the pain, the pain...

"I want Mommy to kill him."

He almost smiles at the determined voice of his young sweetie.

"Me, too, hon. Me, too."

CHAPTER 42

SPECIAL AGENT Rosaria Vasquez steps out of her car as she sees the young Army officer, Lieutenant Preston Baker, walk away from his rusted red Nissan Sentra to the front door of the apartment complex he lives in, nearly an hour away from Fort Belvoir. Scanning the sad-looking two-story structure that has its siblings scattered around beyond distant parking lots, she sees the entire story of the place. The house was slapped up in a hurry when Fort Belvoir expanded years ago, meeting minimum building codes and using cheap lumber and materials, and the roof is now peeling shingles, the clapboards are warped and shedding paint, and the front lawns—which should have been maintained over the years by the property owners—are merely trampled-down dirt decorated with swing sets, barbecue stations, and broken toys.

It's a familiar place, bringing back memories of when she briefly resided in such buildings, as a young ward of the state of Maryland.

She briskly walks forward, wanting to catch up with Lieutenant Baker before he passes through the lobby area. He's slim and freckle-faced, has short red hair, and is wearing the standard ACUs. She knows why he's here, so far from base. Better to be on your own off-property than to be known around your station as a "base rat," one who refuses to leave the base boundaries.

He notices her and Rosaria flashes her badge. "Lieutenant Baker? Special Agent Vasquez, CID. I need a few minutes of your time."

He just nods and his shoulders sag a bit, like he had always anticipated this happening, a CID agent wanting to talk to him.

"Sure," he says. "Right this way."

The inside of his small apartment surprises her, for it's neat and tidy. The furniture is old and dented, no doubt salvaged from Goodwill or the Salvation Army, but the old carpet looks like it's been freshly vacuumed, and there's a small TV and homemade bookshelves, lengths of wood and concrete blocks jammed full of paperback books. Rosaria has spent enough time on previous interviews with male service personnel, wading through ankle-deep piles of trash—porn magazines, empty pizza boxes, crushed takeout containers—that this is a nice change of pace.

She sits across from him, and he answers her initial questions with ease and no sign of the earlier concern. Born in Washington, local schools, community college. One day, on a 9/11 anniversary, he spent hours glued to the television, seeing the old footage of the collapsing towers, the burning Pentagon, and the smoking hole in the ground in Pennsylvania.

So he enlisted and eventually entered the military's famed language school in Monterey, learned Pashto, and after additional intelligence training, was sent off to Afghanistan.

"I was assigned to be with Captain Cornwall," he says, his pale, freckled hands holding his Army cover between his knees. "We were at FOB Healy in Kunduz Province…the place was named after a Navy

SEAL hero who died a number of years back. You ever been at a forward operating base, ma'am?"

"No, I haven't," she says. "What's it like?"

"Like...you're on the surface of the moon. Desolate for klicks and klicks in every direction—rock and sand and scrub brush. Rough mountains where the Taliban would set up mortar positions and drop rounds on us every now and then. A handful of villages off in each direction. Week to week, you never knew which village supported the government or the Taliban. It was...like nothing I've ever seen. Nothing. Reinforcements and supplies came in by chopper. We were entirely cut off."

Even in this safe living room in Virginia, Rosaria could sense the fear and memories coming forth from the young lieutenant. "What was your MOS?"

"Zero-nine-lima, ma'am," he says, "translator for whatever prisoners came our way, either captured by our patrols or the government forces. I was with Captain Cornwall when she was doing her interrogations."

"Interesting work?"

He shakes his head. "Most times it was goat herders or poppy farmers who said they weren't Taliban, that they was just carrying AK-47s for personal protection, stuff like that. Most of the time we just took their photos, fingerprints, DNA swabs, and either sent them on their way or gave 'em back to the government forces."

Rosaria looks down at the thin file that contains the notes and paperwork for the Cornwall investigation. "But there was one prisoner that stood out, am I right?"

He quickly nods. "That's right, ma'am. This guy... his name was Mohammed Something-or-another. He was different."

"Different how?"

"He was older, that's what. Maybe in his forties, fifties. Pretty well-dressed, in good health...I mean, some of these villages, you see a guy that looks like a grandpa who's been smoking cigars and eating raw sugar all his life, and you find out he's only thirty. It's a hard place. But this guy looked okay. And he spoke English."

Rosaria pauses. That wasn't in the initial investigative report. "Really? How well did he speak it?"

Baker smiles. "Crap, better than me. Almost an English accent, like he went to some fancy school in Britain or someplace like that."

"Why was he picked up?"

"Some tribal leader from one of the villages, he narked him. Said this Mohammed didn't belong, was from far away, was from the Taliban. But Mohammed said that wasn't true. He said he was a simple farmer...was just passing through to visit relatives in some other village."

"Did Cornwall believe him?"

"No," Baker says.

"Why?"

"Because of his feet."

Rosaria says, "His feet?"

Another slight smile. "Yeah, his feet. He claimed that he was a simple, poor farmer, did a lot of walking and riding on horses or mules, but Captain Cornwall, she made him take his boots off. And his feet was nice and soft. Not covered with calluses and thick skin like you'd expect."

"What happened next?"

"The old guy, he kept on smiling. But he shut up. And he was put in one of the cages...and came out the next day for another go-around, and kept his mouth shut, and then another day...and Captain Cornwall, she was getting a lot of calls from up the chain. Demanding answers. Leads. Like I said, this guy didn't fit in. A farmer? His hands were almost as smooth as his feet. The captain's superiors...they thought he was a real catch. She was under a lot of pressure to break him."

Those last two words, *break him,* catch her attention. "Did she do that, then? Break him?"

"Well..."

"Lieutenant, need I remind you of your responsibility here, to answer my questions fully and faithfully?"

Baker just nods at that, swallowing hard. "It's like this...she got really pissed and said she was going to his cage, to talk to him, one-on-one, to get what she needed...and then a while later, the call came out. Medics were brought in. The guy...they hauled him out in a wire basket, and I caught a look. His face was bruised, there was blood coming out of his mouth, and his eyes were wide open, staring up."

Rosaria waits, and then Baker says one more sentence.

"Ma'am," Baker says, "Captain Cornwall, she killed that prisoner."

CHAPTER 43

I CHECK my watch, see I have two hours to make my phone call to the kidnapper of my beloveds, and I'm only an hour away from Three Rivers, Texas. That gives me sixty minutes to scope out the address, do a brief surveillance, and then get the job done— freeing a prisoner from that house and taking him…well, taking him to the criminal who took my Tom and my Denise.

I allow myself a brief moment of satisfaction. The drive down from Alabama through Mississippi, Louisiana, and now Texas has been grueling. I was able to stop and sleep for a while, but there's not much on the interstate to break up the monotony but flat farmland, swampland, and industrial landscapes clouding up the horizon. Somewhere along the way I also stopped off at a huge Walmart Supercenter to steal and switch out license plates. Not much of a camouflage, but it's the best I can do. Twice road construction has slowed me down, but I've been able to make up the time without getting the attention of any law enforcement.

Now I've passed through the high-rise obscenity that's Houston, and I'm on US Highway 59, heading southwest through heavy rain. Earlier I spotted the anvil shapes of heavy thunderstorm clouds racing across the flat fields, and the torrential rain has been pacing me for at least twenty minutes, the flashes of lightning in the near-black clouds reminding me of those long, dark nights at FOB Healy in Afghanistan, seeing tracer rounds emerge from the nearby rocks and ravines, as the Taliban continued their daily quest to eject the newest invaders from their homeland.

As I hear the booming thunder, I try to suppress the memories of the rocket and mortar attacks, the explosive rounds dropping in and exploding while I huddled in the bomb shelter with the other noncombatants.

The traffic has been light in the past hour or so, but now it starts to thicken. I sit up and try to stretch my aching back.

Up ahead, more taillights flickering red.

I don't like it.

I see my speed start dropping, from seventy miles per hour to sixty to fifty and now in the forties, and I really don't like it.

What the hell is going on?

I try to peer to the side and just see the traffic slowing down even more, the taillights flickering red and then staying steady red.

The Wrangler's speed continues to drop.

Thirty-two.

Twenty-nine.

Twenty.

Ten.

Three.

Full stop.

Damn it!

Horns around me blare, and I just squeeze the steering wheel hard, knowing honking my horn won't do a damn thing.

But I honk it anyway.

I wait.

All right.

Maybe a traffic accident, or a jackknifed truck, or a sinkhole in the road.

Something.

Check my watch.

Five minutes have passed. That means I'm already five miles behind.

We stay stock-still.

Then the Subaru station wagon ahead of me with a DON'T MESS WITH TEXAS bumper sticker moves ahead a few feet and stops.

More waiting.

I lower the driver's-side window, stick my head out, get drenched.

All I see ahead of me are the line of cars and the red taillights.

Another five minutes slip by.

Another five miles lost.

I roll up the window, lean over to the passenger's seat, take out my atlas and a road map of this part of Texas that I got from a service station an hour ago. There's got to be another way out of here. With my four-wheel drive I could scoot across the grass median, get on the highway heading northeast, find a state road that will at least get me headed in the right direction.

Somebody hammers at my window.

I yelp in surprise, drop the maps, thrust my hand into my open leather bag, and grab my revolver.

CHAPTER 44

A HISPANIC male, thin mustache, black hair flattened down by the rain, eyes wide with fear or terror, wearing a soaked checked shirt and blue jeans, slams both hands again on my window.

"Por favor!" he yells. "Please! *Mi familia!* My family! They're drowning!"

I roll down the window, keeping the other hand with the revolver hidden. "What?"

He points down at the length of stalled cars. *"Mi familia!* They are in my car! *Por favor!* Help me rescue them! Your Jeep! Please!"

My first thought is brutally honest and real. *Sucks to be you,* I immediately think, because I need to get moving to rescue my Tom and Denise. A few hours ago I almost murdered an innocent Tennessee police officer, up close and personal. It wouldn't take much to abandon this terrified father and husband.

Then, just as quickly, I'm ashamed of what just went through my mind, and a calmer voice makes an appearance: *Help this guy out right now, you can get the traffic moving, it'll be faster than trying to puzzle out the maps to find an alternate route.*

I shout, "Get in!" and I toss the maps in the back, along with my revolver, now in my leather bag. He runs past the front of my Wrangler, gets into the passenger's side, soaking everything, and he says, "Hurry! *Rápido! Rápido!* Please!"

I put the Jeep into reverse, slam it into first, start driving down the side of the road, half of the Wrangler on pavement, the other half on the muddy median. Up ahead two pickup trucks have pulled over and I roll up, and there are a couple of men there, in cowboy hats and long yellow rain slickers, and they wave me on, past torn-up grass and dirt where it looks like a vehicle has skidded off the highway.

As I slow down, my passenger jumps out and I put the Jeep into park, step out.

The rain's heavier.

I take in the scene in one long, hard glance.

To the right is a plain concrete bridge, two-lane, spanning what was probably a trickling stream, but not today. It's a roaring, racing river, with torrents and whitecaps and sprays of spume, and down the muddy grass embankment, there is a line of people, holding hands, trying to get to an overturned red Chevrolet in the rapids.

The would-be rescuers are not going to make it.

The water's moving too fast, too hard. It will knock all of them off their feet.

I get back into my Jeep, make a muddy U-turn, and back my way down the embankment, looking at the rearview mirror and side mirror, trying to gauge where I am.

I brake hard, get out, and go to the tailgate, slam it open.

Nestled under an old blanket, a fire extinguisher, and a toolbox is a length of chain. I always keep a chain in my Jeep for those few times each winter when an inch of snow causes Virginia to collapse in chaos, with cars and trucks off the freeway.

I hook the chain onto the trailer hitch, and the Hispanic man, eager to help, grabs the other end of the chain, goes down to the overturned car, fastens it to the rear axle.

He waves at me. "*Rápido!* Please!"

I get back into the Wrangler, shift it into low, and then look at the side-view mirror, get a glimpse of the chain, and see it move up and get taut.

Now.

I hit the accelerator, the wheels churn and spin, and I make a few feet of progress. I look up again and the Chevrolet is moving. It's moving.

Damn!

The current has grabbed the Chevy and is taking it downstream.

And me along with it.

The Wrangler stumbles back, I shift again, pumping the accelerator, and I don't think I'm going to make it. In my mind's eye, I can see it all, the Chevy dragging me in, the fastened chain linking my Wrangler, no way to get out, nothing to do but open the door right now and dive out onto the soggy embankment.

Damn it!

I see quick movement.

Men and women are in the water, holding on to the floating Chevy, pushing it to shore, and I hit the accelerator again, and now I'm going, now I'm going. I drag the overturned vehicle a few meters and stop.

The Chevrolet is out of the water. The driver's-side door flops open. Water streams from it. The Hispanic father has a hammer in his hand, and he's joined by a bulky woman in dungarees with a crowbar, and both of them attack the windows.

I get out and slop through the mud, and by the time I get to the car, a young woman, a little girl, and a little boy have been dragged out.

They're coughing, they're choking, but they're alive.

I stop in knee-deep water, breathing hard, as the sirens start wailing in the distance.

A local volunteer fire department and its ambulance arrive, along with a number of volunteers with flashing red lights in their vehicles' grilles. Then a Texas state trooper arrives, and names are taken, and photographs, and statements, and the Hispanic father — named Carlos — keeps on hugging me, and hugging me, and all the while I'm thinking, *I've got to go, but I can't race away, because that will raise too many questions.*

The rain finally lets up as I get away from the crowd of rescuers, onlookers, EMS, and law enforcement, and with wet and muddy boots, I get back into the Wrangler.

The thought comes to me, like a sweet taste of wine, that I've rescued a family.

I check my watch.

I have thirty minutes to call the kidnapper with the word that I've fulfilled his demands.

And I'm an hour away from Three Rivers.

I've saved this family.

And killed my own.

CHAPTER 45

WITH HIS trusted associate Casper Khourery at his side, Pelayo Abboud unlocks the basement door and strolls in to check on his guests. Coming in behind Casper is the woman doctor from Afghanistan, named Bahara. Even in this heat, the woman insists on wearing a loose black robe nearly covering her plump body, and a distant, human part of Pelayo admires such piousness.

The inside of the room stinks—from fear, burnt tissue, and a foul scent from the area of the chemical toilet. The little girl cries out as they come in, and the poor man backpedals his way across the bed, until his back is up against the cement wall, his eyes wide, holding up his injured arm in an awkward position.

"Please," Pelayo says. "Let the doctor examine you."

Tom's face is red and his eyes are swollen from all the weeping and sobbing, and even though Pelayo can sense the fear in the broken man, Tom does as he's told and gingerly presents the burnt arm to the doctor.

She sits across from Tom on the girl's bed, whispers to the girl, and little Denise turns her head and looks to the wall. Tom groans a couple of times as the doctor goes through her large black valise and begins to work on Tom's arm. It looks like a raw, bloody business, and Pelayo—who fondly recalls killing a school bully back in Veracruz by shoving a mechanical pencil in the teen boy's right ear, said pencil having been gifted to him on his twelfth birthday by his grandfather — doesn't flinch.

Eventually a gauze bandage is loosely wrapped around the burnt arm, and Bahara gets up, rearranging her black robe. She steps away and whispers to Pelayo, "I…this is not what I agreed to do. This is evil work."

Pelayo shrugs. "Then you may leave, if you wish."

The Afghan doctor's eyes widen. "For real?"

"Certainly," Pelayo says. "But you cannot fly or drive. So if you can determine a way of walking back to your cursed country, go. If not, stay quiet, woman, and do your job."

Tom Cornwall sees the doctor scurry out, and he can feel the fear and terror spread inside of him, like a splotch of oil slowly spreading across a blank pavement. With the woman in the room, there was a bit of reassurance that nothing bad would happen to him and Denise, but now, it's his kidnapper and the other well-dressed man who is his deputy.

Pelayo Abboud sighs, sniffs, and says something in Spanish to the other man, and he leaves as well.

Now he is alone with the man who had earlier blowtorched his arm.

"My apologies," Pelayo says.

Tom grits his teeth. "For what? Burning my arm?"

The man grins. "Of course not." He gestures to where the chemical toilet is hidden in the small cell. "It appears your sanitary facilities are failing. I will ensure it is taken care of, very shortly."

Tom looks at his bandaged left arm. The nice woman doctor — still not saying a word to him — had cleaned the large broken blister, applied some sort of ointment, and gently wrapped it with clean white gauze. She left him with a pack of painkillers.

"May...may I ask you a question?"

Pelayo nods. "Go ahead."

He pauses, tries to gather his thoughts. In his newspaper career, he thinks he has interviewed a number of evil men, from a weapons smuggler in the Philippines to a proud blood diamond traitor in Liberia, but compared to this quiet, well-dressed man with the cold gray eyes in front of him, they were Boy Scouts.

The man's assistant comes back into the room, whispers into Pelayo's ear, and then he says, *"Bueno,"* and returns to looking at Tom.

Tom finally says, "You...who are you?"

Pelayo says, "Dear me. I was expecting a better question. You know who I am. I know you've spent enough time doing research about me and my career."

Pelayo gets off the bed, and Tom surprises himself by saying, "No, wait. Don't go. I meant, who are you beyond that? Beyond what I've found out? What's going on here?"

His kidnapper chuckles. "I thought it would have been apparent, considering what you *norteamericanos* think any time you hear a Mexican accent."

"But...I've heard Spanish, all right. But the men who grabbed my daughter and me, I think they spoke Farsi. And I've heard Pashto, as well. What are you doing?"

Pelayo pauses. "Now I'm impressed. That's an adult question. I will spare some of my time to give you the answer."

He sits back on the bed. Tom glances at Denise. She is desperately holding her Tigger in one arm, and is trying to ignore the adult world so scarily nearby by working on a coloring book with her free hand.

Pelayo sits down. "But please, Tom Cornwall. Look at the facts. You are a dinosaur working for an industry and in a world that's already dead, but you don't know it. You still believe in that old-fashioned thought of a free press, operating in a world with set rules and boundaries. That world is gone. National interest is gone. What remains are the conglomerates, the corporations, the cartels. The three Cs, as it would be. There is no such thing left as governments. It's a mere shadow play and puppets, done so well that most people still believe those illusions."

"But…"

"But what?"

Tom forces the word out. "You're evil."

Pelayo laughs. "Compared to what? If one of my associates machine-guns down a competitor and six of his workers at a café in Mexico City, that's a national disgrace, a world story with large headlines about the barbarians operating beyond the fringes of the law. But when an oil company's action incinerates a hundred or so Nigerians in the course of a day's work, well, that small story is buried somewhere deep inside your newspapers. Am I right?"

The man's assistant stands there. Pelayo sits comfortably on the bed. It's so quiet Tom hears the *scritch-scritch* of his daughter coloring in her book. He moves his left arm some and the pain still hits him behind his eyes.

"You may be correct," he says. "But it's not right."

Pelayo smiles, leans over, gives him a gentle slap on the knee. "For a while there was a world where you and your kind struggled to report the truth. That's now gone. Every newspaper and television network is now handcuffed to their ideology, their way of looking at the world. Governments once pretended they worked for the poor common man. That's gone as well. Your elected representatives in this so-called democracy won't pass legislation because their paymaster lobbyists tell them what to do."

Pelayo stands up, shakes his head, brushes each hand as if there was some sort of dust or contaminant there. "In some ways I admire you, Tom Cornwall, still bravely struggling to stay alive and pertinent in this world. But in reality, you're playing in the shadows, thinking it's real. None of it's real."

Tom says, "Someday, you and your kind will be stopped."

"Not today, not ever," Pelayo says, now glancing at his watch. "And you best pray that your wife has not been stopped. She has…eleven minutes to contact me."

Tom looks to his daughter and asks the question. "What happens at the twelve-minute mark?"

Pelayo says softly and with great courtesy, "Please, Tom, not in front of the little girl."

CHAPTER 46

AT SOME point just outside of Three Rivers, Texas, the deadline passes.

But my mission still goes on.

The destination town is flat, with a two-lane state road passing through, and as I go by the Y intersection of Route 72 (King David Drive) and Route 281 (North Harborth Avenue), there's a McDonald's restaurant with flapping, colorful banners saying JUST OPENED PLEASE STOP BY.

The homes are all single story, in tidy square yards with scraggly brown and green lawns. There's not much here, but there's enough, and I slowly go down what appears to be the main road, North Harborth Avenue. There are a couple of service stations, a dollar store, and little stores here and there set back from the road. This is what my supposed betters call fly over country, even though the people in that part of the country pump the oil, grow the food, and mine the ore.

My supposed betters should hope they never band together and go on strike.

I don't have time, and I don't have what I need—an idea of where Linden Street is located. I also don't have much money, which I discovered about thirty minutes ago, when I was making a fast refueling in the previous town, called Kenedy. There I found that my wallet had been stripped of the cash from my go bag—probably by one of the bystanders back at the river rescue—and I made an equally fast withdrawal from a Bank of America ATM.

A risky move, but I needed the money and I also did it for another reason.

So low on cash, not knowing where I'm going, beyond the deadline.

Pretty crappy.

For some reason my overworked mind flashes back to the history of the Israeli-Arab war of 1967, the one called the Six-Day War. It was small Israel versus twelve Arab nations, and instead of waiting around to get slaughtered, the Israelis conducted a preemptive strike. Before the jets flew and the tanks rolled, an Israeli armored-division commander said, *Each unit will push forward as fast as it can. Pay no attention to your flanks. Give no thought to resupply. If you lose nine tanks out of ten, keep advancing with the tenth. Stop for nothing.*

Right now I'm my own unit, Task Force Cornwall, and I'm stopping for nothing.

Up ahead I see two young women walking by the side of the road, and I pull over. In a few seconds, after spinning a tale of woe about some shithead boyfriend who dumped me for parts unknown, I now know where Linden Street is located. I say thanks and get back to my driving.

My loved ones may be dead by now. Or the kidnapper could be secretly extending the deadline. Or the kidnapper could have choked on a chicken bone last night and be dead. Or Tom and Denise could have escaped on their own.

I don't know.

As an intelligence officer, I need to deal with facts

and figures. Making assumptions is forbidden. So are most educated guesses.

So I go on.

Less than five minutes later, I come to Linden Street. It's off another main street in this little town, called North School Road, because—wow, it has a school. I resist the urge to drive down Linden. Instead, I drive a few more meters, stop, and turn around so I can get a look.

The street seems reasonably new and well-paved, with a half dozen homes on each side, and then the road dribbles out to a dirt path with some exposed foundations. A housing development that ran out of money?

Possible.

But which one is holding the prize, the key that will get my family free?

From my glove box I pull out a pair of nice compact Zeiss binoculars, give the street a quick glance.

Then I know.

The last house on the right looks like every other house, a one-story structure with a carport on one side, some thin shrubbery, and twisted trees that look doomed to only grow a few feet or so.

But that last house has a huge pickup truck parked in the small driveway, the kind of truck with big tires and overhead roll bars fitted with lights. It also has an extended cab.

That truck is sending a signal, although its owners probably don't realize it.

The signal is that there are men in that house, more than one, and they have the confidence and money to strut around in such a big, visible vehicle.

Like I said, the owners don't realize they've set up a signal.

But I do.

I shove the binoculars back into the glove box, resume my driving.

A few minutes later I'm parked in the shade behind a three-store strip that has a Laundromat, a dollar store, and a liquor store. I'm scribbling some notes, recreating what I just saw on Linden Street and how best to approach it.

I know my time deadline is far and away gone, like New Year's Eve hats and banners from several months ago.

But like that Israeli general said more than a half century ago, I'm stopping for nothing.

I realize the stacked odds against me have gotten higher and higher with each passing hour, from the time delay to being robbed of all of my cash.

But I'm still not stopping.

If in the next hour or so, I get out of here with my guy in my Wrangler, I'll make the call and find out where to deliver him for the trade.

Oh, yes, I'll make the drive, and I'll make the trade.

No matter what happens, I'll bring my own kidnap victim to the criminal who's taken my husband and daughter, and if Tom and Denise aren't produced alive and breathing, then I'll blow out the man's brains in front of said criminal.

And I'll drop my weapon, and if I'm instantly killed or eventually sent to prison, it won't matter a bit to me.

Without my family, I'm dead anyway.

CHAPTER 47

AFTER GETTING off the phone with his mom, who is still living near Seattle with his increasingly ill father, Army Lieutenant Preston Baker goes for a walk to clear his head and stretch his legs.

The call did not go well. A year ago, his dad, a retired engineer from Boeing, was diagnosed with early-onset Alzheimer's, and in the past few months, his situation has gotten worse. There was a time when Preston's dad would impress friends and family with his ability to multiply two-digit numbers by other two-digit numbers quickly in his head and always have the right answer, but now that's gone.

For the past couple of months, his father has managed to muddle through by reading little Post-it notes around the house, reminding him to zip up his pants, comb his hair, and brush his teeth, but now, as his mother tearfully said, "his doctors think we need to put him in a facility. Oh, Presty, we don't have that kind of money!"

And neither do I, he thinks, as he walks along the roads near his apartment complex, wearing jeans and a faded blue polo shirt, taking his time, going from one busy intersection to another.

To anyone out there, it would look like Preston was wandering aimlessly, but there is a point to his walk, and after fifteen minutes he gets to a dingy-looking 7-Eleven next to a Shell station. The area around the gas station is littered with plastic bottles, plastic bags, fast-food wrappers, and other trash, but the 7-Eleven is relatively clean, because the guy running it—an immigrant from New Delhi—is an old-fashioned sort who wants to keep his place tidy.

Preston ducks around the corner. Another way the guy is old-fashioned is that he likes to maintain a pay phone on the outside, even now, in a time when one could pick up a cheap burner phone for just a few bucks.

But Preston isn't looking to save a few bucks.

He's looking to save his career in the Army.

He drops a fistful of quarters into the phone, which has bright stickers in English, Spanish, and Portuguese, announcing its wonderful calling plans, and dials a number.

It rings once, twice, and then is picked up.

"Yes?" comes a familiar voice, from a man he's never met.

"She came by yesterday, the woman you talked about."

"And?"

Preston turns away, as if trying to hide his face from anyone walking by with their Slim Jims or Slurpees. "I told her the story. The one you wanted me to say."

"Did it go all right?"

"Yes."

"Do you think she was satisfied?"

"I...think so. She didn't stay that long. It was like she just wanted to confirm what she already knew. Or suspected."

The man says, "You did good. There'll be a wire transfer to your account within the next twelve hours. Anything else?"

"I...well, suppose she comes back?"

"Stick to the story."

"But suppose she asks lots more questions."

"Stick to the story."

"Yeah, I know, but—"

There's a *click* and the man has hung up.

He replaces the battered gray receiver with stickers and decals on it, wanders off to the rear of the store, which has two green dumpsters waiting to be picked up. Preston stares at the overflowing containers and thinks, *Wouldn't it be nice if the garbage inside of me could eventually be dumped like that, clean everything out inside?*

Yeah, right.

Some garbage inside will stay there, no matter what.

Preston turns and starts the long walk back to his apartment, and then, on impulse, checks how much change he has left.

Barely enough, but enough to make it happen.

He goes back to the pay phone, slides in the rest of his quarters, dials another number, and when a timid woman's voice answers, Preston says, "Ma, I think I can get the money to take care of you and Dad."

CHAPTER 48

ROSARIA VASQUEZ has just left the Corpus Christi International Airport and is speeding north across the flattest landscape she has ever seen in her life. There are cities off the distant horizon, steam and smoke plumes from industries at work in the Gulf of Mexico, and stunted, twisted trees that look like they've been transplanted from some old horror film.

Several hours earlier she was ready to jump into the shower and have an afternoon to herself, when she got a phone call from her boss, whose message was clear and to the point: "Get your butt to Corpus Christi and call me when you get on the highway."

Now she is on Interstate 37, speeding along at eighty miles an hour, plenty of other traffic zipping past her—including a grocery truck from an outfit called HEB Plus—and with a practiced reach of her hand on her cell phone, she makes the call to her boss, Senior Warrant Officer Fred McCarthy.

He wastes no time.

"We've finally got Lieutenant Cornwall's trail," he says. "A Tennessee highway patrolman was assaulted by her yesterday on Interstate 75, just north of Chattanooga."

"Did he make a traffic stop? Had she been speeding?"

"No on both counts," her boss says. "She was just pulled over, like she was taking a pee break or something. The trooper says she was traveling alone, and was going to meet up with a girlfriend in Chattanooga. He tried to search her car and then she took him down."

"Then why am I in Texas?"

"Because she never stopped in Chattanooga, best I can find out, and because now she's in Texas," McCarthy says sharply. "This afternoon she was helping pull a car out of a flooded stream on a stretch of road on some empty landscape on Highway 59. Texas Highway Patrol took down her name and the license plate number...but the license plate was from Tennessee, not Virginia. And a few minutes ago, we got a hit from a Bank of America ATM in some little town called Kenedy. She withdrew four hundred dollars. Surveillance footage shows it was her. You head up there, find out what you can."

"But boss..."

"What?"

"Where are you getting this intelligence?"

Even though she is hundreds of miles away from Quantico, she can feel the chill in her boss's voice. "It's good intelligence, that's all you need to know."

She thinks it's probably great intelligence, but its sourcing stinks. Somehow her boss has either tapped into a domestic network or has been informed of Cornwall's travels by others in the dark intelligence arts. Getting police reports from state troopers in two states, getting an ATM hit plus video surveillance of same, that is way, way out of CID traditional information systems.

"Understood, boss," she finally replies. "But..."

"But what?"

"I've gone through her service record. She has relatives in Maine. Her husband has relatives in Ohio.

She's never been stationed in Texas. Why would she be going there?"

McCarthy says, "Sounds like questions only a trained investigator like you can find out. So find it the hell out."

"Yes, sir," she says.

"Good," he says. "Just so you know, Kenedy is spelled with one *n*. Get back to me soonest with whatever you can find."

"Yes, sir," she says, and that's that.

She keeps on speeding along, thinking of a little historical display she noted at the airport while waiting to get her rental car. About a hundred years ago, a category 4 hurricane had struck right here, scouring the coast clean and killing up to a thousand people.

Rosaria glances up at the rearview mirror. Sunny blue sky back there. No clouds. No rain. No storm surge racing up behind her to take her away from this dark day and even darker job.

She pushes the Ford's accelerator down as her speed jumps to ninety.

CHAPTER 49

IN A small house on a quiet street in Three Rivers, Texas, Antonio Garcia is pacing through the small, dirty kitchen, living room, his small bedroom, past the closed door of the other bedroom, and then back out to the kitchen. He has on stonewashed, pressed Levi's jeans, a bright-yellow Lacoste polo shirt—one size too small to show off his sculpted figure—and specially crafted Lucchese cowboy boots worth nearly two thousand American dollars. He is carrying a Smith & Wesson Model 500 .44 revolver, one of the most powerful handguns in the world, in a Bianchi shoulder holster.

The revolver is crap for shooting at long distances, but Antonio's work has always been up close and personal, and besides, carrying a small cannon like this scares the shit out of most folks he encounters in his work. He remembers seeing a Clint Eastwood movie when he was much younger, and how handsome Clint used such a revolver to cut down anyone who got in his way.

On the couch in the dingy living room, ignoring the television that's showing a telenovela DVD, reading the Bible and carefully taking notes on a legal pad of yellow paper, is one of the other three men in this house, Pepe. Antonio doesn't like Pepe because a month ago, Pepe found Jesus Christ and is now studying the ways he can save his soul. Slim and well-groomed Pepe says based on what he's done and what he will be doing, he hopes if he knows enough about Jesus, his soul might be saved after all when his time eventually comes.

Antonio doesn't know about souls, lost his belief in Jesus and God years back, and if Pepe were to go soft on him, he'd blow his head off. But so far, Pepe has done his job, and Antonio leaves him alone. He also leaves Ramon alone, who is sleeping in the second bedroom, along with the fourth person in this house, the chicken.

Back again on his trek, small kitchen, living room, his small bedroom, and back to the kitchen. He remembers as a boy, his father affording one day to take him and his sister to the Chapultepec Zoo outside of Mexico City, and he remembers a big black bear. The bear was pacing back and forth, back and forth, and he felt sad for the big guy. He should have been out in the wilderness, killing other creatures, eating what he wanted, humping any female bear in range.

Instead the bear was trapped.

Just like Antonio.

He goes back to his pacing.

This job isn't like any other job he's done for his *jefe*. He's done lots of kidnapping jobs, and except for a few, most of them involved working over the victim and torturing him until his family came up with the money that the *jefe* was demanding.

But not this job.

This job is full of rules, and Antonio hates rules.

Don't leave the house. Don't draw attention to yourself. Keep things quiet. One of you to be awake at all times. No drinking. No drugs.

And worst of all…*Don't mark, harm, or even touch the chicken you are guarding.*

Where's the fun in that?

Most of the fun in jobs like this is seeing the fear in the chicken's eyes, seeing how much he screams when a finger or toe is lopped off, how he begs and begs for mercy, and how friendly and forgiving he becomes at the end, when he is told that the ransom is paid and he will be released in just a short while.

Sweet Mary, the chicken—even if short toes or fingers—will hug and kiss them all, forgiving them for doing a dirty and necessary job, and he will be in a cheerful mood until Antonio and his associates drive him to an empty cornfield and toss him into a drainage ditch and shoot him in the head.

But not this chicken.

He is protected, and he is to stay here until some *norteamericano* knocks on the door, says a certain phrase, and then the chicken is to be released into this stranger's care. Antonio, Pepe, and Ramon will leave a half hour later, cross the border, and go home to Ciudad Juárez, and then have a week off to make up for the monastic existence they've been suffering.

Back in the kitchen, Antonio stops, feeling hungry, thirsty, antsy. He opens the refrigerator, sees water and nothing else. Up in the freezer is a pile of frozen dinners—he's come to hate frozen dinners. Most times the gas stove here either overcooks or under-cooks the frozen chunks of pasta or white frozen meat pretending to be chicken.

He slams the door shut, goes back out to the living room. Pepe looks up at him. Pepe's skin is darker than his and Ramon's, and he's got a beak of a nose that marks some Aztec blood, but that blood must be thinned out some for Pepe to have found Jesus.

He says to Antonio, "What's up?"

"I'm going out."

Pepe pauses, Bible in his lap, pen in his hand. "You can't."

"Watch me."

"The *jefe* won't like it."

"The *jefe* is hundreds of kilometers away," Antonio says, picking up a light-tan jacket from the couch to wear over his polo shirt and his Smith & Wesson. "When we came here a few days ago, there was a McDonald's that just opened up. It's only five minutes away."

Pepe says, "The *jefe* won't like it."

"Yeah, but I don't like that crap we're forced to eat," Antonio says. "I'm going up there, get some fries, two Big Macs, a nice cold drink. You can sit here and thump that Bible. I won't be gone long."

He goes to the door, feeling the truck keys in the jacket pocket. Like some deranged talking doll or toy, Pepe calls out, "Antonio, the *jefe* won't like it!"

Antonio opens the door and says to Pepe, "He won't find out. If he does find out, I will blame you. And if that happens, dear Pepe, I'll make sure you meet Jesus at the end of the day."

CHAPTER 50

PELAYO ABBOUD returns to the room in the upper-floor suite that's been converted into his own little communications center, and a distressed-looking Casper Khourery looks to him and says, "Sir…the deadline has passed by an hour. We've not heard from the Army captain."

"Ah," he says, walking into the room, gently touching and slapping the bulky shoulders of the other three men working here on his behalf, sitting in front of keyboards, computer consoles, and radio equipment. "Do we have a view of the Three Rivers house?"

A young lad named Alejandro says, "Sir, over here, if you please."

Pelayo bends over and takes in the view from the large monitor. It's an amazing sight, like he's taking in a view from a sparrow or a hawk, circling over the small house. The place looks empty, looks quiet. A few bits of shrubbery are scattered across the flat yard.

The driveway is empty.

That's not good.

He says, "There is supposed to be a truck there, am I right?"

"Yes, *jefe,*" Casper says, coming over to join him. "We saw it leave about three minutes ago."

"I don't like that," Pelayo says. "You should have told me."

"There was only one man who came out from the house," Casper explains. "We could see his size and shape. It was clear that he was not the one we're interested in."

"I see."

The airborne drone circles and circles over the small house. It's an amazing thing, what the scientists and engineers can do, if given enough money and resources.

Pelayo says, "Are we sure that this drone cannot be spotted?"

Alejandro says, "This aerial platform, *jefe*, was developed for the American CIA. It is nearly impossible to detect. Four were given on loan to our Centro de Investigación y Seguridad Nacional." The young man smiles. "Officially, one was destroyed in a training accident…but as you can see, it has recovered quite nicely."

"Good," Pelayo says.

Casper steps closer to him, lowers his voice. "About the Army captain…the deadline has passed. What shall we do?"

Pelayo says, "We give her another hour. Why not? Sometimes it is to your advantage to show mercy."

Alejandro leans over and whispers something to the man next to him, and the man laughs. Pelayo grips Alejandro's left shoulder. "I'm so sorry, would you care to repeat that?"

"Er, it was nothing, *jefe*."

"Oh, it must have been something, for your friend there to laugh so loud. Please. Share it with me."

"*Jefe*…"

Pelayo squeezes harder. Alejandro gets the message. He stammers and says, "It was…just a joke. That's all. I just said…good for you that Miguel isn't here to hear the talk of mercy."

He releases his grip on the young man's shoulder, gives him a reassuring pat. "Ah, yes. My cousin Miguel. I suppose everyone knows about him, what he's done, what he's capable of doing. Even though he professes to be a religious man. And if he were to know that I just extended this deadline, it would not go well for me, would not go well for my company. Because Miguel would see any sign of mercy as a weakness, am I correct?"

Alejandro whispers, "Yes, you're correct."

Pelayo moves around so he's face-to-face with Alejandro. Everyone in this small room is now staring at what's going on.

He reaches out and gently taps the side of the young man's cheek. "What, you think I'm so small, so weak, that I cannot take a joke? Do you?"

Alejandro just shakes his head no.

Pelayo smiles, says to Casper. "This man…he's a brave one, and smart. He will go far. Come with me, Alejandro, will you?"

The young man is smiling at his fellow workers and follows Pelayo out to the main room of the suite, where Pelayo says, "Get two Coca-Colas from the refrigerator and join up with me."

Pelayo goes to the far balcony and takes in the sparkling view of the Gulf of Mexico. Another perfect day. He hears the door slide open and a shy voice, *"Jefe?"*

He smiles, takes the open Coke bottle from the young man, already open and with a straw in it. He clinks his bottle with Alejandro's and says, "Well done, Alejandro."

"Thank you, *jefe.*"

Pelayo looks over the grounds that belong to him. Below is a narrow parking lot and a loading dock, and there are two mothers trying to herd about a half dozen youngsters in bathing suits to the nearby swimming pool.

He says, "Again, I admire your skills, your sense of humor. Too often there are organizations that are…too rigid. Too formal. Subordinates afraid to tell their superiors what's really going on, what kind of challenges are out there. Do you understand?"

"Yes, *jefe*."

"Excellent!" He takes another sip of the cold, biting, and so satisfying drink. The two mothers and their children are still moving as slow as a turtle carrying a cement block on its back.

He says, "Tell me…you're in that room, day in, day out. How do your coworkers feel about working here, about working for me?"

Alejandro smiles. "We all love it. The pay is generous, the working conditions are fine…We know you are strict in your rules, about women, about the drink, about the drugs. But that is to be expected…to be so high up, to be working for such a man with such a future."

Pelayo puts his bottle down on the railing. He looks over. The mothers and the children are gone.

He says, "Young man, there is one more thing you must know, and that is the role of the king. The king must be above it all, must be seen as all-knowing, all-powerful, and to be respected. Especially the respect. Otherwise words will be muttered, rumors will spread, and plots will commence."

Alejandro's eyes grow frightened, and Pelayo decides to show him mercy.

By not making him wait in fear anymore.

Pelayo leans in, punches Alejandro in the groin, making him double over and gasp, grabs the man's shirt collar with his left hand, and pushes him up and over the balcony railing using the strength of his right shoulder and his hand on Alejandro's waist.

A brief yelp, a heavy thump that he can almost feel in his feet, and it's over.

Pelayo picks up his glass bottle, gives the ground one more glance.

Good.

The two mothers and their children weren't there to witness what has just happened.

Mercy, he ponders, *can show many forms.*

CHAPTER 51

THE LITTLE mantra of *We're out of time, we're out of time*, is marching through my mind, but then it stops as I see what's just happened. I'm hunkered down near a low and wide bush at the rear yard of the target house, binoculars in hand, gathering intelligence, and then there's a little roar of an engine, and the big Ford pickup with the extended cab pulls out and goes down Linden Street, connecting with North School Road, and then it's gone. I spot one bulky guy behind the steering wheel.

Well.

I'm in a dry field of low grass and scrub brush, with some trees scattered here and there. It's good cover, about one of the few breaks that I've gotten on this heartrending mission to Texas. There's a soft whir of insects flying around me, and I do my best to ignore them.

Think, intelligence officer, think.

The home is one story, like most of the homes scattered up and down the street. Probably a small living room right off the front door. There are propane tanks facing me, meaning the kitchen is right there, to the right of the living room. Bathroom, not more than two bedrooms. Even though I've never been in that house, I can visualize the floor plan.

How many people can you fit in a house like that?

Person being held, that I need to steal away. That's one.

Three, maybe four guards, but four is pushing it. That'd be five people in that small house. Where would you put all of them? And five people eat a lot. I can't see these guys trucking to the local supermarket every other day to stock up. Too many eyes and ears in this small town.

So they're hunkering down.

Waiting.

Not for me, I hope, but waiting for somebody else.

All right.

Let's call it four guys in that house, one being the guy I need to grab.

That leaves three armed guards, watching over things.

And one has just left.

The firepower in that house has just decreased by 33 percent.

The guy that's gone…maybe he's out for a grocery run, or a beer run, or maybe he's off to church. But I don't know how much longer he's going to be gone.

Time to move.

I slip the small binoculars into my coat pocket, take out my SIG Sauer 9mm, make sure there's a round in the chamber, and off I go.

I have no illusions.

There are armed men in that house, and there will be shooting.

But I have surprise on my side, and one other thing.

Almost all armed men who do bad things can never see a woman as a possible threat. It's just not in their DNA or in the way they think or how they've learned.

And I'm about ninety seconds away from giving them one hell of a lesson otherwise.

CHAPTER 52

PEPE TORRES is struggling with a certain phrase of St. Paul's in his letter to the Romans when Ramon Hernandez walks in, face red, wearing a tight black tank top and black shorts, peeling off white workout gloves. There's a small weight set in one of the bedrooms, and he's been dedicated to his daily workout routine. Ramon's head is shaved and most of his body is covered with badly inked tattoos he got while in prisons like La Mesa or El Hongo. He picks up a dirty towel from a chair and wipes his hands and face.

"How goes it, Christian?" he asks.

Pepe says, "I'm working...working very hard. How is our guest?"

"Snoozing. I don't know anyone who can sleep so much. I envy him. His mind must be very innocent to be able to sleep with no worries."

Pepe scribbles one last note. "I need to go to the bathroom. Can you stay here for a few minutes?"

"Sure, just don't stink up the place, all right?" Ramon plops down on the couch next to Pepe and slaps his knee with his hand. "Where did Antonio go?"

"He was hungry. He went to the new McDonald's to get something to eat."

"Oh, the *jefe* won't like that."

"Well, I won't tell him."

"Neither will I," Ramon says. "That Antonio, he needs to chill, am I right? Here we are, we don't have the best food or bedding, but hey, we don't have to worry about some *chicos* coming by, strafing us with iron bananas."

Pepe puts his notepad to the side, carefully closes the Bible, thinking, *Yes, Ramon is right,* even using the slang for AK-47s, iron bananas. His bladder is full and he needs to go, and as he stands up, Ramon says, "Hey, did Antonio say he'd bring anything back?"

"No," Pepe says, walking out of the living room.

"Figures, that stingy bastard. Hey, you taking the Good Book to the crapper?"

Pepe says, "Why not?"

Ramon laughs, picks up the control for the television. "I don't know, it just seems...bad, bringing the Bible into the crapper."

Pepe moves along. "Jesus is everywhere, even in the bathroom."

As he goes into the bathroom and closes the door, he thinks he hears a knock but pays it no mind.

Ramon can handle anything out there.

CHAPTER 53

RAMON HERNANDEZ checks the telenovela DVD playing on the old color television and frowns. It's a good one, *La Reina del Sur*, starring that knock-out actress with legs that go on forever, Kate del Castillo, but he's seen this series at least twice. That *chica* Kate plays an innocent woman who gets involved in cartels and smuggling, and Ramon loves that shit, and—

Ah, no harm in watching it a third time.

There's a knock on the door.

He pauses the DVD.

Another knock.

He reaches under a couch cushion, takes out a Beretta Model 12 9mm pistol, one of the many weapons hidden in the house. He walks off to the side, looks through the window.

No traffic. No cars parked in front.

He can barely make out a shape on the front stone steps.

One person, then.

Is it the *norteamericano*, the pickup guy for their guest?

Could be, and then he and Pepe and Antonio can get the hell out of here and get back to work. It's been nice to relax and do some workouts and weight lifting, but that crappy frozen food and lumpy bed are starting to get to him.

The knock comes again.

"Hold on!" he calls out in English.

He moves slowly to the door and peers out through the peephole.

Small guy standing there, shoulders hunched up, wearing a black baseball cap, hands hanging down, empty. He's got on blue jeans with some sort of silvery stripes on them.

That's it.

Ramon thinks briefly of waiting until Pepe shows up, after he·wipes his bum, and thinks, *No, just one small guy out there*. Besides, if it is their contact, won't Antonio be pissed that he missed the handoff! Let him try to explain to the *jefe* why he wasn't here.

He slides the pistol into the side of his tight black shorts, opens the door.

CHAPTER 54

AFTER I knock at the house again, turned sideways so whoever's inside can't get a good look at me, I'm racing through a lot of options and choices in my mind. Maybe I should have waited some more. Maybe I should have just tossed a cement block through the rear sliding-glass door. Maybe going in through the front door isn't the best idea.

Too late.

I'm committed.

The door opens up, and unlike my comrades in the service, who more often than not can practice and re-practice and practice yet again a raid on a compound or a heavily defended house, I'm going in cold, as they say, making up shit as I go along.

I turn to see who's there, and holy God, it's one bulky and scary-looking guy. Hispanic, shaved head, tattoos up and down his thick biceps and legs, even on his hair-less and muscular chest, and he's wearing black shorts and a tank top, and now, I've got to hit him, now.

"Yes?" he says in accented English. "What do you want?"

My hand quickly goes to my coat pocket and his eyes widen and he steps back, reaching to his side where I see the handle of a pistol, but I'm faster and I come out with the same canister of pepper spray I took from the trooper in Tennessee, and I push for-ward, aim it right at his face, and thumb the trigger.

A slight hiss.

Nothing happens.

Nothing comes out.

It's empty!

The guy pauses and then bursts out laughing at me, and I know what's going through his mind: *Silly girl can't do anything right*.

So I punch him hard in the throat, still holding the metal canister in my hand.

He coughs, stumbles back, and I punch him again in the throat, and he lifts both hands to his neck, starts gurgling, his eyes slightly bulging, and I know that my allotted seconds to get this done are sliding away, so I give a good whirl on my left foot, kick out with my right, and catch him behind the near knee.

He tumbles to the floor, damn near making the room shake.

I put the useless canister back into my jacket pocket, pull off one of the strips of silver duct tape I earlier placed on both pant legs, and with a knee to the small of his back, I work quickly to get his wrists bound behind him. I grab the pistol from his waistband, toss it to one corner of the room, and then I tape his bare lower legs, and I'm thinking, *Fast, have to go faster,* and then I look up and a skinny guy is coming into the room, holding a black leather book with a gold cross on the cover.

We stare at each other for a second.

He ducks back into the kitchen and I get up and move fast, and he's turning around in the kitchen, spinning, and the book is now a pistol, and he's bringing it up, shooting at me.

I react within seconds, pulling out my SIG Sauer, remembering the long hours on the range — "Better to get off an imperfect shot than wait to make a perfect shot and get your head blown off "—and my first round misses, the second one catches him in the upper right thigh, and the next one strikes him dead center in the chest.

He falls against the near cabinets, making one door pop open, and dishes and glassware fall out, and his moans and the sound of the shattering glass nearly drown out the bellowing from behind me.

I whirl and the big guy has torn away the strips of duct tape and is grabbing another pistol from under the couch, and he brings up his weapon and I shoot again, and I catch him right in his mouth. He falls right back in a spray of blood and knocks over the television set, increasing its volume, and some sort of Mexican music starts echoing through the house, overpowering the ringing in my ears.

I'm shaking now, and I go forward and grab the big guy's pistol from the floor, stick it in my waistband, and then retrieve the weapon from the skinny guy in the kitchen, put it in the opposite waistband of my jeans, and I'm panting, trying to get some sort of semblance of calm, because if there's another gunman in here, he'd have to be as deaf as the biggest bat in the world not to hear all the loud noise coming from this horrid gunfight.

But nobody else is coming at me.

I go up a short hallway, hammer open a door to a bedroom, check under the bed, and then the closet. Lots of piles of smelly clothes and porn magazines. I go to the other bedroom and it's a twin of its mate, this time with weight equipment. Again, under the bed, and in the small closet.

Nobody else is here.

CHAPTER 55

THEN I curse myself again for being so thick—thank God I'm not a platoon leader, because I'd probably end up decimating my troops on our first mission—and I go back down the short hallway, kick open the door to the bathroom, and there's a man, huddled in the bathtub, holding up hands that are shaking like tall grass in the wind.

I recall what the man on the phone said when he called me about the kidnapping of Tom and Denise.

You'll know him when you see him. He'll be the one without a weapon.

By God, he's right.

The man in the bathtub seems to be in his late sixties, early seventies. He's wearing a two-piece dark-blue suit with a white shirt. His thin white hair is carefully combed, and he has a nicely trimmed white beard.

His hands are empty, and they are quivering.

I say, "Come on, let's go, let's move it."

He doesn't move.

I step forward, roughly grab his wrist. "Amigo, buddy, whoever the hell you are, let's get going!"

With some difficulty, he clambers out of the tub, and I shove him forward, and we go through the bloody kitchen—now smelly as the dead skinny guy becomes even more dead—and I get the sliding door open, and we're off on a rear patio. I grab his wrist again, and start running.

We run for a few minutes until I get to the grove of trees and scrub brush where I parked my Jeep. I open the passenger door, shove him in, and as I do that, I drop the two pistols I had gotten from the house after wiping them down.

To hell with the extra firepower. Too much to carry around.

I go around and start up the Wrangler; my hands, neck, and lower back are soaked with sweat that is quickly turning cold. A few minutes ago I just killed two men. Two men and their dreams and their lives and their hopes and their history, I've just snuffed out.

I guess I should feel guilty, but the first guy I shot, he shot first, and the second guy I shot, well, based on his tatts and his attitude, he was no Boy Scout, either.

No guilt, then. At least not now.

I pull out and get on a side road that runs parallel to Linden, then drive up to North School Road, and make a left. I see flashing blue lights in my rearview mirror.

That was quick.

Must be some very attentive neighbors back there.

I keep my speed low, keep on driving, and look up in the mirror again.

I see one cruiser, and it looks like another is coming down North School Road, and I think, *All right, one cruiser will probably go down Linden.*

And what will the second cruiser do?

Join the first one?

Or come after the only other moving vehicle on North School Road?

Me.

One more glance. A couple of curious folks emerge from their small houses, putting their hands up to their foreheads, blocking the sun, looking at the action.

The first cruiser turns, and then the second.

The road behind me is empty.

So is the one in front of me.

I take a deep breath, let it out, glance at my passenger. He is gently rearranging his coat and his shirt, and then he looks around and grabs the seat belt, pulls it over, and clicks it shut.

"Hey," I say. "You okay? You didn't get hurt, did you?"

He gives me a look, almost...

Sad?

Tired?

A look of pity?

Then he turns and looks out the windshield.

I make a right, take out my iPhone, check my cell phone signal.

Pretty weak.

I need to make the most important phone call of my life to that man out there who has my family, and I'm not going to take a chance on losing the call over a bad signal.

I put the phone in my lap, keep on driving.

I say to the man next to me, "I'm sorry I'm doing this to you. Very, very sorry."

He doesn't say a word.

No matter, I think.

One way or another, he's valuable to me, the key to get Tom and Denise freed, and if he wants to stay quiet, fine. In fact, more than fine. It's perfect. I don't need to hear him begging or pleading to be let go as I take him to the man who wants him.

I look at my iPhone.

The signal is getting stronger.

Good.

I pull over and dial that number from memory.

In less than three seconds, it's answered, and I recognize the voice. "Yes?"

"Got him," I say.

There's an all-knowing chuckle from the phone.

"I know."

CHAPTER 56

ANTONIO GARCIA belches in satisfaction and looks at the nice porn movie he's watching on his Galaxy with the bigger screen he got last year, with his belly full of two Big Macs and a large order of french fries. He's parked in the lot of the new McDonald's, and he wishes he had come here earlier. The frozen foods back at their place...ugh.

He sips on a big cup of orange Fanta and wonders if he should go back in for something else to top off his meal, perhaps one of those grilled chicken sandwiches.

Chicken.

No, he really should get back to the house, before Pepe decides it would be the Christian thing to tell their *jefe* that he has violated orders and has left the place. The earlier Pepe would have never squealed like that, but the new Pepe...who knows. Once a man starts believing in the gods, anything can happen.

He sucks in the Fanta and finishes it, tosses the empty cardboard cup in the rear. Coming through the border crossing a week ago was so easy, even when the Border Patrol took them aside for a detailed search. Of course, the look of them made the *norteamericanos* suspicious— he, Pepe, and Ramon, looking the way they did, escorting a man who was so well-dressed and polite he looked like a retired television star.

The truck was pulled apart, two bitch dogs sniffed

around and poked, and nothing was found. Nothing. Not a seed, not a trace of powder, not a single 9mm round.

So they were sent on their way, and when they arrived in this little crap hole in Texas, they found that weapons, DVDs, and food had been stocked up in that little house.

He peeks down at the screen of his Galaxy phone and sighs. A sweet movie. It is about a busty housewife wearing a skimpy bikini who invites three bulky men into her home to clean the pool. Oh, yeah, a lot of cleaning was going on, but none of it involved chemicals or skimmers. The four of them had started poolside nice and gentle, and now they were in the wide living room of the house, and the housewife was being tossed around like a doll with flexible limbs.

Antonio watches for a few more minutes—the movie is great but he's seen some real stuff, the video quality not so great but what was being filmed could never be sold in public— but you take what you can get.

When the movie is done, he slides his Galaxy off, feels his stomach grumble.

Oh, one more sandwich. Why not.

He pulls around and goes through the drive-through, and a sweet little blond Anglo girl with a big bust under her ugly uniform passes over his order. She's cute but her face has broken out with acne, but so what. That's what pillows or paper bags are made for.

He smiles at her, says, *"Gracias,"* in his most polite and sweet voice, and drives off with his second McDonald's meal of the day. God, the scent of that food…he starts eating before he even leaves the parking lot, and when he gets on North School Road, he wipes his fingers with a bunch of paper napkins, steering with his knees.

Up ahead a police cruiser is coming straight at him, lights on, siren wailing.

What?

He checks his speed, sees he's right at the speed limit, as he always drives—how many of his friends have come here to the States and ended up in jail because of speeding or having a broken taillight? —and he just keeps on going.

The cruiser slides into a turn, heading right down—

Linden Street!

He swears softly, thoroughly, and with great enthusiasm, and he slows down just a bit more.

All right.

Slow enough not to get attention, but fast enough to look like an innocent resident, wondering what all the excitement is.

Madre de dios!

There are two police cruisers pulled up in front of their house, and an ambulance and fire truck are parked nearby. Cops are there, weapons drawn, huddled behind the police cruisers.

What the hell happened in the short time since he left?

More curses.

The warm and tasty food in his belly has just turned into heavy, wet, cold cement.

He has screwed up.

The words of his *jefe* come back to him.

Don't draw attention to yourself. Keep things quiet. One of you to be awake at all times. No drinking. No drugs.

And most of all…

Don't leave the house.

Another siren cuts through him, and he sees another cruiser fishtailing around another corner, heading straight toward Linden Street.

Like a good, law-abiding citizen, he pulls over.

Don't leave the house.

All right.

Something has happened, something bad.

He chews on his lower lip.

He can still make it work.

He'll call the *jefe* and tell him…something. He had to leave because…

Because the chicken was ill.

That's right.

Their guest was ill, and he had to get medicine at the local drugstore.

While he was there, something bad happened.

It was a stroke of fortune, to be out of the house, so he could tell the *jefe* what happened, be a witness.

His boss will be angry, but will be understanding, Antonio is sure. For the *jefe*'s concern was that the old man be kept safe and secure until the *norteamericano* showed up.

And considering the police response—Jesus, is that another siren he is hearing?—there certainly wasn't anything polite or quiet going on down there during the past several minutes.

He resumes driving, turns onto St. Mary's Street, starts rehearsing what he's about to tell the *jefe*.

A pause.

But what about Pepe?

Pepe knew exactly where he was going.

Not off to get medicine, but to get some hot McDonald's food.

He ponders some more.

Considering what he's seen, Pepe is wounded, dead, or alive in police custody.

If he's in police custody, Pepe will know the rules. Keep quiet, no phone call—which can be tapped—and wait for someone from the cartel to come retrieve him.

If he's wounded, then he'll be in a local hospital. Antonio can track him down and then…take care of him.

And if Antonio is very, very lucky, then Pepe is dead and is now explaining himself to the God he believed in.

Antonio doesn't believe in God but believes in his *jefe*, and now it's time to make a confession of sorts.

He picks up his phone and then freezes.

No signal.

CHAPTER 57

PELAYO ABBOUD is relaxing on a couch in his expansive suite, reading the *Economist,* when Casper slips out of a door and gestures to him. He puts the *Economist* down and strolls over to his trusted deputy, and Casper whispers to him, "There's something going on at Three Rivers. Quickly, please."

He steps in and Casper gently escorts him to a wide computer screen that has the feed coming in from the ex-CIA drone that now belongs to Pelayo and his organization. Once again, he is taken aback by the details he can see from the aerial platform.

"Are we sure this cannot be seen?"

One of the technical men who replaced the unfortunate Alejandro quietly says, "Fairly certain, *jefe*. It has what is known as a chameleon liquid outer shell. The drone adjusts its own color to match the sky and flying clouds. For someone on the ground, they might hear the buzzing sound, and that will be all."

"Your name, son?"

"Ferdinand."

He gently squeezes the young man's shoulder. "Well said, Ferdinand." He leans over and asks Casper, "What, then, is going on?"

Casper takes a pen and places it on the screen, lower right, where there seem to be low trees and brush. He taps the screen and says, "A few minutes ago, we saw a person crawl into this brush. It seems like the house is under surveillance."

"I see."

Pelayo looks to the house. "And the truck is still gone."

"Yes," Casper says.

"Then—"

Pelayo stops talking as a figure emerges from the brush and walks quickly to the nearby road, and then strolls up to the front of the house.

"Well," Pelayo says.

With reluctance the young man says, *"Jefe?"*

"Yes? Don't be shy."

"If you want, I can lower the drone's altitude...which may make it easier for it to be seen. But there is a microphone. We might be able to hear voices."

"Do it," he says.

The young man manipulates the keyboard and the view tightens in on the house, looking down from above, and Pelayo imagines the possibilities of having several drones like this, perhaps armed with weapons. An avenging angel, overseeing his enemies.

He likes that idea.

Sound crackles from the speakers set next to the computer screen. He can hear a car horn, the sound of wind. The figure, wearing a baseball cap and regular clothes, comes to the front door and knocks.

Casper says, "Could that be the Army captain?"

"It might," Pelayo says.

There's another knock on the door. And then, a third.

"Could the house be empty?" Casper asks.

Pelayo says, "Don't even think of such a thing."

Then...voices. He can actually hear a voice and—

The figure disappears into the house.

Gunshots.

Pow!

Pow!

Three more rapid gunshots in a row.

Then another one.

Pelayo leans over some more, like he's now part of the drone, watching everything unfold beneath him.

Two figures emerge from the rear of the house, run across the yard. Ferdinand manipulates the keyboard one more time, and they watch as the two people go into a grove of trees.

A minute later, what looks to be a Jeep drives out and onto a road.

The drone follows the Jeep's progress.

With pleasure in his voice, Casper says, "The Army captain…she drives a Jeep."

"So she does," Pelayo says. "I guess that was the Army captain after all, eh?"

He watches as the Jeep maneuvers its way through some streets and then pulls over.

Pelayo says, "The phone, if you please."

Casper passes it over to him.

He holds it.

Waits a few minutes.

It rings. He answers.

"Yes?"

The woman's voice comes through clear and strong.

"Got him," she says.

Pelayo chuckles.

"I know."

He puts the phone against his chest so she can't hear what he says to his crew, for he knows that they are still worried and disturbed by the day's earlier events, and the fact that one chair in this room is blatantly empty.

With a smile to his crew, Pelayo says, "You see? Sometimes it pays to be merciful."

CHAPTER 58

SO THE son of a bitch knows already, which doesn't surprise me that much. Having committed at least a half dozen serious capital crimes in kidnapping and threatening my family, there's obviously something very big on the line for him, so it stands to reason he'd be keeping track of me.

But he doesn't realize the mistake he's made in revealing this information, which now gives me some hard intelligence I didn't have before, knowing for a fact I'm being tracked.

That's the thing with civilians. They watch some History Channel documentaries, read a bio of a Navy SEAL or two, along with Sun Tzu, and they think they're a goddamn strategic genius.

I say, "All right. I've got him. What now?"

"Let's verify you have the right person. Will you describe him?"

I give my silent passenger one good look and say, "Gentleman in his late sixties, early seventies. Well-dressed, well-groomed. White beard and hair. Brown eyes. Wearing a nice suit, no necktie. You want I should ask him his blood type?"

Another chuckle. "That won't be necessary."

I hear another siren coming in from another direction. This place is hot and is going to get much hotter, and I need to get moving before some smart cop starts setting up roadblocks.

"What now?" I ask.

"You're to bring him to me, in good health. You're to drive east, to a town called Beachside, Florida. It's off Route 98, just below Miramar Beach and above another town called Seaside. If you were to drive non-stop, it should take you just about thirteen hours. But as you can tell, I'm in a giving mood. Your deadline is exactly twenty-four hours from now."

"Where in Beachside?"

"There's a small plaza in the center of town, with a little open music hall and fountain. Park there and call me, and then I'll give you further instructions."

"Why is this…old man so important to you?"

"Really, Captain Cornwall, do you expect me to answer that question?"

"I'm a hopeful gal."

"So you are," he says.

The man next to me is staring ahead with a mournful look. What has brought him here, and why is he so needed in Florida?

Sorry, I don't care.

I say, "I need to talk to Tom, right now."

"I'm sorry, that's not possible."

A sharp shard of cold ice has just been shoved into my chest.

"Make it possible," I say, slowly and with emphasis.

"I'm not in a position to do that at this time," he says.

"Then change your position."

He says, "I give you my word that they are safe. But they are also in a secure location that is sometimes difficult to access. But I promise you this. When you get to Beachside, and before the exchange, you will be able to talk to him."

I look to the quiet and nice-looking man sitting

next to me. "Hey!" I yell in his direction, and he's startled.

Great.

That means he can hear, and is going to hear what I'm saying next.

"Okay. I don't trust you or your worthless word, but we'll have an understanding, okay? When I get to Beachside and phone you, I will hear from Tom directly. I will also hear from Denise, directly and separately. I will be able to ask them both questions to ensure that they are safe and are ready for me to pick them up."

"Meaning?"

"Meaning I want to know that they're in the area, all right? I don't want them to be somewhere in Georgia or Alabama or someplace else. So you need to come up with some sort of solution that tells me they're nearby."

"Or else?" he asks.

I look to the man who's now staring at me with his soft brown eyes.

"Or else I take the man you desire so much, stand him next to the fountain you mentioned, and blow his goddamn head off."

I disconnect the call.

The old man's gaze doesn't flinch.

I start up the Jeep and say to him, "In case you didn't notice, I shot two men dead in your house back there, all in order to get my family back. No offense, buster, but if I don't get my family back, safe and sound, you're not living out tomorrow."

Then I shift into drive and do my best to get out of town.

CHAPTER 59

WHEN THE Army captain hangs up her phone, Pelayo says aloud, "My, she's a feisty one, isn't she?"

Some nervous laughter from his workers, and Casper steps closer to him and says, "I...I just need to ask this. And no offense."

Pelayo puts his arm around his deputy's shoulders. "Casper, you have served me well, for many years. How could you say anything offensive to me? Please. Tell me what's on your mind."

"It's...well, I've always wondered. Since you learned what was going on with Tom Cornwall, and you also learned who was being kept at that house in Three Rivers, why did you send in that man's wife? Wouldn't it have been easier, and quicker, to use our own people?"

He gives Casper a reassuring squeeze. "That's good thinking, and I admire you so. But these are complicated times. Sometimes it's best to contract out a job like this, in case it goes wrong. If we were to send our own resources...they might stand out. They might be witnessed, it being a small town and such. Besides, it's always fun to blame the Americans, in case it did go wrong and the Army captain died, and if our subject died, well, that would be God's will."

Another squeeze to Casper's thick shoulder. "Besides, having everything in one place, within easy reach, makes cleanup so much easier. Best to have the

American family and our absent friend all within easy reach."

Casper says, "Don't you think the Army captain will be suspicious?"

Pelayo says, "I'm counting on it."

CHAPTER 60

ROSARIA VASQUEZ is doing her best to navigate her way in the very small town of Three Rivers, Texas. Earlier she had been sent by her boss to go to the equally small town of Kenedy, where Captain Cornwall had used a Bank of America ATM to make a cash withdrawal, but an unexpected and quick phone call from Senior Warrant Officer McCarthy changed that.

"There've been shootings at a home in Three Rivers," he said. "Next town over from Kenedy. Go check it out."

"Do you have information that Captain Cornwall was involved?"

And McCarthy said, "Hell, no, but you're going to find out. She was in Kenedy not too long ago, and now there are dead people in the small town next door. On Linden Street. And I don't believe in coincidences."

Vasquez checks her rental car's GPS, which sometimes winks in and out, like there's some sort of communications foul-up in this town. Even though she's never been in Three Rivers before in her life, it feels very familiar. In her investigations over the years, visiting small towns like this to talk to soldiers either on leave or recently discharged, it was always the same. A struggling, proud small town that doesn't have much opportunity for recent graduates, except for the military.

The GPS sends her down North School Road, and up ahead, a police cruiser races toward her, then makes a sudden turn to the right.

The GPS quits on her.

No matter.

She knows where she's going.

Up ahead she sees the sign for Linden, makes a left, and then pulls her rental car over. There is a mess of people and police cruisers down the street, along with a fire truck and ambulance, and she knows she has to take this one easy. For one thing, Captain Cornwall might not be connected to this in any way. And for another, locals are always suspicious, and rightfully so, about having the Feds—FBI, ICE, military police— come in and stomp over everything.

Rosaria steps out, puts on her jacket, and slings her black leather bag over her shoulder. She starts walking down the street, retrieving her Army CID shield as she does so, walking by the fire truck and ambulance. Clustered around the plain one-story house are two black-and-white police cruisers belonging to the Three Rivers Police Department, one white cruiser belonging to the McMullen County Sheriff's Department, and another black cruiser with a white hood from the Texas State Police.

Officers with drawn weapons are slowly going through the yard, and one officer comes out of the house—also with weapon in hand—and yells out, "Clear, but for Christ's sake, we got a goddamn bloodbath in there. Anybody know when the chief will get here?"

Someone answers him, and Rosaria pushes her way through a handful of civilians, until she comes up to a heavyset Three Rivers officer, wearing a dark-blue uniform, holding his arms out.

"Sorry," he says. "This is an active crime scene. Nobody's allowed through."

Rosaria shows her badge. "Warrant Officer Rosaria Vasquez, US Army. I'm a special agent with the Criminal Investigation Command."

He eyes her badge and identification, and almost looks relieved. "Sweet Jesus, what a mess we got."

"I'm involved in an investigation that might have a connection to what's happened here," she says, still keeping her identification in hand. "May I ask who's in charge?"

"That'd be Sergeant Morales, over there by the door."

"Your name, Officer?"

"Puntez."

She smiles, one Hispanic to another, helping out. "Thanks, Officer Puntez, I appreciate the cooperation."

Rosaria walks by him just as another officer trots up, quickly unspooling the traditional black-and-yellow crime scene tape, and as she gets closer to the house, there are a lot of loud voices, cursing, and more loud voices, until a woman's voice cuts through and says, "That's enough. Right now we got two victims inside, and nothing's getting moved or touched until the chief and our own crime scene investigator show up."

The woman is Sergeant Morales, skinny and short but wearing her dark uniform with pride and, now, with anger. She's glaring at the other officers—two from the county and one from the state—and then notices Rosaria.

"And where the hell are you from?" she demands. "Border Patrol?"

Rosaria displays her identification and badge, and

Morales nods and says, "Nice. The Army. Why the hell not? Add more confusion and jurisdictional pissing to this mess. What brings you here?"

Rosaria sees the other officers looking on with interest, and Morales sees that as well and says, "All right, I get it. C'mon, let's duck around the corner."

At the corner of the house Rosaria sees two other officers slowly going across the field, and Morales says, "The chief goes out of town for a doctor's appointment, and look at the shitstorm that just got dumped over my head. So... Vasquez, is that it?"

"Yes, Sergeant."

"What's going on with the Army?"

Rosaria says, "If I tell you, will you tell me what happened here?"

"Christ, yes. In fact, I'd love to bundle it up in a big box and bow and pass it over to you. I can't tell you the last time we had a homicide in Three Rivers, and I grew up here. And now we got a double homicide. Damn."

Rosaria puts her identification away. "I'm investigating an AWOL Army officer. She was last spotted in a town called Kenedy."

"Sure, right down the highway."

"Well, I was on my way to Kenedy when I got the information about the shootings here in Three Rivers."

Morales frowns. "What, you got some crazy vet, suffering from PTSD, going on some sort of killing rampage?"

"No, not at all," Rosaria says.

"Good. I got two nephews, good boys both, who've been to Iraq and Afghanistan. I won't stand for that shit, anybody dissing our veterans. So why do you think there's a connection?"

"I don't know if there's a connection," she says. "That's why I'm here. It just seems…odd, that my AWOL officer would be spotted in Kenedy, and then there's a shooting here, not long after."

"Your officer a combat veteran?"

"No, she's an intelligence officer."

"She got family around here?"

"No, she's originally from Maine. She's never been to Texas, has never been stationed in Texas."

"She got somebody here she might have a grudge against?"

"Not that I know of."

"And you don't know of any connection between her and my town?"

"Not at all."

Morales slaps at a buzzing fly and says, "Fair enough, you've been up front with me. Now it's my turn. We got a nine-one-one call about twenty minutes ago, saying there were shots fired at this house. No big deal, hearing gunshots, but the caller said the shots came from within the house, and that she had spotted two people running away from the scene. First responder came in, saw bodies and blood, and that's where we stand."

"Any identification of the victims?"

"Two adult males, that's all we know. Both died from gunshot wounds."

"They rent or own the place?"

"That's being tracked down."

Rosaria nods. "Mind if I take a peek inside?"

Morales says, "Think you can stand it?"

"No," Rosaria says. "I know I can stand it."

CHAPTER 61

AT THE steps leading into the house, a young male Three Rivers police officer holds a clipboard in his slightly trembling hands, and near his feet there's an open black plastic case. The door to the house is propped open with a rock.

Morales bends over the case, comes back up, and hands over a set of light-blue paper booties and latex gloves. As Rosaria and the sergeant start getting dressed, another Three Rivers officer comes over, nearly breathless, and says, "Mister Houston, up two houses, he says the folks who were here had a big black pickup truck, extended cab, with those overhead lights. He said it drove out a while ago, he's not sure of the time."

Morales says, "Okay, then, put it out. I'm busy here."

Once they are both dressed, Morales says, "I know you're a pro, but I still have to say it: be careful where you step, and before you touch anything, ask me first. Savvy?"

"You got it."

At the open door, the officer notes the time and writes down Morales's name, and Rosaria presents her identification. After the recording is done—essential at any homicide scene to keep track of the traffic—Morales goes in, and Rosaria closely follows.

The police sergeant stops, and Rosaria takes in the

bloody scene. The smell of death is here in this room, and unlike other crime scenes she's visited over the years, this one is relatively fresh. Too soon for body decomp to have set in, though there's the aroma of discharged firearms mixed in with the pungent scent of bodies having just been ripped apart by bullets traveling at several thousand feet per second.

The dead man in this small living room is huge, bulked-up, and Rosaria can imagine the house shuddering when he hit the ground. He's wearing black shorts and a wrestler-type tank top, and there are torn and twisted strips of gray duct tape around his ankles and wrists.

What's visible on his skin are a lot of tattoos, and Morales notices Rosaria's interest as she leans over the dead man and says, "Rough ink work, right? That's Mexican prison stuff, right there. Our dead guy here has a lot of blood and bullets under his belt."

Rosaria says quietly, "Yeah, plus one through the mouth. Good shooting."

"Or accidental. Once bullets start flying, you never know where they'll end up."

A television is on its side, the sound and picture still on, and Rosaria cants her head, says, "Looks like a telenovela."

"Good call."

Rosaria straightens up and says, "This guy…he wasn't shot right off when the intruder came to the door. He either recognized the intruder or didn't think he or she was a threat. And the intruder…violent death wasn't the goal."

Morales nods. "Yeah. The duct tape. Looks like the big guy here got caught or stunned, was secured by the duct tape, but was strong enough and pissed enough to tear himself free. And look at this."

Morales steps over the dead man's thick and out-stretched legs, points down to the floor between him and the couch. "Don't touch it, but it looks like a Beretta nine mill down there. I did a quick check before you showed up. There's weapons stashed all over the place. Way I figure it, he was down for the count but managed to break free, find a weapon, and he was zapped before he could use it."

"All right," Rosaria says, noting the bloody and gaping wound in the man's mouth and head. Flies are starting to come in and buzz around. Morales goes into the tiny kitchen and Rosaria follows, careful to keep her footsteps slow and careful. It wouldn't do to slip on the paper booties and fall on your ass in front of a local.

In the kitchen is another dead man, also shot, splayed out against a kitchen counter, broken dishes and glass-ware on the floor. This one is younger and slimmer than his companion in the living room. Morales says, "Looks like junior here took the brunt of the assault. At least three wounds I can see, and no duct tape."

Rosaria nods, says to Morales, "Mind if I check the refrigerator and cabinets?"

"Sure. You hungry?"

"Not yet."

The cabinets are mostly empty, save for bags of potato chips and tortilla chips, some containers of salsa. The refrigerator is nearly empty as well, but the freezer is full of Swanson frozen meals.

Rosaria says, "Temporary quarters for temporary guests."

"You got it."

She sees a book on the floor, near the dead man. It's a Spanish-language Bible. "What do you think of this?" Rosaria asks.

Morales says, "Looks like the guy had a 'come to Jesus' moment before the bullets started flying."

Rosaria says, "I wonder what Jesus might be saying to him now."

Rosaria carefully goes through the rest of the house. Another siren in the distance. Two bedrooms, each with a bed and a mattress on the floor.

"Looks like four guys," she says. "Waiting...but for what?"

"Not for a hit," Morales says. "But really..."

The sound of the siren grows louder.

"Go on," Rosaria says. "What were you going to say?"

"It wasn't a hit, it was a snatch," she says. "We got a report of two guys running across the field after the shooting started. We got two dead guys here. That means our two runners were probably the shooter and somebody else. And if you were just coming in to hit the residents, you wouldn't be running away with another guy in tow."

Rosaria says, "You got sleeping arrangements for four."

"Yeah, and we also know that a large tricked-out pickup truck left before the shooting started. Maybe that guy betrayed his friends here. Went out to make a phone call, and then the hit comes. Might be halfway to the border by now."

Rosaria nods and just walks quietly out of the house and, on the worn, beaten-down brown lawn, tugs off the gloves and the booties. Morales keeps hers on. Rosaria says, "But it certainly wasn't a hit."

"How are you so sure?" Morales asks.

"The guy with the duct tape. It means the shooter came in with mercy on her mind. She didn't want to kill anybody right off. But she killed when she had to…and then she left with the man she was here to take. If this had been a hit, there would have been no duct tape…just a shooter coming in with an M4 or an Uzi or AK-47, just hose down every room."

Morales says, "I like the way you think."

Rosaria smiles. "So do I." With her warm and moist hands, she reaches into her jacket, removes a business card, passes it over. "You and I both know that in a few minutes, your chief is going to show up, your crime scene folks, maybe more state troopers and the Texas Rangers. But I would sure love to talk to you directly, without having to go through the chain of command. Especially if you can get an idea of who the victims were, why they were here, and what they were protecting."

Morales nods, passes over her own business card. "When did you know it was your Army officer?"

"What?"

Morales says, "A few minutes ago, you said the shooter was a she. Earlier, you said him or her. What made you decide?"

Rosaria gives her a wide smile, and Morales smiles in return when she says, "Female intuition, what else?"

Morales takes one more glance at the house. "Sad, isn't it?"

"The two dead guys?"

"No, this nice little house. Once upon a time, it was probably a sweet home for a nice family, raising kids, watching them grow up and succeed. Know what I mean?"

"No," Rosaria says.

Five minutes later, Rosaria is back in her rental car and she feels like she needs to brief her boss, but first, she needs a cold drink, and as she's driving up the main road in Three Rivers, she spots a McDonald's and pulls in.

And then she sees something else, and her SIG Sauer is in her hand, at her side in the car.

Parked at the rear of the McDonald's lot, partially hidden by a green dumpster, is a black pickup truck with an extended cab and overhead light rack.

CHAPTER 62

AFTER WORKING for his first *jefe*, Antonio Garcia no longer believes in Jesus, the Blessed Virgin, the Holy Saints, or nearly anybody else, but he's beginning to reconsider his atheism as his day proceeds. Back here in the McDonald's parking lot he finds a strong signal for his cell phone, and with dread in his bones, he calls his *jefe* to tell him how everything has gone wrong.

But his boss isn't home!

On the phone is one of his lieutenants, a grim, sour little man called Pedro, and Pedro is demanding to know why Antonio is calling, but he won't answer the man's questions. Each day working for the *jefe* is a balancing act, keeping him happy, watching the rivals in the organization who will stab you in your back— literally!—if the opportunity arises.

Antonio says, "Look, when will he be back?"

Pedro swears and says, "How should I know? All I know is that he had the urge to go visit his wife and do some serious drinking and humping, and now he's gone."

Antonio says, "Which wife?" and he's not joking, for like most cartel heads in Mexico, strong men with strong appetites have three or four wives scattered across the country or in the States.

Pedro says, "I think the one in Puerto Vallarta.

She's the one that he likes seeing in those dental-floss bathing suits."

Antonio swivels in his seat, to see if any police are in the area. No, just a McDonald's worker, a woman in one of those brown shirts, walking from car to car, holding a brown paper bag.

Other than that, clear.

He says, "All right, do you have a number for him?"

"I do, but you're not getting it unless you tell me why you need it."

Antonio swears at Pedro and says, "Look, I'm not getting into some school dispute with you, *amigo*. It'll be on you when the *jefe* finds out you've been dicking around."

Pedro laughs. "We'll see," and his *jefe*'s man disconnects the call.

Okay, then.

Antonio feels much, much better. Any delay in telling his boss what happened here in this town will be on Pedro. And the delay now gives him time to get a story together.

What kind of story?

Any kind of story that will leave Antonio innocent of any foul-ups or wrongdoing.

A knock on his window makes him jump.

He turns, his heavy revolver in his right hand.

It's the woman from McDonald's, holding up the paper bag, a dumb grin on her face. "Sir, is this yours? Is this order yours?"

Antonio snaps, "Go away."

She shakes her head, still smiling. "Sir, please, I've checked everyone in the parking lot. You're the last one here. It must be yours."

He swears and the woman taps her ear with a

free hand. "Sorry, sir, I can't hear that well. What did you say?"

Antonio wants to get rid of this bitch as soon as he can, so he lowers the window and starts to talk.

And he chokes, with a pistol barrel now crowding his mouth.

CHAPTER 63

AFTER SPENDING a few bucks for a Quarter Pounder meal and persuading the manager to lend her a worker's shirt—by flashing her Army identification and spinning a tale of hunting an ISIS spy— Rosaria is now by the open driver's-side window, her SIG Sauer in the man's mouth.

He's well-built, flashy-looking, and an empty leather shoulder holster is visible. No real evidence that he was the guy at the house back there, because there must be lots of pickup trucks like this roaming around this part of Texas, but Rosaria has a gut feeling it must be him.

He's Hispanic, eyes wide but not afraid, like he's used to having a gun drawn on him.

Rosaria feels like one of those zoo workers who has successfully grabbed a deadly and angry rattlesnake by the head, only a slip or two away from being poisoned.

She needs to be careful.

Rosaria drops the McDonald's bag on the asphalt and says, "Both hands up, touching the roof. Now."

The man slowly complies, both arms lifting up, shirt and jacket sleeves sliding off, to reveal the same type of prison tattoos as the dead guy on Linden Street, plus some gold jewelry and a heavy-looking watch.

Rosaria spots what looks to be a hand cannon on

his lap, and with her left hand, reaches in through the open window, picks up the heavy revolver, and tosses it into the bushes behind her, where it makes one hell of a crashing noise.

"Now," she says, "I'm coming in to join you. When I come in, you're going to slide right over."

Again, moving slowly, she opens the door while removing the pistol from the man's mouth, and in a quick maneuver, she slides her way in, and then quickly pushes her weapon into his side.

Now she's in.

The pistol is jammed into the man's ribs just below his left armpit.

She says, "Hands behind your head, interlock your fingers. I promise, this won't take long."

The man spits at her. *"Puta."*

"Really? That's the best you can do?"

She shoves the gun in harder.

"This won't take long. But you do anything funny, I'll pull the trigger, and before you can blink, your heart is going to turn into mush. Do I have your attention?"

The man just nods, eyes lit with hate and fury, and Rosaria stares right back, hoping he can't tell how goddamn scared she is.

CHAPTER 64

A WOMAN! Antonio can't believe it. A woman has a gun on him...No matter how this turns out, he will make sure this woman ends up dead. There's no way in hell that he will let her live, to be in a position to tell someone, who will tell someone else, such that the information eventually ends up with the *jefe*.

Not on your life. Or anyone's life.

He stares at her and says, "Put me under arrest, if you can. And then I want a lawyer."

Then another surprise comes to him when she speaks.

"Who says I'm police?" she says, jamming the gun harder into his ribs. "I'm looking for information, that's all. I don't care about you, or what you've done, or what you might be doing. A few answers and then I'll be on my way, and you can go on yours."

"Go to hell."

The woman fumbles for a moment in her pocket, pulls out a cell phone, and her thumb is on the glass screen. "Here's the deal, no talking, no negotiating."

He stares, hands behind him, clasped against his head. The bitch doesn't know it, but his fingers aren't interlocked. They are resting plain and open on his head...Now, if he could just slap her suddenly—women don't like being hit in the face—but she speaks again, interrupting his thoughts.

"This is pre-dialed to nine-one-one. I just press my thumb and in a minute or so, this parking lot is going to be full of police officers, eager to talk to you. Or, you can be stupid and try to hit me or something, and my other finger presses, and you die in this pretty truck."

Antonio waits and waits. He can't have her call the police, not with all the sirens in the distance.

He also can't have her live.

Rosaria says, "Oh, and if I find later you've been lying to me, I won't be happy. I'll find out in a day, or a week, or a month."

She takes the cell phone up, and there's a *whir-whir-whir,* and she says, "By then, I'll know who you are, and who your friends are, dead back at the house, and I'll also know who you work for. You think he'll be impressed if these pictures arrive to him, showing you being held at gunpoint? By a girl?"

Antonio says, "They're dead? All of them?"

Rosaria says, "Now that's something to say. Define all."

"What?"

"How many were in the house besides you?"

"Three."

"Two are dead," she says. "That means one is missing. Who's missing?"

Antonio is thinking things through. All right, he will work this to his advantage. So what if he tells her what has happened? She will give him the facts that he can use later to talk to the *jefe* and explain what happened...all to Antonio's benefit.

"Was there an old man in the house?"

"No."

"Then someone came in and took him."

The bitch asks, "Who is the old man?"

The chicken is gone, Antonio thinks. It was supposed to be easy. A quick exchange. The old man was going to be peacefully turned over to an American who was to say a phrase, and then the three of them could go home over the border.

"Somebody that my boss wanted us to protect."

"Who is he?"

"We don't know."

"What? For real?"

Stupid puta, he thinks. "Our *jefe* ... our boss. If he tells us to guard someone, we guard him. It could be a priest, a child, a farmworker, a billionaire. We don't care. We don't ask. It's ... a chicken, that's all. To be kept well and alive until the exchange."

"But he is somebody important."

"Quite. We were told never to hurt him, or cause him concern, and to protect him."

"But you were to give him to someone else? Is that true?"

"Yes. We were told it would be peaceful. No need to be alert. No need to be suspicious."

"But who were you going to turn him over to?"

Antonio is thinking through even more. Yes, if he reveals the details to this woman, then he can still find a way to use it to his advantage.

The deal was supposed to be peaceful.

It didn't happen that way.

That certainly wasn't Antonio's fault. In fact, the *jefe* will be pleased to know that he has survived, to tell what really happened. Or at least what happened that would put Antonio into the *jefe*'s favor.

"A man," he says. "We were to turn him over to a man, after he told us a code word. Then ... we would leave and go back over the border."

Antonio moves his hands a few centimeters. Close.

He could still slap away the woman's weapon and take charge.

"Who is the man? Do you know who he is?"

Antonio shrugs. "An American. Named Tom Cornwall."

CHAPTER 65

ROSARIA KEEPS her face firm and placid, but she blinks hard at hearing those two words.

Tom Cornwall.

"Who's Tom Cornwall?" she asks, although she certainly knows who he is. "Why were you to hand over this old man to him?"

The cartel gang member just stares at her with hate and contempt. "I told you before. Can't you hear? We do our job. That's it."

That's it.

Rosaria thinks that's the perfect phrase for now.

That's it.

She draws back quickly, kicks the door open, and is now outside, holding her pistol on the man with one hand, her Galaxy phone with the other.

"I'm out of here," she says. "You were cooperative, so I'm not calling the police. But you better get going…"

He sits there, slowly lowers his hands, and mutters a long, nasty string of expletives, and Rosaria says, "I never knew who my mom was, so that's a waste of breath."

Then she backs away from the truck and does her best to move quickly in reverse, keeping an eye on the vehicle. She scrambles inside her rental car and drives out, remembering only five miles later that she's still terribly thirsty.

*   *   *

Antonio goes to the driver's side, starts up the truck, and then runs into the brush, looking for his revolver. He kneels down, scrambling around, scratching his hands, until yes, there it is.

He grabs it and then starts back to his truck. Get in and get out.

That's all.

Then call his *jefe,* but only after he's back over the border.

"Hey!" comes a sharp voice.

Standing to either side of his truck are two cops, wearing white cowboy hats, neckties, and white shirts, both holding pistols in their hands.

"Drop the weapon, buddy, drop it!" the one on the left says.

Antonio smiles, thinks, *Just like Clint Eastwood,* then quickly brings up his heavy revolver. Before he can get a single shot off, he's hammered hard in his chest and falls back, everything going dark in seconds.

CHAPTER 66

CLOSE TO two hours after I've driven out of Three Rivers, Texas, I'm just past the city of Victoria, and I've pulled off Highway 59 at some scraggly motel with half of the neon letters on its sign burnt out, and I know when I drive out at dawn, I'll have forgotten this little place of refuge within ten miles of driving.

It's a typical one-story stretch of motel rooms, and in the small office, a chubby young Pakistani man holds a controller in his hands and is playing some sort of shoot-'em-up video game. He pauses the game only twice: once to pass over a registration card and key, and then to take my American dollars. I fill out the card with a fake name, address, make and model of vehicle, and license plate number, and the young man doesn't even give the card a glance before going back to his game.

I step out into the thick night air and go to my Wrangler, which is parked in front of the office and where I could keep a close eye on things, and my older charge is calmly sitting there, slightly wrinkled hands folded in his lap, seat belt still in place. I get in and drive my Wrangler down to the end of the bumpy parking lot and park in the rear. My headlights pick up a scrawny creature that races into the underbrush, a starving dog or coyote, I can't tell.

The room has two twin beds, worn-down green carpeting, a small bathroom that smells of bleach, and a television on a low counter, kept in place by a thick chain and combination lock.

I drop my bag on the floor, motion to the bathroom. "All yours. Have at it."

He nods and goes in, shuts the door, and I hear water running.

I sit on the edge of the bed, lower my head into my hands.

The shakes begin.

A cool, comforting voice tries to tell me, *You didn't go in there to kill, you went in there to get this old man, you went in to save your family. It was bloody, horrible, and awful, and you'll feel guilty for the rest of your life, but what choice did you have?*

What choice?

I could have gone to the police. I could have gone to my superior officer. I could have gone to the CID. I could have gone to the FBI.

But I have no time.

No time.

The shakes continue.

The smell of burnt gunpowder, the yells, grunts, the way the pistol jumped in my hand, the frantic run through the small house...

The run to the Wrangler, dragging this old man along with me.

I'll never, ever forget it.

It's in my memory, my skin, and my bones. And it'll be there forever.

What choice?

I hear the toilet flush, more running water, and then the slight old man comes out into the motel room, looking at me.

"Still not talking, eh?" I ask.

He doesn't say anything, doesn't even make a gesture. He sits down on the edge of the other sagging bed, his hands on his knees.

"How long were you in that house?"

No reply.

"Who was keeping you there?"

Silence.

"Why are you so important to someone on the Gulf Coast of Florida?"

Quiet.

I notice my hand is throbbing deeply, and I can't figure out why, until I remember punching that big tattooed guy twice in the throat while holding an empty metal canister of pepper spray.

"Do you know my husband, Tom Cornwall? He's a journalist."

Stillness.

I shift around on the bed. It's sagging deeply in the middle. I'm thinking I might take a blanket out of the Wrangler and sleep on top of the covers, leave my charge to his own devices.

I say, "Why me, and why you? I have nothing to do with Texas, Mexico, or drug dealers. No offense if you're Mexican, but the two men back at that house didn't look like Mormon missionaries from a small town in Utah. And Tom...I don't think he's ever been to Mexico. Or Texas. He covers the Middle East. Saudi Arabia. Syria. Iraq. Parts of Africa and Afghanistan."

Something whispers to me there, some sort of idle fact, and I try to think it through and it slips away.

"But you're not going to tell me, are you?"

I can only hear the drone of the traffic from the nearby interstate. In between our single beds is a scratched and dinged-up nightstand with a lamp and a telephone. There's a drawer underneath and I slide it open, revealing a Gideon Bible and a very thin phone book. I pull the phone book out and show it to my new friend.

"See this?" I ask. "Old-time New York cop once taught me this…long time ago, when things were stretched thin and even retirees in the Reserves were being called up. You take a phone book, even a skinny one like this, and you can beat a suspect with it until he's crying and begging for mercy, and for some reason, it doesn't leave a bruise. No evidence you were tortured to get information."

The old man stares at me with dignity and calmness, like one of those old Christian martyrs in the Coliseum, kneeling before a hungry lion to meet his fate.

I toss the book back into the drawer.

"Not the way I operate," I say. "Before this little misadventure began, I was being investigated for doing something like this to an alleged farmer, all the way over in Afghanistan, ending in his death."

I close the drawer hard, making a loud *bang* in the room.

I say, "I didn't do it over there, and I'm not about to do it over here."

CHAPTER 67

MAJOR BRUNO Wenner, executive officer to Lieutenant Colonel Hugh Denton of the 297th Military Intelligence Battalion at Fort Belvoir, Virginia, is preparing for his 0800 morning meeting with the colonel when the intercom in his office buzzes. He picks up the phone and it's Mrs. Bouchard, the colonel's civilian secretary, and she says, "The colonel wants to see you right now…and I'm sorry, Bruno, he's in a pissy mood."

"Thanks for the heads-up, Mrs. B," he replies, before hanging up and grabbing a legal pad, his iPad, and the folder with the colonel's schedule and other necessary paperwork for the day.

The usual morning meeting is set to begin in nineteen minutes, he thinks, as he hustles his way to his boss's office. What could be so important?

Then a little chill settles around his heart, about something he did yesterday for Captain Ted Cooper, one of the intelligence officers assigned to the battalion. What he did wasn't particularly illegal or against Army regulations, but still…the colonel likes to claim he runs a tight ship, and what Wenner did yesterday could be considered mutiny, even if this is an Army outfit and not the Navy.

He goes into Denton's office, gets a sharp grunt as a greeting, and he sits down, carefully balancing the folder, legal pad, and iPad on his lap. Denton is reading a sheet of paper, shaking his head as he does so, and that little cold chill around Wenner's heart starts getting chillier.

Denton looks up. "Bruno."

"Sir."

"It's the little things that can cripple a unit, that can hurt a commanding officer, don't you agree?"

He has no idea what Denton is going to say next, but the safest thing is just to play along. "Certainly, sir."

"The minor things, the items and information that can slip through the cracks. They often can come back and bite an officer right in the ass, even if he had no knowledge of them. Even if they weren't his fault. But because something untoward happened to somebody under his purview, he takes the ultimate responsibility. And the ultimate fall."

Crap, Wenner thinks. Denton has found out about what he did for Captain Cooper. One of Denton's big commandments for the officers and soldiers in his battalion is staying free of too much debt, and if he ever finds out anyone in his battalion is behind in car payments, mortgage, or credit card bills, he will throw a tantrum and possibly cripple an officer's career. In the overall scheme of things, Denton is right to be concerned, because overdue bills make someone vulnerable to blackmail or extortion, but the way he always goes at it…

Captain Cooper had earlier come to him, pleading for help to stave off an imminent car repossession, and Wenner had lent him the necessary funds—with the typical tearful promise to make it all good with the next pay period—but Denton will be ripshit if he knows Wenner did this behind his back.

Wenner feels like his heart is now encased in a heavy block of ice.

Denton picks up the offending sheet of paper. "It's like this, Bruno—I don't like being surprised by... unexpected developments."

"Sir," is all he can come up with.

Denton purses his lips and says, "I have information here concerning our missing Captain Amy Cornwall."

"Sir," he says again, but this time, the word is full of relief and relaxation. So this will have nothing to do with his loan to Captain Cooper.

"Tell me the latest you know about her location."

Wenner goes to his paperwork. "Yesterday she was at a Bank of America ATM in Kenedy, Texas, at 6:03 p.m. EST, where she withdrew four hundred dollars. Prior to that, she took part in a river rescue near a bridge on US 59. The Jeep Wrangler she was driving was bearing stolen license plates. Earlier... well, you'll recall her assault on the Tennessee state trooper."

Wenner pauses. He certainly recalls it well, for when he told the colonel that bit of nasty news yesterday, Denton exploded, yelling, face red, hand pounding the desk and then sweeping paper and folders to the floor.

"Go on," Denton says.

"That's all I have now, sir. CID out of Quantico is still working to find her. I've got a good working relationship with one of their XOs over there."

Denton rubs at his eyes. "Then all they need is to go online and check the news out of Texas."

"Sir?" Wenner feels a little worm of worry drop in for a visit. Something bad has happened in Texas, something bad enough to make the news.

"Two Mexican nationals were shot and killed in Three Rivers, a town adjacent to Kenedy," Denton says, speaking in a low and surprisingly calm voice.

"There was no immediate identification of the shooter, but a black Jeep Wrangler was seen leaving the area."

Wenner can't help himself. "Shit."

Denton goes on. "So far our intelligence officer's possible involvement in this horror show hasn't made the news. But when and if it does...there'll be a hammer coming down on the 297th Military Intelligence Battalion that will make the Abu Ghraib prison scandal look like a fraternity prank gone awry. Do you understand? I'll be gone, you'll be gone, and probably every line officer in the unit. The investigation into that Afghan prisoner Cornwall supposedly killed? Forget it. The American media don't care about one more dead Afghan."

He pauses. "But have something violent happen in this country, by what appears to be a rogue American military officer, brutally killing two innocent Mexican nationals...holy God, the media, the bloggers, the columnists...they'll camp out at the base's gates until I'm crucified, and you'll be right there next to me. It'll be more than a story, it'll be a sociological event, representing the evil American military empire, the vicious nature of our intelligence services, blah blah blah. All because of one bitch who's gone crazy."

Wenner doesn't know what to say, so he says nothing. He knows he should probably stand up for Captain Cornwall, but this is neither the time nor the place, not with his commanding officer so spun up.

Denton asks, "Have I ever told you about my uncle Willard?"

Say what? Wenner thinks. "No, sir."

"He was a nineteen-year-old draftee, sent to Vietnam, assigned to the Twenty-Third Infantry Division, the Americal Division."

"Oh."

"Yeah, the one with the platoon that committed the My Lai Massacre. Uncle Willard didn't take part in that, thank God, but he got there a year later. A terrible time. The policy back then was that troops and officers were rotated out after a year's service…which meant no unit cohesion. And let's say you're a poor kid, you've got a month left in-country, and some hard-charging fresh lieutenant comes in and starts risking your life and the lives of your buddies for stupid missions. What do you do then?"

"I'm not sure, sir," Wenner says.

"Yeah. Fragging. Know the term?"

"Ah…"

Denton says, "You got a green lieutenant who's about to get you and others killed, he goes into a latrine, somebody tosses in a fragmentation grenade. Boom. The official story is that he was hit by a VC mortar round or the latrine blew up because of a methane gas buildup, but the new L-T who came in will no longer be a problem, as brutal as it is. And his replacement will catch the news of what happened to his predecessor and will act accordingly."

Denton picks up the piece of paper he had been reading from and crushes it in a hand, tosses it in a nearby black wastebasket. The crumpled-up piece of paper hits the rim and falls to the carpet.

He says, "Fragging. A brutal method, to be sure, but it solved the problem. Now we have the problem of Captain Cornwall, whose desertion and actions are threatening you, me, this unit, and the Army." He pauses. "It makes you think—dream, actually—that a troubled officer like that can face the same discipline."

Wenner can't believe what he's hearing. "Sir, really, I—"

Denton holds up a hand. "Dismissed."

"Sir."

Wenner gets up and Denton says, "I know who you are, Bruno, and I know your reputation in this unit. You're a fixer."

He just nods.

Denton says one more thing, like he's repeating something heard earlier.

"Fix this," he says. "Fix it now."

CHAPTER 68

BENITO ZAMORA is from Nogales in Sonora, just across the border from Arizona. He has always worked with tools and his hands, having started out working for his uncle at one of the local trucking companies, doing all sorts of maintenance. He knows he's considered a simple man with simple talents, which is fine, because it has led him to his latest job, working for a business in Florida.

The climate is wonderful, the pay is superb, but he's under no illusions about the men he works for, and has worked for, in the years since his uncle's trucking firm went bankrupt. He maintains a strict focus, keeps his mouth shut, and never gossips or talks about his work.

This morning he is in a small cement-lined room in the basement of a new hotel that is under construction, and is accompanied by one of the young, hard men who also work here. Inside the room is an Anglo male who has a bandaged arm and a sweet-looking blond girl Benito assumes is his daughter. He has been told to fix a toilet in this room, and with a tool belt around his ample waist and a toolbox in his callused right hand, he goes to work.

He won't look at the two Anglos. That will gain him nothing, though he will say a prayer for their souls when he leaves here and goes to the little room that he has been gifted to live in while working here.

He has nothing against Americans, although he doesn't like their arrogance and how they blame his country for the drug trade, though without their own appetites, the drug traffic would collapse in a month.

Benito also remembers a phrase his local priest had said over and over again, *Poor Mexico. So far from God, so close to the United States.*

The priest was a good man, teaching classes at night about economics and politics, and he took particular interest in Benito, telling him that he shared the same name as Benito Juárez, a past president of Mexico and one of its greatest leaders, as well as a child of Zapotec peasants. He taught Benito and others to have pride in their poor nation, to have hopes for its future, and their neighborhood dearly missed the priest after the army came in one night and took him away forever.

He lays out his tools, gets to work, uses some rags to mop up some of the leaking water. It looks like a simple repair job, and Benito should be out of here in a few minutes. He accidentally looks toward the two beds. The Anglo male is sitting on a bed, his back against the wall, his face puffy and red, looking like a defeated man.

The blond girl is cute, and Benito feels a sharp pang, remembering his own little girl, Gabriela. Oh, such a black-haired beauty, and he has to pause for a moment, remembering the year after she graduated from high school, how she went to work for a cousin in Ciudad Juárez, across the river from El Paso, Texas. She worked as a restaurant manager, was young, beautiful, with her whole life ahead of her…

He wipes at his eyes. One night she went out with some friends, driving a car across the border as a "favor" for someone. The car was part of a mule effort, smuggling cocaine across to the United States, and the car passed through the border checkpoints without any problem. The real problem came when the car was to be delivered to some sort of dealer in El Paso but ended up being seized by his rivals. The drugs were taken, the car was driven into the desert, and young, sweet Gabriela and her three friends were shot in the car and burnt.

"Hey!" comes a little girl's voice. "Hey, mister!"

He ignores the girl's voice. The toilet seems to have shifted on its base, which has led to leaking and a backup, and with a soft shove from his shoulder, the toilet returns to the proper place.

"Mister, please! Look at me! C'mon, look at me!"

Benito doesn't want to look, but the pleading tone of the girl's voice makes him turn his head. The cute Anglo blonde is standing straight up on her tiptoes, arms stretched out, and then she does a perfect cartwheel on the cement floor.

She stands, smiling, arms back straight up.

"Did you see? Did you?"

Benito nods and turns away, eyes filling with tears. He doesn't want to think of what will happen to this sweetie at some point. Her father, sitting on the edge of the bed now, a dead look on his face… well, Benito thinks he is here because of something he has done. He is the guilty one. The little girl?

She is an innocent.

"Look! Please! Look again!"

And damn it, he does look again, and even the hard man standing guard looks, glancing up from his cell phone where he's been playing some game, and the girl spins out again in a cartwheel, and her foot slips and she falls in a tumble.

She screeches and her father comes down and

checks her, and she cries out for a moment, and says, "It's okay, Daddy, it's okay. I'm fine."

He picks her up and gives her a hard, squeezing hug, and Benito's hands shake as he gathers up his tools and nods to the other man.

"I'm finished," he says.

The hard man goes to the door, unlocks it, and Benito follows behind him and keeps on walking, for he never wants to see that man and his daughter ever again.

The air in the room is still stuffy and smells lousy, but Tom doesn't care. His little girl is safe, she's with him, and that's all that counts.

He says, "You okay?"

She nods and pulls away. "I am. You can put me down now."

He gently puts her on the bed. Her face is dirty where she's cried, and her pretty nose has dripped snot, but she's smiling.

"Did you do it, Daddy, did you?"

From under his shirt he pulls out what he had seen earlier, what he had grabbed from the Hispanic man's toolbox: a wooden-handled cutting tool used for linoleum, with a curved, razor-sharp blade.

With one arm he hugs his little girl. "Thanks to you, I did."

"What now?" she asks, wiping her nose with her hand.

"You know how you wanted Mommy to kill them?"

"Yes."

Tom examines the blade again. "I'm not going to wait."

CHAPTER 69

FOLLOWING ANOTHER bit of thievery this morning—taking Texas license plates from a dented white Subaru wagon and putting them on my Wrangler— my new best friend and I stop for a quick drive-through meal from McDonald's.

He still hasn't said a word. I tell him what I'm going to have for breakfast—coffee, OJ, and Egg McMuffin—and he just shrugs, so I double the order that is our morning meal. Following directions from a helpful senior citizen out for his morning walk, we're on North Main Street, pulling up to the Victoria Public Library. The area around the squat, bare concrete building has small homes and one-story businesses, with lots of trees. I park my Wrangler in a nearby parking lot, hiding it from the main street, and after shutting off the engine, I give the old man a good, long look.

I say, "So we have a situation, you and I. I need to spend some time in the library, doing research. But I can't leave you here alone. So you're coming in with me."

He doesn't say anything, but his eyes look intelligent, so I'm sure he's understanding what I'm saying.

I say, "I'll be as quick as I can, but you've got to be at my side. I can't have you running away while I'm in the library. You see…"

My voice catches for a moment.

But just a moment.

"Somebody has taken my husband and my daughter, and to get them free, I need you as a trade. And we're going to do that in Florida. But don't try to run away. Back at Three Rivers, I killed two men to get you. Trust me when I say I'm not going to let you run away."

He just looks at me.

I reach for the door. "If you try to run away, I won't kill you. But I'll break your arm. And you'll be hurting all the way to Florida."

Getting to a computer terminal at the nice library takes some work on my part, since they require a library card and PIN to get access to a computer, but some sweet-talking and showing my Armed Forces identification card persuades the cheerful young lady librarian with a strong Texas accent and black hair to let me in. She's a bit overweight but wears it proudly, with tight black slacks and a bright-red blouse.

God love the South. I grew up in chilly Maine, and I long ago gave up the soft bigotry most northerners have for those living below the Mason-Dixon line, for I've found most of them unerringly charming, polite, and, in the army, stone-cold killers.

I sit down at one of the terminals and make sure my companion is sitting behind me. "You know," I tell him, "I can't keep on saying 'Hey you' when I'm talking to you."

Of course he says nothing.

"You don't look like him, but you have the charm of an older Cary Grant," I say. "So I shall call you Archie. Archie, stay put while I get to work."

I dig in and decide to start where my destination is going to be, Beachside, Florida. I've never heard of the town, and as I start Googling my way hither and yon,

I learn a lot. It's a very new town, a "planned community" for retirees, for budget travelers, and for corporate retreats. I get a map of the streets and arrange to have it printed out at a nearby printer. The population is about three thousand or so, and...

It has no police department.

Interesting.

It has a top-of-the-line full-time fire department, but any law enforcement requirements are fulfilled by the Walton County Sheriff's Department.

So how and why did this little town spring up on the Gulf Coast of Florida?

There's not much about its history or construction, but I do find a throwaway line in an old story that makes me sit back and swallow hard.

The place was mostly financed by a bank.

A bank in Mexico.

First Republic Global Bank, NA, based in Guadalajara.

The same bank that owns the Learjet that took away Tom and Denise.

I let my fingers float across the keyboard, look to my rear, and Archie is sitting there, quiet and calm.

"Time for a gamble," I say, and I go to Gmail and sign into my personal email account to see what information might be waiting for me, and to also do something else dangerous, but necessary.

Good God, look at all those unread messages that have piled up in the past few days...with a good chunk from Major Bruno Wenner, pleading and then demanding to know where I am and what's going on. If Wenner is using my personal email account in addition to my standard Army account, he and Colonel Denton must be really going berserk.

Then there's the regular email mishmash of spam, a couple of messages from old friends of mine in the service, and some reminders from Amazon and Staples.

But no messages from Tom.

Or Denise.

I check out Archie again. "A gamble. You never know how and where it's going to pay off."

Archie doesn't look away, and I shake my head and say, "Just so you know, I'm one to keep my promises, to keep my oath. No matter the pressure, no matter the temptations. When I was in college, my roommate, Marcia, cheated on her boyfriend. She asked me to keep that secret. Save for you now, I've never told anyone, even my husband, even my best friends in the service."

My throat thickens. "I'm about to violate a promise I made to my husband, a long, long time ago. I've been tempted here and there to break that promise, but now...well, it's an emergency. I have to do it. You understand? I have to do it."

I turn back to the keyboard, stop wasting time with Archie. I minimize the open screen that has my Gmail account, get back to work. Within a few minutes, I locate Tom's Cloud account in Google. I feel sick at what I'm doing. For a long time I've known his log-in data to get access to his Cloud storage—as an intelligence officer, how could I not?—but I've never, ever gone into it. When we were first dating, Tom said to me, "Hon, I know how talented you are...in lots of ways, but especially in the Army. But Amy, please. My work has a lot of sources and confidential information in it. Please don't ever try to find out what I'm doing, all right?"

And of course I promised to do that, and now, I am

breaking that promise. At some point, I hope he will forgive me.

Tom's office at home is a mess of papers, folders, books, and piles of old newspapers and clippings, but I'm pleased to see he's not a slob on the Internet. I start going through his files, looking at his notes, and using a function that allows me to see the most recent information. I'm stunned at how quickly I find what I'm looking for, and what it means.

"Oh, Tom," I whisper. "You damn, damn, damn fool."

I can't believe what I'm seeing there, in plain text on a plain screen, but it's apparent. And thorough. And deadly stupid.

Now I know why he was picked up. And my Denise as well. And although I don't know the identity of the man behind me, I know his background as well.

Oh, Tom.

I shake my head in disgust and turn around to leave.

Behind me is an empty chair.

Archie is gone.

CHAPTER 70

AT THE George Bush Intercontinental Airport in Houston, Warrant Officer Rosaria Vasquez is quickly walking to the service kiosk for Hertz when a familiar man in civilian clothes steps out from a news shop and says, "A minute, Vasquez."

She halts in her tracks, stunned. Her boss, Senior Warrant Officer Fred McCarthy, who should be back at Quantico in Virginia, is here, deep in the heart of Texas.

"Sir?"

"This way," he says, walking to a food court, where he takes a chair and gestures her to sit down.

She takes the chair and says, "Is this where you're going to tell me why I'm in Houston?"

"You want coffee or something?" he asks. His usually tanned and fit face looks pale and anxious, and as always, he's wearing a dark-gray suit that doesn't fit him well. Senior Warrant Officer McCarthy is tall and loose-limbed, and Rosaria doubts that even the best tailor from Hong Kong or London could ever make a suit fit him.

She says, "No, I don't want coffee. I want to know what the hell is going on."

"You first, Vasquez," he says. "What's the latest on the Three Rivers shootings?"

Rosaria really doesn't need her notebook but pulls it out for appearance's sake. "Shooting broke out at a rental residence on Linden Street. Two Mexican nationals killed. A person—male or female, not sure—was seen fleeing the residence, dragging an older gentleman along. That person's identity is also unknown. A black Jeep Wrangler was seen leaving the area shortly thereafter. No confirmation of how many people were inside. And the license plate wasn't noted, either."

"Forensics?"

"Too soon," she says. "It's a small but professional department, but even a big-town department would have a challenge handling three shootings in one afternoon."

"Three? Who was the third one?"

She turns over a page. "Approximately thirty minutes after the first shootings, Texas State Police responding to the scene found a tricked-out black Ford pickup truck with extended cab that had earlier been seen at the Linden Street residence. The truck was seen at a nearby McDonald's restaurant. The driver of the truck, armed with a revolver, was spotted nearby. He refused to drop his weapon. He was killed in a shootout."

"Another Mexican national?" he asks.

Rosaria says, "That's right."

McCarthy rubs at his large chin. "Hoo boy, the nearest Mexican consulate is going to have their hands full. Besides the fact that Captain Cornwall drives a Jeep Wrangler, and was seen earlier in the next town, is there any specific, credible evidence linking her to these two shootings?"

Rosaria has thought this through, again and again, thinking of what she learned from the third gunman. That the older man kept there was to be turned over to American journalist Tom Cornwall when he arrived.

And instead of journalist Cornwall arriving, apparently his wife did, taking the man and killing two in the process. Rosaria is convinced that's what happened. As to why...no idea.

But her boss has asked her for specific, credible evidence linking the missing captain to the shootings. And Rosaria can always say later that she didn't believe a bulked-up gangbanger armed with one big-ass revolver to be credible, which was why she never mentioned meeting him.

Thin ice indeed, but she's been there before.

"Nothing that I've heard from the police," she says.

"You got a good contact with the Three Rivers police?"

Sergeant Morales's business card is safely secured in her travel bag. "I do."

"Good." He rubs at his massive chin and says, "We have good intelligence that she's heading east. Alone or with someone, we don't know. But she's definitely heading east, most likely on Highway 59, coming from either Three Rivers or Kenedy. That's why you were ordered to Houston."

"Where did you get this information from, boss?"

"From a good source."

She doesn't like the sound of that.

"Sir..."

"A good source," he repeats. "That's all you're getting. So you're going to get into a rental car, and start heading east on Fifty-Nine. Once we get better information on where she is, or where she's going, you'll be in a position to intercept."

The din and movement of people around her in this busy terminal gradually fades away until all she can see and hear is the senior warrant officer sitting in front of her. On the table, there's a crumpled napkin at his elbow and two half-circle rings from where earlier travelers deposited their drinks.

"By myself?" she asks. "With no backup?"

He says, "You can hook up with any local law enforcement if needed. In this state, they'll trip over themselves trying to help the Army."

She literally cannot believe what she's hearing. "Sir…she assaulted a state trooper in Tennessee. She's a good suspect for a kidnapping and a double homicide. She's a deserter. And you want me to go after her…by myself?"

He nods. Doesn't say anything.

"It doesn't make sense!" she says, her voice rising.

McCarthy's tired eyes flicker. "It might not make sense to you, Vasquez, but to certain higher-ups and the Army, it makes perfect sense. So do your job."

Something else comes to her quickly, and she's nauseated at the realization. "Boss…you could have told me all of this over the phone. By text. Or email. Why did you waste your time coming to Texas?"

McCarthy says, almost in a whisper, "Because it makes sense, that's why."

It feels like a passenger ambling by has just hit her between the shoulder blades with a sledgehammer. Higher-ups and the Army have just made a determination this is one horrible case and a potential national embarrassment, and that someone has to be sacrificed to either solve the case or make it go away. And her superior has flown here to tell her, face-to-face, so there's no paper or email trail, no evidence, nothing save her word against his.

"Yes, sir," she says quietly. "I'll do my job."

McCarthy looks relieved as he stands up. "Good. I'll be in touch with any additional information that comes my way."

He walks away, and in a very few seconds, is lost in the moving and shifting lines of travelers passing through this fine airport on this fine day.

Rosaria stands up, starts going in the direction of the Hertz terminal, and she goes three steps and starts weeping, goes three more before she realizes why she's crying.

She's just lost her family.

CHAPTER 71

WITH ARCHIE'S disappearance, I try not to panic.

So what do I do?

I panic.

I leap away from the chair in front of the computer terminal and race out to the center part of the library. A few quiet patrons are there, but there's no well-dressed man with white hair and beard.

Damn!

I head outside, figuring if he's still in the building, I have a chance of going back and finding him in there, and I slam through the door and nearly run over a young mom and her two young boys, and she yells a very well-deserved curse at me as I step out on North Main Street, frantically looking up and down the sidewalks.

Nobody.

I run to the shaded parking lot, hoping that Archie got bored and decided to return to my Jeep.

I skid up next to the Wrangler.

The interior is cluttered and filthy, but no Archie.

Damn it again!

I look around the parking lot, duck and look under the vehicles, trot over to the rear of the library. I disturb a few pigeons and that's it.

You've lost him, comes the nagging voice. *You've lost the key to freeing your family, and they're going to die because of you.*

I run back to the library.

* * *

Special Agent Rosaria Vasquez is driving as fast as she can in downtown Victoria, Texas, looking for the library. About fifteen minutes ago she got a quick and very frantic phone call from Senior Warrant Officer McCarthy.

"Nailed her," he said. "She's using a computer at the city library in Victoria, Texas, address is three-oh-two North Main Street."

"Got it," she replied, and hung up. What else was there to say?

The GPS on her Hertz vehicle is working like a charm. Up ahead is the square cement library, plopped right down in what looks to be a sparsely populated residential and light business district. Despite all that's going on, Rosaria gets a warm feeling at seeing a public library. This one has a nice sign out front, the lined concrete looks warm and inviting— because there are books inside, no doubt—and the lawn is bright green and closely trimmed. In her troubled years growing up, it was never certain if there was going to be food in the house, or if your foster sisters would steal your stuff, or if your foster father would stare at you at bedtime, but one thing was certain: there would always be a building nearby that would take you in and would let you read as many books as you wanted, all for free.

Rosaria spends less than two minutes circling the library and then drives into its nearby parking lot.

Nearly slams on the brakes.

Black Jeep Wrangler, pulled into a space, under the shade of a tree.

Hidden from the street and backed in so someone could drive out quickly.

Rosaria slowly drives past the Jeep.

It's empty.

She reaches for her leather bag, pulls out her SIG Sauer, lays it across her lap.

What now?

Phone the cops? ID herself as an Army CID investigator and ask for interagency assistance? Would they speedily respond or would they take their time, checking her out?

Rosaria circles around and returns to the Wrangler. She could park in front of it, <u>prevent it from leaving.</u>

She checks the license plates and sees they're from Texas.

So. Stolen or legit? And if she were blocking a legit citizen, that could cause a stink, which would cause attention, and she doesn't need attention now.

Rosaria pulls into an empty spot, steps out with her pistol at her side.

What she needs is to go into that library and find her AWOL officer.

Now.

CHAPTER 72

SLIGHTLY OUT of breath, I go up to the helpful young lady at the front desk and say, "Have you seen my grandfather?"

She looks up from her computer terminal. "Who?"

"The older man I came in with," I say, and hold out my hand. "About this tall, white beard and hair, doesn't talk, has on a nice suit."

She shakes her head. "No...but I've been pretty busy these past few minutes. He might have slipped out without me seeing. Is everything okay?"

I look around at the tall book stacks and the doors marking study areas or small conference rooms. "No, not really," I say. "He easily gets confused. I'm going to take a look around the stacks. If you see him, could you just try to keep him here, at your desk? Honest, he's very gentle."

My cooperative librarian says, "Should I call the police, ma'am?"

Hell, no, is what I think.

"Not yet," I say, and then I walk fast into the areas near the closest bookcases.

Rosaria steps into the air-conditioned library and takes an appreciative sniff of the smell of books. Nothing like it in the world. Before she goes up to the main desk she slides her small SIG Sauer into the right pocket of her jacket, checking at her hip to make sure she has her handcuffs. When she gets to the desk a sweet, young heavyset lady steps up from her terminal and says, "Can I help you?"

She displays her gold shield and identification card. "Special Agent Rosaria Vasquez," she says. "I'm looking for—"

The librarian smiles. "Oh, your friend must have called you then, am I right?"

Rosaria is still holding on to her IDs. "My friend?"

"Sure," the librarian says. "I forgot her name, but she came in a while ago with her grandfather, a quiet old man, and asked if she could use one of the computers. They're reserved for residents of Victoria, but she showed me her…that special ID, the one with the funny green letters."

She puts away her identification. "Her Armed Forces identification card."

"That's the one!"

Rosaria takes in the open areas and the book stacks. "Do you know where she is?"

"Oh, out back there somewhere," the librarian says. "She was looking for her grandfather. I guess he wandered off. She must have called you to come in and help, right?"

Rosaria slides her hand into the coat pocket holding her firearm. "You could say that. Just so I know how to help her, are there any other exits from this building?"

"This is the main one," she says. "There's a fire door on the other side…but you can't go through there. If you do, it'll set off one heck of a ruckus."

"Thanks," she says.

The librarian asks, "If your friend comes back, should I tell her you're here?"

"No worries," Rosaria says. "I'm sure I'll catch up with her on my own."

I've gone up and down four long lengths of bookshelves and have only come across a young girl, splayed out on the floor, reading a Harry Potter book. I can't tell which one it is. I step over her long legs and have a pang of fear, thinking about Denise.

When I get to a point where I can look back at the main door and the lobby, I freeze.

A woman is talking to the cheerful and helpful young lady at the main desk. The woman has on plain black slacks, black jacket, white blouse. She has a dull-looking leather bag over one arm and she's got a serious look on her face as she talks.

I wish I could read lips, so I knew what she is saying.

But whatever she's saying, her entire presence and demeanor say one thing to me: cop.

I duck back into the stacks.

Rosaria turns and freezes.

A shape has just moved back into the near stacks.

It looked like an adult. Hard to tell if it was a man or woman.

But the shape moved pretty fast, like it didn't want to be spotted.

"Thanks, ma'am," she says to the librarian, and steps quickly away from the curved desk.

Her hand is still gripping her SIG Sauer, and she makes another quick check at her waist, making sure her handcuffs are ready for use.

If she's very, very lucky, she will end this in a few minutes.

*   *   *

I'm moving as fast as I can, slipping from one set of stacks to another. I can sense I'm being tracked, and there's not much I can do. The cop out there has my trail here among the volumes depicting civilized life, and I'm running out of places to hide. At least there are no civilians back here to get in the way.

And where the hell is Archie?

I feel like I'm making a house out of a deck of cards, and one by one, the cards are slipping away.

I come to a wall, see a small alcove with books and book carts, and I turn.

The shadow is coming closer.

Damn.

If I duck to the left or to the right, I'll be spotted.

I head to the alcove.

Rosaria sees movement.

She's getting closer.

This will end now, she thinks. It will end now, and she will prove to her boss and anybody else out there that she can do a job, no matter how abandoned and alone she is. The shadow and shape flick before her. She senses she's coming to a corner of the building and Captain Cornwall will be trapped, and then it will be done.

She turns around the end of one full bookcase and finds…

No one there.

What the hell?

She steps closer.

Wait.

There's an alcove with three book carts shoved in, the ones used to return books to the shelves.

They're not in a line.

They've been moved around, like they're hiding something.

She lifts up her SIG Sauer. "Captain Cornwall? Are you there? Please come out, with your hands showing."

No answer.

She hears a murmur of the librarian talking to someone way behind her.

"Captain Cornwall?"

She slowly moves forward, hugging the wall, knowing Cornwall has taken down a Tennessee state trooper and has probably killed two Mexican drug cartel members, and she's not taking any chances by leaving herself exposed.

Then…

Rosaria grabs the end of one book cart, quickly pulls it out, steps into the alcove.

Empty.

Nothing here but books.

Damn!

She steps out of the alcove and starts back to the stacks when something heavy slams into her and drives her into the floor.

CHAPTER 73

LUCKILY THE bookcases here are securely bolted to the concrete floor, so they don't move as I climb up on top of them, and they even stay in place with my weight when the armed woman calling out my name passes underneath me.

I roll over and hit her right on the shoulders, and she drops with a surprised "Oof!" I grab a shoulder, roll her over, and shove the muzzle end of my .357 Ruger up against her chin.

Her eyes widen and she stares up at me as I shift position and kneel on her chest, locate her pistol, and shove it into my coat. A quick frisk and I come away with her handcuffs.

I shove the muzzle in another quarter inch and whisper, "Hands above your head, right now."

The woman does as she's told. I'm both grateful and surprised. I was expecting some resistance, but the day still isn't over.

I snap the handcuffs securely on her wrists, stand up, and haul her up as well. My revolver is now pressed against her sternum, and I whisper again, "We're going to have a sixty-second talk. If you murmur, yell, struggle, I'll kill you. All right? I will pull this trigger and the center of your chest will be turned into a bloody mess."

I push her into the alcove, shove her to her butt, and kneel back into her, my revolver back under her chin.

"Talk," I say. "Don't waste my time."

*   *   *

Rosaria is both shocked and stunned that this woman—a bookworm intelligence officer!—has managed to surprise, overwhelm, disarm, and secure her in just a matter of seconds. And then a cold clarity comes to her: this bookworm also successfully passed Ranger training. Her initial thought was stupid. The metal of the revolver muzzle is harsh and cold under her chin, and Captain Amy Cornwall bears little resemblance to her official photo, sitting in front of an American flag in full-dress uniform, smiling confidently into the camera's lens.

Cornwall's hair is disheveled, her eyes are swollen and red-rimmed, and she smells of little sleep, bad food, and long hours on the road.

"Talk," she orders.

Rosaria keeps quiet. Maybe somebody out there heard something. Maybe a library worker or even an off-duty cop might walk by.

The muzzle is shoved harder. "Talk. You know my name, I don't know yours. Doesn't seem fair, does it?"

The steel barrel is twisted into her skin. "Who are you? Army? FBI?"

Rosaria doesn't like the woman's look or her tone of voice. "Warrant Officer Vasquez. CID special agent. Out of Quantico."

That gets Cornwall's attention. Her eyes sharpen and she says, "Why are you after me?"

Rosaria says, "You're absent without leave, Captain."

Cornwall has a sharp, bitter laugh. "AWOL? For real? I've been gone from base less than three days and I got a CID officer from Virginia tracking me in Texas? That's crap. Why are you after me?"

Rosaria's not sure what she can say, so she tries the truth. "Orders."

"From whom?"

"My boss," she says. "Who else?"

"And what has he told you?"

Rosaria doesn't want to say any more, but Cornwall checks her watch. "About thirty seconds left. Make your time count."

And then, in this small alcove in an out-of-the-way library in the middle of Texas, so far away from home and the Army, Rosaria makes a decision.

"My boss has hardly told me anything," she says. "Besides what I've learned, they've been tracking your movements."

"Of course they have," she says. "Hell, I made an ATM withdrawal yesterday, stayed logged on my private email account here, practically sent up a goddamn flare."

Rosaria thinks that through. "You…you did that, knowing you'd be tracked."

"That's right," she says. "I got a crew following me already. I wanted to know who else is dogging me, and now I know. Civilians and military. I'm surprised you guys haven't bumped into each other yet. Now, you said you've learned stuff on your own. Like what?"

A hesitation, and then Rosaria goes all out.

"I know you hit a house yesterday in Three Rivers. I know you took someone from there. And I also know you shot and killed two men."

She was hoping that last bit of news would shock Cornwall, but her expression doesn't change.

"They were bad men," she says. "I've been fighting bad men for most of my adult life. I really don't care."

Rosaria says, "Maybe you'll care about this. The

man being held at that house, the one you took…he was supposed to be turned over to your husband, Tom Cornwall."

Now there's a shocked look on the Army captain's face.

Even though she's handcuffed and has a revolver pointed at her, Rosaria feels a sense of satisfaction at doing that.

CHAPTER 74

THIS DAMN CID officer has just confirmed something I found out less than thirty minutes ago, that my Tom has been involved in some very dark and dangerous work.

I try not to show my shock or dismay, and I say, "How do you know about my husband?"

"Is it true?"

"How do you know that?" I say, poking her once more with my Ruger.

She says, "Like I said. I've found some information on my own."

"What else?"

"That's all you're getting." Her voice now growing defiant. "Captain Cornwall, what the hell is going on? That man you kidnapped...who is he? Why did your husband need him?"

I decide we're done.

I push her against her chest, shove her back deeper into the alcove, and I grab her cuffed arms, pull them up, and loop them over a valve fitting for a sprinkler pipe. She squirms and doesn't say anything from the sudden shift in position and the strain that's on her arms.

I'm impressed.

I hold the revolver between her eyes, touching her forehead, her thick hair about her shoulders.

"I'll say this low and slow, so there's no misunderstanding." And for emphasis' sake, I tap the cold steel on her olive skin. "I'm headed out of here. If you follow me, if you try to track me, interfere in any way with what I'm doing, I will shoot you dead." Another brief tap to her moist forehead. "If I even get the slightest hint that you might be out there, trying to find me, I'll kill you. And if somewhere along the way, before I get to where I'm going, if I'm arrested or stopped, I will blame it on you. And when I get out of prison, thirty, forty, fifty years down the road…I'll find you and shoot you dead. Do we have an understanding?"

The CID officer calmly says, "You're doing this for your family, aren't you? They're in some sort of trouble. Your husband, Tom…he was working on a story that got the wrong attention. That's why you're doing this."

I'm not going to give her the benefit of an answer. I tap her forehead again, conscious that I'm in a city library, and at any point, an innocent young library volunteer might stop by and find this disturbing scene.

"Do we have an understanding?"

"Yes," she says. "But one other thing."

"Make it quick."

No hesitation on her part. "I want to help you."

Rosaria sees the surprise in the woman's eyes and stays on message.

"This…case, investigation, whatever it is I'm doing, it's been nuts from the start. I shouldn't be investigating an AWOL officer, not when you've been absent for just a couple of days, and my boss…he's providing intelligence about you and your movements that someone's feeding him. I don't like it. I don't like it at all."

"Welcome to my world," Cornwall says.

She squirms, tries to ease the pain in her stretched arms, fails. "I want to help...I...I can't explain it. But you're doing something beyond regulations, beyond the law. You're trying to save your family."

Cornwall checks her watch. Rosaria says, "Give me your cell phone number, some way of communicating with you, and I'll tip you off."

"You intent on committing career suicide?"

Despite having her hands cuffed and being threatened with a revolver, Rosaria almost laughs. "Career suicide? What career do you think I'm going to have when this is over, one way or the other?"

The captain checks her watch one more time, seems to come to a decision. "Warrant Officer...that's the best offer I've had in days. If it's a true offer." She pauses. "But in the end, I don't know you. I can't trust you. I can't trust anyone."

She moves her hand, and Rosaria starts to cry out in fear when a wad of rolled-up tissue is shoved into her mouth.

I move quickly away from the cuffed CID officer and shove a couple of book carts in place, to conceal her, and then I slip the revolver into my bag and retrace my steps back through the library. In intelligence work sometimes information comes in bits and pieces, dribs and drabs, and sometimes information flies out at you like water coming from a fire hose.

I've just been soaked with lots of information, but I need to stick to my primary goal, my primary mission, and I don't know how I'm going to pull it off with a CID officer bound back there who's eventually going to get discovered.

What to do?

Another sweep of the library, of course, and then

another, wider sweep outside, because I've got to get my hands on Archie right now, if not sooner. And if cops roll in as I'm leaving, and I don't have Archie, well, I don't know what I'm going to do.

I'm heading back to the main desk area, hoping that the polite and cheerful woman back there has some information for me, and I approach two doors, one marked MEN and the other marked WOMEN, and I feel like I've just lost a hundred pounds of weight on my shoulders, for Archie is placidly standing in front of the door marked MEN.

I roughly grab his upper arm and we start heading out, and I whisper in his ear, "The next time you have to make a bathroom visit, let me know. Even if you have to tap on my shoulder and play charades. You pull something like this again, you'll be going to Florida with two broken arms, not one."

He doesn't say a word, of course, but he puts up no resistance as we head out of the library. The woman at the main desk calls out cheerfully, "Oh, you found your grandfather! Lucky you!"

"You know it," I say, as we quickly stroll past her and the curved desk.

She says, "Did your friend find you? The other Army officer?"

We're at the doors.

"No, I'm afraid she didn't," I say.

One more foot to go and we're free.

The librarian tries to have the last word. "Oh, too bad. Are you sure you can't stay here until she shows up?"

I turn and smile. "I think the poor dear got herself lost back there."

CHAPTER 75

IN A small meeting room at the Victoria Public Library, Rosaria Vasquez rubs one more time at her wrists, where her own handcuffs had dug into her flesh during the long minutes when she waited to be rescued. Truth is, though, it didn't take that long, for while she couldn't say anything with her mouth gagged, her legs were free, and she kicked and kicked until the book carts in front of her fell, and a library worker came over to check out just what in God's name was making all that noise.

Before her is Paul Santiago, a detective from the Victoria Police Department's Assault Crimes Unit, and he's scratching at the side of his bald head with a pen as he tries to make sense of what he has just encountered here with Rosaria and Captain Cornwall. A small notebook is open on the table in front of him.

"I'm sorry if I sound confused," he says, "but tell me again why you were here in Victoria."

She rubs at her wrists but keeps them below the table, out of view of the detective so he can't see. "Like I said before, I was tracking Captain Amy Cornwall. I had received information that she was in this facility."

"Information from whom?"

"My boss at our base in Quantico, Virginia."

"And you didn't think to contact us first?"

"No."

"Why?"

"You know why," she says. "The case was moving quickly. I didn't have time to contact you, or to contact anyone else."

"And what kind of case is this?"

A nightmare case that could kill me or kill my career, she thinks. "Captain Cornwall is AWOL. Absent without leave."

"So that's why you came in the library by yourself. Because you were concerned that she might leave the premises and that you would lose her trail."

"Correct."

He scratches at the side of his head again. He has a thick brown mustache and brown eyes that are sharp and to the point.

"All by yourself."

Rosaria says, "Repeating yourself doesn't change the facts."

"Yeah, you're right," he says. "Tell me this, Miss—"

"Special Agent Vasquez, please."

He doesn't smile or react, just says, "Tell me this, Special Agent Vasquez, it seems that your Captain Amy Cornwall is considered a suspect in a double homicide yesterday afternoon in Three Rivers. Is that true?"

Rosaria stops rubbing her wrists. "I'm not aware of that information."

"Really?"

Scritch-scritch comes the sound of the pen rubbing against his head. "Three Rivers is about ninety miles from here. Not much of a drive. And we received a BOLO this morning about Captain Cornwall. Before I spoke to you, I talked to Miss Chambers who works at the library. I showed her a photo of Captain Cornwall. Miss Chambers readily identified her."

"That's...interesting."

"Yep."

He lowers his pen and says, "I also chatted up a police captain over there in Three Rivers. You can imagine they're quite busy, investigating a double homicide. It seems your Captain Cornwall drove all the way from Virginia, to a tiny town that hardly anybody has heard of, to assault that house, kill two well-armed men, and then leave, with another person in tow. Pretty unusual, don't you think?"

Rosaria says, "I can't think of anything more unusual that I've heard of lately."

Santiago picks up his pen, starts scratching the other side of his head, just above his left ear, where there's a line of faint brown stubble, looking like a farmer's field of corn after harvesttime. Rosaria is trying to war-game what's going to happen here, what she's going to tell her boss, and most of all, how to extricate herself from Victoria without being subject to more interviews, more interrogations.

She needs to get out and get working.

"Another unusual bit of information," Santiago continues, "is learning that yesterday afternoon, another Army officer was found at the scene. Asking questions. Going into the house. Looking at the crime scene."

He pauses with the *scritch-scritch*. "Her name was not available to the Three Rivers police captain, but he's pretty sure she was an Army cop. From the Criminal Investigation Command. That's your unit, isn't it?"

Damn. "Yes, it is."

Finally, Detective Santiago says, "Special Agent Vasquez."

"Still here, sir."

"Just so you know, I have two nephews currently deployed overseas, one in Qatar, the other in Afghanistan. My father did his thirty in the Navy.

One of my uncles died in Vietnam. My family has deep love and respect for the military."

"Thank you," she says.

He slowly and carefully puts his notebook and the pen that he's been using as a scratcher back into his pocket. "Is it safe to say that you believe Captain Cornwall has left Victoria...for parts currently unknown?"

That isn't exactly 100 percent, but Rosaria isn't going to correct him.

"That's a very insightful observation."

"I see." He rubs his hands together and says, "The only crime I see here has been an assault."

Rosaria says, "I don't intend to press charges."

Santiago shakes his head. "That's not your choice, Special Agent Vasquez. Assault is a felony, and we don't need your say-so to proceed toward an investigation and an eventual indictment."

"I see."

There's a quiet moment, and Rosaria is wondering what the detective is thinking, but he doesn't keep her in suspense long.

"If, however, you don't intend to stay here in my city, such that it would be a chore and challenge to contact you for further interviews and questions, then this case might just quietly die away. Do you see what I mean?"

"I certainly do."

She rubs at her sore wrists one more time.

He stands up and says, "So excuse me for being blunt, Special Agent Vasquez, but get the hell out of Victoria and never return."

Rosaria tries to hide her relief at Santiago's words.

"On it, Detective," she says, standing up as well.

"Fantastic," he says. "By the way, thank you for your service."

CHAPTER 76

THE DRIVE along the Gulf of Mexico slowly descends into a monotonous vision of various interstates, interspersed with long stretches of rugged driving along state roads or country lanes that parallel the famed American highway system. I switch from state roads to interstates to avoid tollbooths and their surveillance equipment, either closed-circuit cameras or suspicious troopers sitting in idling police cruisers. I'm also being tracked by the evil ones who took my family.

My poor filthy Jeep Wrangler is now bearing license plates from Mississippi, representing the state we're passing through. Earlier she had on plates from Louisiana, and those were dumped off a concrete bridge spanning a muddy stream in a small town once I crossed the state line.

I'm not under any illusion that changing out the plates will save me, but I'm just hoping it will provide me some cover over the next few hours, as I head into Florida with my quiet Archie, who still hasn't uttered a word, even after I hustled him out of that library back in Victoria.

Part of me appreciates seeing the "real America" near the highway, the road joints, shotgun shacks, struggling farms, mobile home parks, the lights of industry and refineries out there on the horizon, but I also realize that while I'm still comfortable time-wise, I'm very uncomfortable knowledge-wise.

We're now on a long length of two-lane highway called Pass Road, which is flat and offers tobacco and beer stores, used car lots, Dollar Generals, and other merchant hangers-on a few miles away from the warm promises of the Gulf Coast.

I say to Archie, "The worst part about digging into Tom's computer files is finding out that he's been spying on me. Me! His goddamn wife and partner."

We drive past a few pickup trucks heading in the other direction, each hauling a trailer carrying a fishing boat that would probably take a year's salary of mine to purchase.

I go on. "He got a literary agent interested in him last year. The agent was looking for a blockbuster book. Turned down about a half dozen ideas of Tom's. Then Tom hired a hacking firm on the dark web to get access to Army intelligence unit activities, and then my name popped up, what I was doing…and somehow, that led him to two competing drug cartels in Mexico, both of them looking to significantly expand their territory."

I give Archie a sideways glance. "Cartel number one was offering you as an information source to Tom. Out of the goodness of their dark hearts? Hardly. They were using you as an informational tool to take down cartel number two…with Tom's knowledge and assistance. All for a blockbuster book. But cartel number two apparently found out about it, kidnapped him and Denise, and is using me to bring you to them."

I drive on. At some point I'll need to get this cursed little task force onto a highway.

"But for God's sake," I say, "what is the possible connection between Central Asia and Mexico? What could they possibly have in common?"

And he turns and gives me a look that expresses…

Intelligence?

Awareness?

Knowledge?

"Oh, damn it, it was right in front of my face, all the goddamn time!" I yell, and I pull over the Wrangler in a used car lot, and fumble through my leather bag.

In his cubicle at Fort Belvoir, Lieutenant Preston Baker is in a good mood. A while ago he had a nice talk with his mother back home in Washington, and unlike previous calls that ended with sobs and cries of despair, this one ended with a cheerful "Good-bye, Pres, love you," because at long last there's progress in helping out Dad.

The good mood lasts exactly three more seconds.

His phone rings, he answers, "Baker," and there's a static-filled call coming in.

"Hello?"

The familiar woman's voice comes through. "Baker? It's Captain Cornwall."

Preston swivels in his chair so no one strolling by can see the shocked look on his face.

"C-captain Cornwall?" he stammers. "Ah...how are you, ma'am? Where are you?"

Her voice sounds strained and tired. "Lieutenant, I need for you to do something for me, straightaway."

"Yes, ma'am."

"I need you to retrieve the investigative file on that prisoner you helped me interrogate at FOB Healy. The one named Mohammed."

He tries a joke and fails. "They're all called Mohammed, you know how it is."

She ignores the attempt at humor. "The one who claimed he was a farmer. The one who ended up dead."

"Ah, sure, ma'am, I remember that one," he says,

closing his eyes in frustration. Just a few seconds ago everything was falling into place—the promised large deposit into his checking account had come through, Mom had gotten a meeting set up for a long-term care facility for Dad, and now…this.

"Good," she says. "I need you to get the investigative file and retrieve something for me. It's vitally important. Can you get to the file? The sooner the better, Lieutenant."

Preston looks at his desk. The thick file on Mohammed the farmer is sitting right there, because he knows there's some sort of CID investigation going on with that death and wanted to be prepared when the interrogator arrived, whoever he or she might be.

Carefully he says, "I think I can get to it in a while. What do you need?"

He thinks he hears a tone of relief in her voice. "That's great, Lieutenant. That's great. Ah…when we first interrogated him, we found a business card in his belongings. There was an international phone number on the card, that's all. The name of a company as well. Something Holdings. Begins with the letter *M*. Remember? The joke was that maybe it was the guy's bail bondsman."

"Sure, Captain, I remember that."

"Good," she says. "At the time the number was checked out and was found to be a fake…but I want you to recheck it, okay? Really dig into it, see what you can find."

He reaches over to the thick file folder, opens it up, and like some talisman or sign, right on top is the creased and dirty business card in a plastic envelope.

"Ah, Captain?"

"Yes?" comes the same tired voice, but now impatient.

What to say to her?

He knows what his instructions are with his anonymous male caller—present certain information to him in exchange for financial assistance and tell him if Cornwall contacts him. The deal has been shaky, underhanded, and he is desperately afraid to get caught. But he knows his caller is in the military, having met him one night on base in a darkened Humvee, and is convinced that his actions aren't going to hurt the country.

Preston is a trained intelligence officer and knows this isn't how things are done, but the man convinced him that in certain times, regulations have to be ignored for the greater good. And although Preston has his doubts about Cornwall's guilt in that farmer's death, the man also showed him video evidence on an iPad that in a moment of fear months ago, Cornwall smoked an entire Afghan family with a Hellfire missile against orders.

What now?

This superior told him not to offer any information to Cornwall if she were to call, but Cornwall…

Lots of memories come back from his tour at FOB Healy with the captain. Her sharing candy and snacks from her packages from home. The time he lost all his socks after washing them, and how she shared her socks with him. And twice when he and she had gone to the shelter when Taliban units had sent mortar fire into the small base, and how scared he was, oh God, and the captain had just put her arm around him and that bit of comfort had seen him through that shelling.

"Lieutenant, what is it? I don't have much time."

He takes a deep, reassuring breath.

"Call me back in ten minutes, Captain. I'll have what you need," he says.

CHAPTER 77

HER WRISTS are still sore, but Rosaria Vasquez is holding the steering wheel firmly as she is driving east to Florida. Why Florida?

Because Senior Warrant Officer Fred McCarthy told her to go there.

She winces, recalling the sharp and cutting words he used as weapons against her, all the way from calling her a useless ROTC officer who went into the Army for three hots and a cot, up to calling her a stupid coward.

"A library!" he shouted. "You got ambushed in a goddamn library?"

Nothing she could have said would have turned back that anger, so she had taken it in silence, until finally there was a quiet moment and he said, "Gulf Coast of Florida. Get your sorry ass out there as soon as possible."

"Then what, sir?"

"Then you'll have actionable intelligence, and you act on it, Vasquez, and when the day is over, I want one of two things in your hand: Cornwall's dog tags, or Cornwall's dog tags and a copy of her toe tag. It finishes today, it finishes now. Got it?"

Rosaria nods in memory as she speeds east on Interstate 10, going through a strip that boasts gun shops, dollar stores, gas stations, hairdressing outfits, and everything and anything else a high-speed traveler needs on his or her way to the beaches of paradise.

She gently moves the steering wheel, wrists still aching, her eyes swollen with tears, her insides empty, only knowing that yes, when she gets to the Gulf Coast, she will end it.

In a quiet wooded area near the Fort Belvoir Country Club, Lieutenant Preston Baker waits, leaning up against the wide trunk of an old oak tree. Thirty minutes earlier he called his contact and followed his directions.

There is movement out there, footsteps, and then the senior officer stands on the other side of the tree trunk, so he can be heard but not seen.

"So she called, then?"

"Yes," Preston says.

"What did she want?"

"Information about the prisoner who died in captivity, over at FOB Healy."

"What kind of information?"

Preston tries to focus on the good news he received today, about a facility being readied for Dad. His father, who had sweated and worked and thought to design and build the aircraft that had defended this nation for decades…abandoned in his time of need, but Preston is going to take care of him.

That's the good news, that will always be the good news.

"She asked about a business card that was found on the farmer when he was brought in. The official report said the business name and the phone number on the card were fake."

"And?" comes the inquiry.

"Captain Cornwall wanted me to recheck it."

"And did you?"

"I did."

"Did you confirm to her what the report said, that the phone number and company name were fake?"

A blue jay skitters to a halt, not more than three meters away. It steps across the ground with proud, jerky moves, and then flies off.

What a gorgeous day.

The officer repeats, "Did you confirm to her what the report said, that the company number and name were fake?"

He takes a sweet breath. "No, I didn't. Captain Cornwall…I don't think you understand what it's like being out there, in an FOB. You learn to depend on each other, have each other's backs, look out for each other."

The officer on the other side of the tree doesn't say anything.

Preston says, "I trust her. I've always trusted her. And she asked me to do something, so I did it."

The voice is flat. "Which was what?"

"I researched the name and phone number on the card."

"What did you find?"

"There was a phone number. Out of Mexico. And the company name…Mercador Holdings. An agricultural firm, in the States and Mexico."

"Anything else?"

"I dug a bit into Mercador Holdings. Its majority owner is a bank out of Mexico. Called First Republic Global Bank."

"What did the captain say when you told her that?"

"She seemed excited, happy," Preston says.

"I'm sure."

There's silence and then the officer says, "You did all right, Lieutenant. No worries."

Preston sighs. This sweet day is back on track. "Thanks."

"Let me ask you one more question."

"Sure."

The man asks, "You ever hear of something called fragging?"

"No, I haven't," he says.

"Funny, you're the second person to say that today."

And Preston hears movement, feels something metallic pressing against his right temple, and then nothing else.

CHAPTER 78

I RUB at the crusts in the corners of my eyes, take an exit off US 98 in Florida, following the signs pointing to my end destination, Beachside. The road is bleached asphalt, and the surrounding land is sandy, with thin grass and spindly green trees.

Archie is sitting next to me, hands folded carefully in his lap, watching the scenery fly by. Since we left Texas some hours ago, he's not said a word to me.

But I can't stand the silence, so I talk to him as we get closer to Beachside.

"I'm a trained Army intelligence officer," I say, as we head south. Even though I can't see it, I can smell the nearby Gulf of Mexico.

"About ninety percent of civilians think all we intelligence officers do is read lots of reports, stare at maps, make educated guesses," I say. "And part of that's correct. We read lots of reports. We look at maps. We make educated guesses. But we also talk to people. Lots of people...like a young engineer from Karachi, very intelligent, very sweet-looking, who was captured after his suicide belt didn't go off in a marketplace in New Delhi. And who politely lets you know that if he ever gets out, he plans to go to the Hindu Kush and get a belt that's designed better, so it works the next time."

The road stretches on. How can anyplace be so damn flat?

"Or a Russian girl, about ten years old, who was sold to…perform. You meet her in a sweet cottage with toys, dolls, and games, and while you try to find out which particular oligarch from Moscow had a hand in her sale, said oligarch also being involved in smuggling weapons-grade uranium to North Korea, she keeps on asking why she hurts so much down there."

There's an intersection. I slow down and take a left. BEACHSIDE TWO MILES, says the sign.

"That's the people you talk to," I go on. "And then there's the films, the videos. You sometimes see them on the cable channels, heavily edited. But because your job is intelligence, no matter how terrifying, how horrible, how bloody, you need to watch it. Again and again. Looking for clues."

My chest is tightening. I'm saying words my husband, Tom, has never heard.

"I saw a video of a captured fighter pilot, stuck in a cage, set ablaze in an Iraqi desert. He burned and burned…and I saw his jaw fall to the ground when the muscles and tendons melted. I saw a video of a Filipino family—mom, dad, five children—lined up in a jungle on an isolated island, beheaded one at a time. And I had to watch that video dozens of times, freeze-framing, trying to see if I could ID the man holding the sword. Dozens of times I saw that family die, saw the mother try to hide her baby under her blouse, saw them both killed…Funny, but every time I replayed the video, part of me was hoping, this time, this time, maybe they live."

I try to clear my throat. "Then they never do. And after watching that beheading video a couple of dozen times, then I leave the base and in twenty minutes, I'm home. I hug Denise and kiss Tom, and look over

Denise's homework and cook dinner for the three of us...and an hour after seeing the blood spurt, seeing the father sob—they save him for last—I'm eating mac and cheese in our dining room, trying to keep a happy face on for my girl and my man."

Up ahead I make out the thin line of the Gulf of Mexico and the low buildings of Beachside. My chest is really tight.

"Then there are the times when you do more than just watch," I say. "You have a hand in it, by pure accident and happenstance." I find it's getting harder to talk, even though I'm not getting any answers back from my passenger.

"You're put in a situation, sitting in a comfortable chair, a computer control in your right hand, and because you're at the ultimate pinnacle of human development and technology, you can flip a switch, take a sip of iced tea, and on the other side of the world, a family is incinerated. Just like that."

Buildings start to appear. Cute one- and two-story structures, made of some sort of cement or rock or adobe, the colors pink, blue, and yellow. Tall palm trees sway in the Gulf breeze. I feel like we've driven onto a movie set for some South Pacific paradise. People are strolling on the sidewalks, most wearing bathing suits, and there are cute little shops selling T-shirts, swimwear, towels, inflatable beach toys.

So damn peaceful.

And I feel so damn out of place.

Then the road comes to a wide four-way boulevard, and as promised and described, there's an oval brick plaza with a fountain and a round bandstand. There's a set of angled parking spots on this side of the plaza, and I drive in and park, out of breath.

I check my watch.

Thirty minutes ahead of schedule.

Well done, a sour voice inside of me says. *Now let's send this quiet old man to his death and get our family back.* I look around the place. Across the wide avenue there's a hotel building that looks to be under construction, flanked by smaller buildings that could be condos or high-priced shops. There's a high pink stone wall and a black metal gate. A blue Mercedes-Benz convertible comes up to the gate, which has a keypad on a metal post. The driver reaches out, punches the keypad, and the gate slides open. There's a large brass numeral 9 attached to the middle of the gate.

To the left of the gate is a smaller entrance for pedestrians, and that gate doesn't have a keypad, for I see some beachgoers head in, carrying coolers and towels in their hands.

So pleasant, so peaceful.

I take my phone out, look to Archie.

"I'm sorry," I say. "I have to do this."

Then I press the keypad on my cell phone, no doubt leading to this man's death by the end of the day.

CHAPTER 79

TOM CORNWALL looks up from his bunk when the door clicks open and one of the men who works here comes in, bearing a tray with two white-plastic-covered dishes, and he reaches over and gently taps Denise's foot. She's snoozing on her side, Tigger up by her chin.

"Hey, wake up, hon, dinner's here," he says.

Then it all goes wrong.

Two bulkier men come in, and there's a dead look in their eyes, and he sits back in the bed, yells, "Denise! Run! Get out of here!"

The men are pros, they spray something in each of their faces, and Tom chokes and Denise screams, and like that horrible day when they were taken from their homes, bags are pulled over their heads.

"Come," a voice says, and strong hands grab his upper arms, and he's propelled out of the room.

I dial the number, hoping to God this is the last time I ever have to remember this demonic series of numerals, and the phone is picked up on the first ring.

"Yes?"

"You know who this is," I say. "I'm here at the little park, bandstand, and fountain."

"So happy to hear from you, Captain Cornwall."

"The feeling isn't mutual," I say. "Let's make this quick. I have my weapon in my lap. Anybody approaches me I will shoot this old man next to me, all right?"

He chuckles. "With that deadly attitude, I'm surprised you're not a general in your Army."

"Give me time," I say. "I need to talk to Tom, and I need to talk to Denise. Otherwise, this man is dead on this plaza."

"For real?"

"Oh, yes, for real," I say. "Besides getting me arrested, I'll also scare a bunch of tourists."

He says, "Fear is a useful thing. All right. I will follow your request. Hold on, please."

I say, "Not too long," but I'm talking to empty air.

I wait.

Look around.

The gate across the way opens up and a white Cadillac, with tinted windows, eases out. With the gate open, I see little areas of tended brush and trees, and a wide beach spotted with beach umbrellas and kids playing.

My caller comes back. "This will be on speakerphone, just so there's no misunderstanding."

I try to speak, but another male voice interrupts me. "Amy?"

I put a fist to my mouth, trying so very hard not to sob in relief.

Tom feels light-headed and woozy, standing on a balcony, sun beating down, holding Denise's hand. The air feels good, but he's also up at a height, maybe five or six stories. The canvas bags have been pulled off their heads, and the man who's been in charge is standing a few feet away, wearing a light-blue-and-white seersucker suit, a cell phone in his beefy right hand.

He says, "This will be on speakerphone, just so there's no misunderstanding."

The phone comes over to Tom, and he takes it, hand shaking, and brings it up near his mouth.

"Amy?"

A slight pause, and her voice comes right out through the speakerphone. "Oh, Tom...Tom, are you okay?"

"I'm fine, honest," he says, ignoring the throbbing pain in his burnt arm, still covered with the bandage the Afghan doctor had put on him. "Denise is with me, too."

"Let me talk to her, just for a moment."

Tom lowers the phone, and Denise, her face as nearly bright as the sun, talks loudly into the phone. "Mommy, Mommy, are you here? Are you here to pick us up?"

"That's right, hon, that's right. Give me back to Daddy."

Tom brings up the phone. "I'm back."

"Good, good," she says, her voice sounding so sweet and wonderful. "Tom, this is very important. What do you see?"

"What?"

"The scenery," she snaps. "Tell me where you are, what you see."

He looks to Pelayo, who offers him a slight nod. He's happy that he can do what Amy asks, but he's still humiliated at being under this man's control.

"Ah...I'm somewhere in Florida, I'm sure. There's a flagpole that's flying the American flag and the Florida flag. I see the beach, the ocean...and on the other side, looks like a wide stretch of downtown..."

"Look at the downtown. What do you see?"

He leans over the balcony a bit. "There's...a band-stand. And a fountain...Hey! There's a black Jeep Wrangler. Is that you?"

The phone goes silent.

"Amy?"

I lose it for a long minute, just sobbing against my clenched fist.

I've made it.

My Tom and Denise are nearby, so very, very close.

The other man's voice comes back onto the phone. "Satisfied?"

"I am," Amy says.

"Very well. The time is now...five thirty p.m. Let's make the exchange in exactly thirty minutes. Six p.m. on the dot. Is that satisfactory to you?"

"Why not now?"

"Because arrangements must be made," the man says. "You've noticed there's a gate nearby. The access code to the gate is one-two-three-two-one. Easy to recall, am I correct? Come into this little gated community and make a left. About a hundred meters down the drive is a store that sells women's beachwear. It's called Yucatan. Go into the store and there's a package waiting for you."

"What kind of package?"

"A bathing suit," the man says, laughing. "A very, very skimpy bathing suit. Once you have that on, you will walk with your...guest, to a small park with four concrete benches. Stand by the closest bench. I will be there in exactly thirty minutes. If you're not there...well, let's not consider that, shall we?"

My breathing starts to quicken.

"All right," I say. "Six p.m. I'll be there. And you'll

be there with Tom and Denise. If I don't see Tom and
Denise, I will—"

"I know, I know, you will kill the man that you
have," he says. "Aren't you ashamed of saying these
threats out loud, so he can hear them?"

"No," I say, and I disconnect the call.

CHAPTER 80

TOM'S EYES are swollen and filled with tears, and he wipes at them, not caring if his captor is seeing this embarrassing display. Pelayo is smiling widely.

"Everything is coming together," he says. "See? Save for some disruption to your life, and an unfortunately burnt arm that is entirely your fault, in just a little while, your family will be reunited." Pelayo reaches over, rubs Denise's head, and Tom feels a sharp bile of anger rise up in him.

"Don't touch my girl," he says.

Pelayo lifts his hand. "I understand. Come, we need to get ready."

Tom takes Denise's hand and starts walking down the balcony, to the open sliding door leading back inside. Pelayo says, "Tom, are you all right? You seem to be limping some."

"Leg cramp," Tom says. "Lying down all day and night will do that to you."

"Oh, I see," Pelayo says, and they are ushered into a wide suite, Tom holding Denise's hand, walking carefully with a limp so the cutting tool hidden in his right sock doesn't fall out.

Rosaria Vasquez swears and bursts into tears. This is too much, just way too much. Her last phone call came from her boss ten minutes ago, sending her to a small town named Beachside, and then there was a *thump,* the right rear of her rental Buick shuddered to the side, and here she is now, with a flat tire and a damn jack that just won't work.

Again she moves the thin handle, and again it slips out, skinning her knuckles. She throws the handle into the dirt, turns and slumps back against the car, draws up her knees, and runs her hands through her now very short hair. She's parked just off US 98, and she hates this stretch of road, hates the state of Florida, and pretty much hates everything. The land is flat, bleached, with trees and brush that look fake.

Traffic roars by, and the occasional tractor-trailer truck buffets her car, rocking against her back.

"Hello?"

Rosaria wipes at her eyes, stands up. Behind her disabled Buick is a dented and rusting blue Audi sedan, and an older Vietnamese woman is looking at her with concern.

"Hi," Rosaria says. "Thanks for stopping, but I think if I—"

The woman, wearing baggy black slacks and a floral blouse down to her thick hips, turns and yells back at the parked sedan. The rear door flies open and two young Vietnamese men and a woman bail out and come to her. Another older male is dozing in the front seat.

The woman points and yells at the three young people, and the two men get right to work, slipping the jack handle in, while the young woman—a sister?—wrestles the spare tire closer to the car.

"Um, hey, I mean—"

The Vietnamese woman shakes her head. "We'll be done soon. You see."

And by God, that's exactly what happens. The two young men manage to get the jack working, get the rear end of the Buick up, while their mother and sister offer advice, criticism, and tips in fast bursts of Vietnamese, and soon enough, the flat tire is tossed into the trunk, the car is lowered down, the jack and handle are put away, and after a round of handshakes, the two young men and woman get back into the car.

Rosaria tries to get to her bag, to offer something to the family, but the woman violently shakes her head.

"No, no," she says. "We're good now. Honest. Go with God, my sister."

Rosaria bows to her. "You, too. Go with God."

And as they leave, horn honking, everyone waving save for the older man still sleeping in the front, Rosaria knows that no matter what happens in the next hour, she will never, ever forget this family and what they did for her.

I check my watch after I leave the Yucatan beachwear store, feeling about as conspicuous as an elephant in a child's wading pool. There was a bathing suit waiting for me, and I'm so self-conscious walking out in public with such a skimpy article of clothing that I'm sure my ears and face are burning. My jiggling butt cheeks are hanging out, my boobs—not impressive but a reasonable size—are oozing out of the sides of the small top, and I hate to look down, seeing my flabby and pale white tummy overhanging the tiny triangle of cloth that is rubbing and tearing at me something fierce.

My watch says I have fifteen minutes before the exchange, and I know why my nameless tormentor has ordered me to dress this way: he wants to make sure I'm not concealing a weapon, and by God, this jet-black suit is so skimpy I don't think I could hide a nail file.

Archie is right next to me, the placid yet mournful

look still on his face. The dressing rooms back there had doors of wooden slats so I could keep watch on him while I changed, but he's been a very good victim.

I only wish I could be a better person.

We walk along the side of the wide parking lot, heading to the place where the concrete benches are placed, and I slip my arm into his for a few feet. I stare ahead and say, "I'm…I'm sorry for what's going to happen. But I have to do this to save my family. I hope you can forgive me."

Then a man's voice quietly says, "You should not trust that man, not at all."

And I come to a halt.

The voice is from Archie.

CHAPTER 81

IN THE basement garage of his new hotel, Pelayo Abboud approaches the black GMC Yukon with his associate Casper keeping pace with him. Tom Cornwall is being helped into the rear of the Yukon, sitting next to the young girl who is on the far side, wearing black tights and an oversized Epcot sweatshirt, Tigger doll in her lap.

Casper says, "The old man and the Army captain, they have left the Yucatan."

"Good," Pelayo says. "Then it will be finished in just a few more minutes."

Casper holds the rear door open, and as another vehicle starts up in the distance, Pelayo cheerfully climbs in and sits next to Tom.

I grab the old man's wrist and pull him closer to a little island of grass and low brush, drag him in for cover, and I say, "You tell me what you know. Now."

Archie sighs. "His name is Pelayo Abboud. He is a killer, a criminal, a very, very bad man who will one day burn in eternity for his sins."

My hand is still on Archie's wrist. "Go on. That's not really a news flash."

He looks out at the warm and wide waters of the Gulf of Mexico, acting almost like a child seeing the ocean for the very first time. "Pelayo is the head of a Mexican cartel, the Veracruz."

"Never heard of it."

"No matter," Archie says. "Like many other cartels, his has a bank under his control. One for which I worked."

"First Republic Global Bank, NA, based in Guadalajara."

"Ah, exactly. You are a very smart woman."

"Not smart enough," I say. "Tom Cornwall…my husband. He's a journalist. He found out about Pelayo and the bank, and made arrangements to interview you."

"True," Archie says, shaking his head. "I was kidnapped by the El Baja cartel, to be turned over to this Tom, so he would write a book about their rivals, the Veracruz cartel. I was to be El Baja's weapon to publicize the Veracruz's activities, to cripple them. But now Pelayo has used you to bring me to him, to disarm his enemies."

I'm running out of time, and sensing that, Archie adds, "One last warning. Do not trust any promises Pelayo has made. They are all false. There will be no exchange, there will be no safety for you or your family. At the right moment for Pelayo, he will kill you all, even your little girl."

That had been my thought right from the start when I had picked up that sheet of paper back home in Virginia, but to have it confirmed by this mild-mannered and elder banker before me chills me so hard and fast in this tropic sunshine that I shiver.

"Why did you keep your mouth shut all this time?"

"What could I say?" he says. "I could have begged to have been released, but that never would have happened, would it? You had a mission, to save your family, and they can only be saved by my presence.

Like any good banker, I knew that someday there would be a final accounting for my sins."

I pause for the briefest of moments. "How do you know this?"

A mournful shrug. "Pelayo is my son."

CHAPTER 82

SITTING IN the rear of the Yukon with Tom Cornwall and the little girl, Pelayo Abboud allows himself a smile of satisfaction. It's going well, better than expected, and in a very few minutes, this complex and very satisfying operation will come to a close.

Driving is one of his men, Paco, whose shoulders are so broad that they nearly rub up against the passenger up front, who is the Afghan boy, Hamid. The young Afghan lad still seems overwhelmed by the sights and sounds of wealthy Florida, and it's now time to bring him back to earth.

"Paco," he says, as the bulky man maneuvers around a slow-moving crowd of beachgoers.

"*Jefe,*" he replies.

In Spanish, Pelayo says, "Tell Hamid that he is doing a wonderful job for me and that he is going to be rewarded, as a true warrior of…God, Allah, whatever it is he believes in."

Paco stops the Yukon for a moment, talks to Hamid in Pashto. The young Afghan turns and smiles at Pelayo, nodding his thanks.

Again in Spanish, Pelayo says, "Tell Hamid that the man sitting here next to me is married to the American woman who killed his family. Tell Hamid that when I call his name out, he has my permission to kill this man, to avenge the deaths of his family."

About halfway through Paco's talking to Hamid,

his expression darkens, his eyes narrow, and he utters something and stares the look of utter death and hatred toward Tom Cornwall.

Paco says, "It is done, boss."

"Bueno," Pelayo says.

He gently pats the upper leg of Tom.

"No worries, Tom. It will be over soon."

Tom says not a word, but his eyes look to be swelling with tears.

The girl next to him also remains quiet.

I'm standing at the arranged meeting site, near a concrete park bench that is empty, still feeling cold and exposed with the skimpy bathing suit I'm wearing, and with Archie at my right, I say again, "Your son? Pelayo is your son?"

Archie says in a quiet voice, "Yes, by blood and birth, the boy is my son. I have disowned him many times…but still, he haunts my life. He knows I have always been a threat to him, and now, he has come to settle accounts, to make sure I will no longer be able to do him harm."

A black Yukon is slowly approaching us. There's no visible sign that this vehicle contains my family or Pelayo, but I can sense something odd and evil about the large black four-wheeler coming my way. Its windows are all tinted, not allowing me to see inside.

Thinking as fast as I can, I say, "When the time comes…and if I have my husband and daughter, run for it. I'll try to protect you."

He shrugs. "Run where? This complex…it is completely owned by Pelayo, and the people here work for him. Even these tourists…they are either workers of his or family members, here on a holiday to repay their work in assisting Pelayo to climb his bloody hill of bodies."

I reach over and grab his hand, give it a squeeze. "I'm so sorry…I'm so, so sorry."

The Yukon pulls around so that the passenger's side is facing us. The Yukon is blocking traffic but I'm sure nobody here is going to complain.

"What's your real name?" I ask.

He chuckles. "It makes no difference. I like Archie. You may keep on using it as long as you wish."

A breeze comes up, and I freeze in terror. No, not a wind, not now. Please God, no wind. Make it remain still.

I see a rear door on the driver's-side open up, and a confident-looking man wearing a seersucker suit with no necktie casually walks around the front of the Yukon, placing himself so the engine block is a shield.

Archie whispers, "There he is. Again, don't trust him, not at all. He has planned this, all of it, and the plan does not include any of you coming out alive."

"But we're in a public place."

He says, "His public. Don't forget that. There are no innocents around here. May God help you."

"And you, too, Archie."

I step forward and hold out my arms, to show I'm not armed.

"I'm here!" I call out. "And so is the old man you wanted."

Pelayo clasps his hands and smiles. "So he is, so he is. Well done, Captain Cornwall."

When he passes the driver's-side door, Paco—even with his impressive bulk—slips out and is now kneeling beside him, by the Yukon's big front tire.

Pelayo whispers to Paco, "Are you ready?"

Paco is holding an H&K MP5 9mm submachine gun at his side. The weapon looks like a toy in his huge hands.

"Yes, *jefe*."

"Good," Pelayo whispers back. "When I'm done talking to the old man, and say, 'It is finished,' then kill the bitch."

"What about the old man?"

Pelayo waves again, smiling. "The old man is mine."

CHAPTER 83

THE MAN called Pelayo is smiling at me, his expression that of a butcher eager to start his day, standing in a wooden chute, ready to kill cow after cow with a bolt to the head. I see his lips moving but don't hear anything, which tells me there's someone else nearby, heavily armed.

He calls out, "Captain Cornwall, why don't you come closer so I don't have to yell?"

I say back, "I like standing in the shade."

"Ah, yes," he says, "underneath the palm fronds and branches. Wanting to cover yourself from any snipers, eh?"

"Where are Tom and Denise?"

He points to the Yukon. "Right in here, of course."

"Show them to me. Now."

He shrugs. "As you wish."

He steps back and the near rear passenger window slides down, and I see my Tom and the top of my little girl's head, and the tears just burst out and I desperately try to keep my cool.

"All right, let's get this over with," I say. "I brought you this old man. Give me my family."

Pelayo is back in front of the Yukon. "But a few words to the old man, if I may."

Pelayo starts speaking in Spanish to his father, but the old bastard, demanding as always, yells back,

"English! Speak to me in English. At least this poor woman should know why I am here, and why you have done so much harm to her and her poor family."

Seeing the arrogant old man standing in front of him stirs up lots of memories that Pelayo thought had been buried deep and long ago, and he recalls the lecturing, the beatings, and most of all, the disappointing looks on his father's face as Pelayo grew older and learned it wasn't love or family that meant anything in this world, only money and power.

He yells, "You're here because of what you've done to me, how you've belittled me, and because you were about to betray me."

The old man shoots back, "Then I'm proud to be here, to face a creature that pretends to be my son. Betray you? I was merely going to tell the world of how you were always a twisted, evil child, and that your despised life has caused death and misery to thousands."

"You have no right!"

The Army captain, looking ridiculous in a skimpy suit perfect for a woman half her age and weight, is standing close to his father, as if she is trying to reassure him as he yells back at Pelayo.

"A father always has the right to tell the truth about his son, especially when he has a heart and soul as dark as a rotten gourd, forgotten in the field at harvesttime."

"It is because of you, old man, that I am like this!"

He grins back. "You have been an adult for many, many years, my son. Are you so weak that you continue to blame me, your mother, and the Church for how you turned out? Like your despised cousin, you have the face and body of a human, but the soul of a monster."

Enough is enough, Pelayo thinks, and he yells out, "It is finished!"

There.

He reaches under his coat to grab his Glock .40-caliber pistol, and then like a jack-in-the-box, Paco leaps up next to him, submachine gun in hand, and as Pelayo brings the pistol up to shoot the old bastard, there's movement and—

The Army woman is pointing a pistol at him!

How is this possible?

Where did she get it?

Where was it hidden?

He warns Paco, "Faster, faster, she's armed!"

And then the bitch shoots first!

CHAPTER 84

AS PELAYO and my friend Archie yell at each other, I'm ignoring the words and instead looking for the threat. I'm looking at the Yukon, knowing there has to be at least a second or third gunman back there. There's no way this cartel leader has come to this supposed swap by himself without extra firepower right next to him.

Movement.

I'm looking for movement.

And here it comes.

Now it's my time.

A wind comes up, and I don't care anymore if the breeze reveals the slit I earlier made in the rear of Archie's suitcoat, which gives me easy access to my SIG Sauer pistol concealed in his rear waistband.

I grab it and it's in my hands as Pelayo whirls out with a pistol, and a beefy-looking guy pops up with a cut-down H&K MP5—*Nice intelligence work there, Amy*, says a voice inside me—and I'm presented with two threats: I go to the deadlier one, the man with the submachine gun, and open fire.

Inside the Yukon, Hamid jerks at hearing the familiar sound of gunfire, and he turns in his seat, ready to slaughter the American behind him when the word comes, but the American is bent over, seemingly crying and sobbing, and Hamid shouts, "Shut up, you bawling woman!"

He has a pistol on him but is going to go with the folding knife that is now in his hand. A bullet to the American's head would kill him and be merciful.

Hamid is not going to be merciful.

The little girl is also crying, and Hamid is ignoring her.

Tom Cornwall is bent at the waist, making noises to signal he's crying and afraid of the gunfire, but he's been in a number of tight places before, and the gunfire is now just part of the background noise, like the yells and the curses he also hears.

With his hands bound in tape, he is desperately working at his left pant leg, which he manages to drag up, revealing his sock and—

God, yes, the cutting tool.

He tries to work with the tool, cutting and slicing at the tight tape, and he winces as the blade twice cuts into his own skin, but he keeps on working.

The gunfire outside continues.

The bitch was using his father to get to him, Pelayo screams inside, and he opens fire, just as Paco aims at the woman, and there's an ugly noise of metal being ripped apart, and then there's a quick "oh" and the side of his face is suddenly soaked, and he spares just the quickest of glances, seeing the pockmarked metal on the Yukon's hood where the woman opened fire in Paco's direction.

It looks like four or five rounds worked their way up the metal, until the last bullet took off the top of Paco's head.

Pelayo fires off two rounds, ducks, and picks up the

MP5, rolls to the left, and the woman is advancing, shooting at him, and Pelayo yells out, "Hamid, Hamid, kill him, kill him!"

Hamid hears the blessed words, and he yells, "American, sit up, look at me in the eye!" and yes, the American comes up, but he has something in his hand which whirls toward Hamid, and then his throat is burning, and he tries to yell something again, but his mouth is full of blood and he falls back.

I have no cover so I'm doing what's called advancing under fire, and I think I get the gunman with the submachine gun and then Pelayo is on the ground, firing back at me, but yeah, like most civilians, he's not used to firing in a prone position, and there's whistling noises as rounds roar by me, and I shoot and shoot and I'm aiming at the Yukon's tire, and then at Pelayo, for my loved ones are in that vehicle and I'm not about to let it head out.

The rear passenger door suddenly pops open, and Tom and Denise tumble out in a confused pile, and I keep on advancing, and another Yukon roars by, front passenger door opening up, and Pelayo runs to it, and I don't care, I let him go. Tom and Denise are right here, and Pelayo can go to the North Pole for all I care, and now I take cover behind the first Yukon and Tom rolls over, eyes wide, covered with blood, and he's struggling to take a piece of tape off his mouth.

And the little girl next to him is in familiar black slacks and an Epcot sweatshirt, and as I reach for her, Tom screams, "That's not Denise! That's not Denise!"

The girl rolls over, eyes wide, tape on her mouth as well.

A hammer blow hits me so hard I think I've been struck by an RPG round.

The girl is not Denise.

I run to the front of the disabled Yukon.

The second Yukon is still there, door open, Pelayo climbing into the passenger's seat, and there's a confusing scramble, and then he shoves out a little girl who screams, "Mommy!" and then she's pulled back in and the door slams and the Yukon roars off.

CHAPTER 85

TOM CORNWALL sits up and wipes at the blood on his face and shirt. His lower legs are still secured by tape. He crawls back into the rear bloody seat of the Yukon, finds the cutting tool, goes back out to the parking lot, works at his legs.

There's a man dying in the front seat, gurgling and coughing, and Tom doesn't want to be near him.

There.

The tape is off and Tom works to free the little girl. She's bawling, and he has no idea who she is—another kidnap victim?—and once her tape is off, she gets up and runs away, screaming.

Tom sees a man on the ground, legs and arms splayed out, and he scrambles over and sees the man's eyes are open, and his mouth is slowly opening and closing, like a fish out of water, slowly suffocating. His white dress shirt is soaked with blood, he has closely trimmed white hair and beard, and moments ago, he was standing next to his wife, Amy.

"Sir, I'm Tom Cornwall," he gasps out. "I'm… damn, I'm so sorry this happened. I swear to God."

Tom leans over as the man softly speaks. "I'm sorry, too, that I can't answer your questions, Mister Cornwall…but…I think you might have enough for a book, eh?"

The man closes his eyes.

*   *   *

A man of his named Georges is driving the second
Yukon, and the screaming little girl is in Pelayo's lap,
and he turns to the rear and says, "My father, did you
see my father?"

Casper is there, pistol in his right hand. "*Jefe,* I saw
him fall. I saw blood on his chest."

The girl is still screaming, and Pelayo slaps his
hand over the brat's mouth.

"Good," he says, as the girl squirms and struggles
on his lap.

Casper sharply says, "Good? For real, *jefe*?"

Pelayo yells to Georges, "Drive faster, fool!"

The young man swerves the Yukon around a
group of children, standing in the middle of the parking lot, and speeds to the gate.

I've dumped the silly flip-flops and I'm racing across
the hot asphalt of the parking lot, then the grass, then
the parking lot again, my SIG Sauer in my right hand,
running, running, running, not letting the Yukon get
out of my sight.

The black vehicle suddenly stops in front of a
group of laughing children, swerves, and then picks
up speed.

Running.

Running.

People are watching and pointing at the chunky
woman spilling out of her teeny-tiny bikini, running,
holding a pistol in her hands, and I ignore them all.

The Yukon is heading right toward the gate.

Running.

Should I stop, aim for the tires?

Can I do that?

But this is no thriller novel, no blow-'em-up movie, no cop show on TV, where the hero can be a hundred yards away and carefully shoot out the rear tires of a racing vehicle. I'm scared, I'm angry, and if I stand and try to shoot, shit, I might take out a tire, a taillight, or —

A high-speed round from my hand, my weapon, could break through the rear window of the Yukon and kill my little girl.

I don't stop.

I keep on running.

Will somebody call the police after seeing this shootout? Will the cavalry ride to the rescue?

Of course not.

This artificial community created by drug money has no police.

Running.

The Yukon makes a turn to the right and I break right as well, and I screech as my right foot is sliced open by something but I don't care.

Now.

The Yukon has stopped.

Finally!

A hand emerges from the left side, works a keypad.

Running.

A stitch starts stabbing hard at my left side.

The pistol feels like it weighs a ton.

My breathing is harsh and ragged.

"Denise!" I scream.

The gate ahead starts rattling to the right.

The taillights of the Yukon blink as the driver takes his foot off the brakes.

In a few seconds the SUV with my kidnapped daughter aboard will quietly go out into traffic and then disappear.

"Denise!"
I bring up my pistol but it feels useless.
I'm too far away.
I'm not going to make it.
"Denise!" I scream one more time.
Oh, God, I'm not going to make it.

CHAPTER 86

GEORGES BRINGS his arm in and the gate starts moving, and Pelayo is confident it will all work out. In just a few minutes, he'll be at a private airstrip to the northeast of Beachside, and with Casper and this little girl with him, they'll head back south to Mexico.

There he'll regroup and think things through.

The little girl is still crying and struggling.

As for her?

Well, he knows that objects can be sent via delivery systems to nearly anywhere in the United States. A small shipping container with frozen dry ice would keep something fresh for several days, until it got to a certain Army captain's home.

Fresh, like a little girl's head.

The gate is open, but the way is blocked by a steady stream of tourists and beachgoers, and Casper calmly says, "The Cornwall woman is back there, running at us."

"Georges!" Pelayo yells. "Move!"

The driver honks the horn, the line of people moves to the left and right, except for one tired-looking, short-haired woman, carrying a folded beach umbrella over her shoulder.

The woman doesn't move.

Casper says, "She's coming closer."

Pelayo leans over, pushes the horn again.

The woman stares and stares at them, and then looks behind the SUV, and back to them.

Pelayo pushes the horn, tells Georges, "Move! Drive over her if you have to!"

Then the woman finally moves to the left.

Drops the beach umbrella.

And pulls out a pump-action shotgun.

For some reason the Yukon isn't moving, and my heart leaps as with each passing second, I get closer and closer.

Damn it!

I'm still not going to make it.

The Yukon honks its horn once, twice, and then I see a woman move around, with short hair, wearing tan shorts and a white T-shirt, and she looks vaguely familiar, and the beach umbrella drops and—

What the hell?

A pump-action shotgun is now in the woman's hands.

I now recognize her.

Vasquez, the CID officer, with her hair shorn. I had taken her pistol but now she's re-armed herself.

Here?

To arrest me?

It's not going to happen.

I make a split-second decision, turning my SIG Sauer in her direction.

But she's faster.

The shotgun is up and aimed.

I don't care. I've turned into a coldhearted bitch, and I warned her to stay away and told her what would happen if she showed up.

I start pulling the trigger.

But...

Her shotgun isn't pointed at me.

It's aimed at the Yukon.

The strange woman with the shotgun fires once, *BOOM!* And the Yukon shudders and there are two more booming gunshots as the woman takes out both the engine and the two front tires.

The engine rattles and dies, red lights appear on the instrument panel, and he yells to Georges, "Shoot her, shoot her, shoot her!"

Georges lowers the window, brings up his pistol, and Pelayo does the same on his side. Before Georges can shoot, the woman shoots again, hitting the side of the door, tossing Georges back.

Pelayo gets off one shot that is insanely loud in the Yukon's interior, and the girl is screaming and forces herself to the rear, and Casper grabs her around the waist, forcing the right rear door open.

Pelayo jumps out, leaving Georges behind, who's now crying with pain, and he leans over the right fender, firing off three shots. The woman with the shotgun spins around and falls to the pavement. Beyond her, people are running away, screaming, and a couple of cars have collided by the fountain in their attempt to drive away.

The glass to the passenger door shatters as another gunshot rings out, and Casper yells, "The Army woman is coming!"

Pelayo whirls, sees the crazed woman coming at them, pistol out in front of her, and Pelayo yells, "Move!"

He breaks away from the Yukon, starts running to a small clump of people, knowing he can slip through them, make a phone call, and then get out of here before the county sheriff or state police roar up.

Another shot snaps out, something stings his leg, but he won't break stride.

He needs to get out of here.

Now.

Pelayo turns, sees Casper breathing hard, trying to catch up, still holding that little brat in his arms, and he calls back, "Shoot her! Shoot her and get going!"

He keeps on running, hears the nearby crack of a gunshot, flips back one more time, sees the crumpled form of the little girl on the ground, Casper now racing faster, and Pelayo thinks, *Yes, we're going to make it.*

The crowd ahead moves apart to let him and Casper escape.

Behind him he hears a woman screaming.

Good.

CHAPTER 87

MY FEET are sore and bleeding and I could not give a shit. I race past the Yukon, turn, and there's Pelayo and another man, holding my Denise, and I brake to a halt, bring up my pistol, and I'm about to scream, "Stop!" but before I can do that, the man…

Lifts up his own pistol.

To my daughter's head.

Pulls the trigger.

My daughter flops.

He drops her to the ground.

I scream so loud I can't hear myself.

Rosaria Vasquez thinks, *Christ, this hurts more than I could ever imagine*.

Will it ever stop?

She's looking up at the blue sky, some palm tree fronds, and she thinks, *Well, good planning*. Earlier she stopped to get her hair closely trimmed to disguise herself, and to purchase a Remington 12-gauge pump-action shotgun, because she no longer trusted anyone in this screwy case, and Amy Cornwall had taken her pistol back at the library.

But maybe she should have gotten a bulletproof vest.

That would have made sense.

She moans.

Jesus, is her chest ever going to stop hurting?

*   *   *

Tom Cornwall is moving toward where he last saw the Yukon driving away, with his wife, Amy, in full pursuit, when he hears Amy yelling, "Denise, Denise," and then gunshots, and then a full-throated scream from his wife.

He starts running harder.

I'm sobbing, yelling, and I feel like I'm going to lose control of my bladder and bowels as I approach the still form of my little girl.

Oh, Denise.

I drop to my knees, scraping them hard, and my girl's head is blackened and there's blood, and I can't see anymore, I'm crying so very, very hard.

Denise!

I reach down and touch my little girl.

And—

"Mommy?"

I break out in one more loud sob.

She's sitting up, rubbing at the side of her face.

"Mommy...my ear hurts. It hurts a lot."

I grab her and squeeze her hard, and if I could, I wouldn't move for the rest of the week.

She says, "Oh, Mommy, you're squeezing me too hard!"

I ignore her, refuse to let her go.

CHAPTER 88

IT HURTS too much to do anything, including keeping her eyes open, and then there's a dim voice above her.

"Special Agent Vasquez? Can you hear me?"

Rosaria manages to get her right eye open. It sort of focuses in, and there's a woman looking down at her, wearing a skimpy bathing suit.

"Yeah, I can hear you," she says. "Who…Captain Cornwall, is that you?"

"Yes, yes," and now the captain is holding her left hand.

"Damn, girl, why are you in a bathing suit?"

Her hand is squeezed. "A long story, Vasquez."

"Then save it for later."

I'm holding Special Agent Vasquez's left hand, and my other arm is tight around my brave little girl, Denise, who isn't sobbing but who's running a hand over and over her scorched hair, near where the muzzle blast of that man's pistol had passed through.

Sirens are in the distance, and there's a circle of people watching us, lots using their cell phones to record this horrible scene.

Tom races up, clothes bloody, and he kneels down next to me, starts squeezing Denise as well.

We're finally together.

"Vasquez," I say. "Why did you do it? Why did you come here?"

Her right eye is the only one open. Even with the bullet wounds in her chest and her soaking-wet T-shirt from her spilling blood, the haircut makes her look ten years younger and oh so vulnerable.

"I told you that, back at the library…I wanted to help…you and your family…"

"You could have done that by staying away or going back to Quantico."

Her eye flutters shut, opens up again.

She manages a smile. Her lower lip is frothy red with blood.

"That would be running away…and I wasn't going to do that…I have no family…I thought for a long time the Army was my family…I was so wrong…They kicked me to the curb like a piece of trash…"

Tom has an arm around me.

The sirens are getting louder.

I squeeze her hand again. "Hang on, Vasquez. The EMTs are coming. Hang on."

She says, "Captain…I need to warn you…need to tell you something…"

A long, drawn-out wheeze.

Tom says, "Isn't there anything we can do?"

"Be quiet," I say to him, and then I squeeze her hand again.

"Vasquez? What is it? What do you want to warn me about?"

Her other eye opens up, and both eyes wander and then lock in on me.

"Captain…is that your husband? Your daughter? Your…family?"

"Yes, yes it is," I say.

"Oh, so beautiful," she whispers. "So beautiful…"

Her eyes close and then she's gone.

CHAPTER 89

IN HIS Army career, Major Bruno Wenner has seen lots of odd things, but he's sure this afternoon's meeting is going to be one of the strangest events he's ever seen, three days after a firefight in Florida brought everything about Captain Amy Cornwall to a fiery head. He and five others are in a small, secure conference room in Fort Belvoir, and they are all waiting on Captain Amy Cornwall, who should have been here five minutes ago.

At the head of the table is his boss, Lieutenant Colonel Hugh Denton, in dress uniform, and with each passing minute of Cornwall's absence, his face grows redder and redder. At his left are a colonel and brigadier general from the Judge Advocate group, a male and female, and across the table are three quiet men in expensive-looking dark-gray suits, white shirts, and red neckties, like they had been dispatched from some government-central tailor shop. The near man, with a pair of horn-rimmed spectacles and blinking eyes that make him look like an owl, says he's from the Department of Defense. In the middle is a quiet man with closely trimmed dark-brown hair, who says he's from the FBI. And the last civilian looks bored and has a dark tan, and claims he's an observer from the Department of the Army.

Nobody in the room believes the last man is from the Department of the Army. Wenner is guessing that he's CIA, but keeps his guess to himself. He's sitting to the right and rear of Colonel Denton.

General Sawyer looks to Colonel Denton and then her watch. "Well, where is she?"

"She should be here any minute."

The general says, "Give her five more minutes, then send out some MPs to drag her sorry ass in here."

"Yes, ma'am," Denton says, and he turns and glares at Wenner, like it's his fault that Captain Cornwall hasn't shown up.

Wenner looks away and then there's a rap at the door; it opens up, and Captain Cornwall comes in, cover in hand, saying, "My apologies, Colonel Denton, and everyone else. I was…unavoidably delayed."

"Sit down, Captain Cornwall," Denton snaps out, and Cornwall sits at the end of the polished conference room table, moving slowly, her feet bandaged, Wenner knows. She looks impressive in her uniform with the badges and ribbons, and Wenner feels sorry for her. Based on the bloody and wild trip she had through the American South, the captain will eventually exchange that uniform for the dull khakis of a prison uniform at Leavenworth.

The room has one door, no windows, and just the table and chairs. There are no photos, paintings, or anything else to cheer up this cheerless room, and Wenner thinks that's part of the plan, for nothing good is going to happen here.

General Sawyer says, "All right, we'll begin this…session. Now that Captain Cornwall has joined us, I'll remind everyone again in this room that there's to be no recording, note taking, or any other official record of what transpires here. Am I clear?"

The only person who says anything is Cornwall, who nods and says, "I understand, ma'am."

Sawyer says, "Again, I want to remind you, Captain Cornwall, that you are appearing here by yourself, without counsel, and that you agree to this... circumstance."

"Yes, ma'am."

Sawyer clasps her hands and says to her fellow JAG officer, "Colonel Patrick, let's begin with the narrative and list of particulars."

Colonel Patrick starts reading from several sheets of paper, and the room is so silent that Wenner can hear the traffic outside and the overhead thrum of a helicopter. At each pause in the narration, General Sawyer looks to the captain and says, "Is that true, Captain?"

"Yes, ma'am."

The list of particulars goes on and on—assaulting a Tennessee state trooper, stealing license plates, crossing state lines for the purpose of committing offenses under the Uniform Code of Military Justice, and then, the first big one.

"In the town of Three Rivers, Texas, that you shot and killed Ramon Hernandez, a citizen of Mexico."

"Yes, sir, that's correct."

"In the town of Three Rivers, Texas, that you shot and killed Pepe Torres, a citizen of Mexico."

"Yes, sir, that's correct."

"In the town of Three Rivers, Texas, that you kidnapped Javier Abboud, a citizen of Mexico."

"That's correct, sir," she says again, in the same flat tone of voice.

"That you did transport Javier Abboud across state lines."

"That's correct, sir."

"That at the public library in Victoria, Texas, you did assault Special Agent Rosaria Vasquez of the CID."

Only then is there a change, as Cornwall's voice seems to catch, and then she says, "That's correct, sir."

The long list of particulars then finally ends five minutes later, in Beachside, Florida, where it is charged that Captain Amy Cornwall illegally fired a nonregistered weapon within the city limits.

"Yes, that's correct," she says.

"And finally," Colonel Patrick says, "while these alleged offenses were taking place, you, Captain Amy Cornwall, were absent without leave."

Cornwall changes her response and says, "Well, that's pretty damn self-evident, isn't it?"

The civilian men smile, but the Army side of the table is not amused. General Sawyer says, "Captain Cornwall, these are incredibly serious charges. I appreciate your willingness to come forward and accept your responsibility...but this is highly unusual."

Cornwall says, "Ma'am, it certainly is highly unusual. And I thank you and Colonel Denton for arranging this session. Now, may I ask your indulgence to speak for five minutes?"

General Sawyer says, "Colonel Denton, do you mind?"

His fists are clenched on the table. "No," he finally says. "Not at all."

"Good," Sawyer says. "Captain Cornwall, proceed...and I hope you choose your words carefully, because at this moment, you're looking at a life sentence in Leavenworth. Do you understand?"

"Yes, ma'am."

"And you intend to make this statement by yourself and with no counsel?"

"Yes, ma'am."

General Sawyer says, "Then you may proceed."

Cornwall says, "Ma'am, all of these events occurred

while I was in the process of rescuing my family. And—"

The general gently raps a knuckle on the table. "I'm sorry, Captain, that's not the Army's concern. Do you have anything else to say?"

The room is silent. Cornwall's face looks like it's been carved out of cold, gray granite.

"You bet your ass I do," she says. "General."

CHAPTER 90

MAYBE THE people in this closed and stuffy office think they're going to intimidate me, but I doubt any of them — with the exception of one — has ever been in a shelter at an FOB in Afghanistan, knowing you're completely surrounded by enemies who would delight in slitting your throat.

So I have nothing to lose. My career in the Army is about to crash in one big, impressive ball of flame and debris, and the next five minutes will determine whether there's going to be a surviving parachute or not.

I say, "General, my apologies for the last statement. I wanted to make sure you and everyone else in this room are paying attention."

With a dry tone in her voice, the general says, "I think you can count on that. Proceed. You have your five minutes."

I look at each and every face — including my boss, Colonel Denton, who looks like he wants to leap across the table and throttle me — and I say, "This entire series of events began at FOB Healy in Afghanistan. A number of months ago, a prisoner in my custody, Mohammed Noor, was found dead in his holding cell. At the time, Mister Noor claimed to have been a simple farmer, but later research on my part revealed that he was an agronomy expert who was in the employ of a transnational organization called Mercador Holdings."

Everyone is paying attention, but it seems the near civilian—with a deep tan—is now paying strict attention indeed.

"Mercador Holdings is linked to a Mexican criminal organization, the Veracruz cartel. Members of this cartel kidnapped my husband and daughter six days ago from our home. I was then contacted by the head of the cartel, a Pelayo Abboud, who at the time was based in Beachside, Florida. In exchange for me kidnapping an individual in the custody of a competing cartel, the El Baja cartel, and bringing him to Abboud in Florida, my husband and Denise would be released."

One of the civilian males says, "And you didn't contact the CID? Or FBI?"

"No," I say. "I was specifically warned not to do so. I had no choice. It was my husband and daughter."

"But why were they taken, and how were you involved?" the same civilian asks.

"My husband, Tom, is a journalist. He was working on a book about the international drug trade, the cartels, and the banks that support them. His work took him to the El Baja cartel. They offered him a former bank official as a news source that knew the intricacies of their rival, the Veracruz cartel. They did this in the hope of crippling their competition. But Abboud of the Veracruz cartel acted first, kidnapping my family and having me, in turn, kidnap the news source to bring him to Abboud."

"And this news source was Pelayo Abboud's father, Javier?" General Sawyer asks.

"Yes, ma'am," I reply.

"Who was killed in the shootout at Beachside?"

"Yes, ma'am."

"Said shooting also resulting in the death of Warrant Officer Rosaria Vasquez, a special agent with the CID, who had been investigating you and your travels?" the general asks.

"Yes, ma'am."

She looks at her watch again. "This is all fascinating, but—"

"General—"

"Yes?"

I think of the last few minutes, and the phone call I had received that had caused me to be late. The unexpected phone call had come from Freddy, a.k.a. Major Fredericka West, executive officer for the Second Ranger Battalion, 75th Ranger Regiment, who had said, "I know your fat ass is in one tight sling, and I'm here to free it up, so just listen."

Which is what I did.

I say, "General, information has come to me concerning more in-depth intelligence about the two cartels, the Afghan farmer who was killed while in my custody, how and why Warrant Officer Vasquez was given information to track me, and how this is all connected. May I proceed?"

Major Wenner is leaning forward, just to the side of Colonel Denton, listening to Captain Cornwall. To him she seems like some sort of robot or android, reciting bits of information over and over again in a flat and emotionless tone even though it will do her no good.

And then General Sawyer says, "Yes, you may proceed."

Cornwall is now staring right in the direction of her superior officer, Colonel Denton, and Wenner feels like the chair he's sitting in has suddenly compressed around him, not allowing him to move an inch.

Cornwall says, "At the initial investigation back in Afghanistan, the farmer named Mohammed Noor was in the possession of a business card with the name of Mercador Holdings and a phone number based in Mexico. At the time, I requested the information on this business card be traced. I was told the company name and the phone number were fake."

Wenner can't breathe anymore, and even Denton is stiff and unmoving next to him.

"That information was wrong," Cornwall says. "The person conducting that research at FOB Healy was hiding the real information from me and the Army. The person who did that is in the employ of the El Baja cartel, and has been so for more than a year."

General Sawyer says, "Who is it?"

Cornwall continues her long and deep stare.

"Major Bruno Wenner," she says. "Who was with my unit in Afghanistan at the time."

CHAPTER 91

I HAVE to give the traitorous son of a bitch credit, for he doesn't flinch or raise his eyebrows, or even yell at me. He just keeps sitting there, to the right and slightly behind our mutual boss, Colonel Hugh Denton.

Colonel Denton starts to speak, but General Sawyer cuts him off. "That's a pretty serious accusation, Captain Cornwall."

"I know," I say.

From my coat pocket I remove a small thumb drive, which I put on the shiny surface of the conference room table and which contains an info dump from my dear friend Freddy.

"On this thumb drive is a video excerpt from a classified surveillance system at FOB Healy. This particular system was observing the only entrance and exit into the server system room that supported the surveillance stations covering all of the interrogation cells located at the base. Major Wenner is shown entering this room and departing sixty seconds later. Maintenance records show that the camera aimed at Mister Noor's cell failed at this time, and that he was beaten to death shortly thereafter."

I refuse to look in Wenner's direction. I say, "Also on this thumb drive are documents, bank statements, and records of phone conversations between cartel representatives and Major Wenner, who has an anonymous numbered bank account in the Cayman Islands. The major was also receiving payments from banks representing both the El Baja and Veracruz cartels. He was playing both ends against the middle. If you excuse the phrasing, Captain Wenner was making a killing."

No word from anyone.

I say, "As part of this arrangement, Major Wenner was also giving information he gathered from both cartels to Senior Warrant Officer Fred McCarthy of the CID in Quantico, who in turn was passing it to Warrant Officer Vasquez. If Vasquez had succeeded in her mission to halt me from freeing the older Mister Abboud, Major Wenner was to be handsomely compensated by the El Baja cartel. If not, his additional compensation would have come from the Veracruz cartel. Payment would have been made, no matter what."

The silence is deathly still.

One of the civilians, the nearest one with the heavy tan, is slowly moving his chair back.

"Finally, I learned yesterday that the body of Lieutenant Preston Baker of my unit was found in a wooded area on this base, an apparent suicide. Lieutenant Baker served with me in Afghanistan and provided me with vital information concerning my prisoner's connection to Mercador Holdings. I would suggest that the appropriate investigators re-examine the circumstances of his death, with a close look at Captain Wenner's whereabouts at the time of the shooting."

Wenner tenses up. The facade he's carefully built over the years to suffer through his military service and leave with a fat bank account has just been blown away, like a Texas trailer park in the middle of a tornado. No time to think of how temptation came his way, how he gladly seized the temptation with both hands, and how he had planned to leave the Army when his latest term of service was up and then disappear forever.

Again, no time to think.

Just burst out of this chair and haul ass before anyone can react. A good run will take him to his car, and then he can roar out before word gets to the gate to block him from leaving

A heavy hand is on his shoulder, squeezing hard. Wenner turns. It's the tanned man that he's certain is from the CIA, and the man leans into him and says, "Move out of this chair and I'll snap your neck, son."

The two civilians at the desk look stunned. Colonel Denton is slumped in his chair. General Sawyer and Colonel Patrick from JAG are looking at each other, as if to say, *What now*? And Major Wenner is sitting like a carved chunk of wood, face pale, and the tanned civilian man has a hand squeezing his right shoulder. That man is looking at me with hard and knowledgeable eyes.

I clear my throat.

"Any questions?"

CHAPTER 92

PELAYO ABBOUD wakes up with a start, wondering where he is, and then he instantly relaxes. He's in a luxurious leather seat in one of his several private jets, somewhere over Mexican airspace. He sighs. At his side is a tumbler of Buchanan's whiskey and ice cubes, and he picks it up and takes a satisfying sip. His usual drink is native Coca-Cola, but this drink is part of a celebration.

He made it out of the States just an hour ago, having spent three days hiding out at a private airfield near Beachside and having the wound in his lower right leg cleaned and dressed.

A lot of things went to hell, but he's alive and breathing and on this jet, and there's plenty of good work waiting to be done.

Across from him, also sitting in the same type of deep leather seat, is Casper Khourery, who is reading that day's *Miami Herald*. Pelayo reaches out with a foot, gently kicks Casper's shin.

He looks up. "Yes, *jefe*?"

"How soon before we land?"

Casper looks at his big watch. "About ten minutes, *jefe*."

"Very good." He looks over at the mountainous and rough terrain of his home nation, and thinks of the riches he and others have managed to wrest from this desperate land. Despite the setbacks, his crew will soon be doing the same in Afghanistan. That poor nation produces 90 percent of the world's opium, and Pelayo plans to grab his share and expand his market beyond the Americas.

He finishes his drink. A very small part of him wishes the old man was alive to see what his cursed son has been able to do, and a very large part of him is looking forward to letting the other cartels and other family members know that he, Pelayo Abboud, would never, ever give up in his quest.

There's a soft *thump-thump* as the landing gear is lowered, and Pelayo puts the empty glass down, tightens his seat belt.

He says, "You did good work there, in Beachside, keeping your cool, doing what had to be done."

Casper says, "Thank you, *jefe*. But we lost so much…several of our workers, sensitive communications equipment, and too many questions being raised about the resort and its financing."

Pelayo leans over, gently pats Casper's closest leg. "Minor issues, that is all. All great firms, all great concerns like ours, can afford to suffer the occasional setback. And with you at my side, well, you did well, in shooting that little girl."

Casper stays quiet, folds up the newspaper, carefully puts it at his side.

Pelayo says, "Tomorrow, a special project, just for you."

"Yes?"

"Track down the Cornwalls, find out where they are, kill them both. Use whatever resources you need, but don't take too much time. I want that matter settled."

"All right."

"Save their heads," Pelayo says with relish, remembering his earlier plan for that young Denise Cornwall. "Freeze them. We will send them to their respective superiors."

"As you wish, *jefe*."

Pelayo looks out again, sees the wide and long pavement of the runway.

He loves his life.

CHAPTER 93

AT A remote lake in central Maine, Tom Cornwall is sitting in an old gray Adirondack chair, watching his family at play. Denise and Amy are swimming and splashing each other, squealing and laughing. There's a small dock with a pontoon boat tied up to it, and a comfortable cottage that has a wonderful view of the lake and the nearby mountains.

There are other residents on the lake, who wave at them as they take the pontoon boat out, or as they walk side by side along the dirt roads linking the cottages on this rural shore.

His wrist itches. He gently traces his fingers over the bandages, wondering how his burnt skin is healing, wondering how the sickness inside of him is healing as well.

The past days have been a blur of packing, flying, driving, and getting used to this slice of country paradise, and along the way, apologies, apologies, apologies.

He apologized to Amy the day he and Denise were rescued at Beachside, and the day after that, and the day after that.

Each time Amy has given him a slim smile, and said, "That's nice, Tom. We'll talk later."

He wonders when and how later will come.

And if the sickness inside of him will ever go away.

He looks at his fingers, tracing the bandage on his

arm, the fingers that held that cutting tool, killing the young Afghan who had been ready to kill him.

One of the many surprises during these past days is feeling no regret or guilt at having done that.

Denise squeals one more time, and then the two of them step out of the water, and Amy wraps Denise in a thick blue towel, rubs herself down with another blue towel, then drops the towel and runs up to Tom, wearing a conservative one-piece dark-red bathing suit. He has a brief memory of seeing her wearing that skimpy bikini, her eyes swollen and red, her feet bleeding, her hands shaking.

Amy comes up to him and suddenly sits in his lap. "Hey," she says.

"Hey," he says, putting his arms around her. With her wet bathing suit she has instantly dampened his shorts and T-shirt, but he won't say a word about it.

He hugs her and he whispers, "Amy, I...I'm sorry. I betrayed you, I put Denise in harm's way, and—"

Amy gently pulls his head into her side, and says in reply, "Tom, I betrayed you, too."

When I come out of the lake, I see Tom's sad face and decide it's time to settle things. I plop myself in his lap and for the tenth or twentieth time, he apologizes to me, and I think I surprise him when I apologize in return.

He pulls his head away, looks up at me. "Apologize? For betraying? What do you mean?"

I stroke his hair. "When we first got married, you asked me never to dig into your work or your computer files. I did that. I had to do that...but I broke a promise. I'm sorry."

His eyes well up. "Amy...compared to what I did, what lies I told, that's nothing. I...was desperate for a book deal. I paid money for a dark-web search. I never asked for a specific search for you or your unit. The facts I learned…they just came up…and I followed them."

I continue lightly stroking his hair, and he says, "If I knew what would happen…"

I lower my hand, put a finger to his lips. "Shhh. We're done. I forgive you."

"I forgive you," he says, voice shaky.

"Good," I say. A helicopter slowly flies over the lake, and it fills me with happiness, knowing there's a sniper aboard, keeping an eye on the lake and the surrounding cottages. Out in the woods and on the rural roads and dirt trails, armed US marshals are keeping watch over me and my family.

And for the future? The Army is gone for me, but when I left that conference room, the deeply tanned man who had kept Major Wenner in place slipped me a plain white business card with a Virginia phone number.

"I like your style," the tanned man said. "Give me a call, anytime."

I hug Tom one more time, look at my little girl peacefully playing in the lake sand, and I think of Rosaria, dying back there in Florida, saving me, saving my family.

I will never forget her, and I will always protect my family.

Tom says, "What now, hon?"

"Now?" I ask. "Now we relax. We have fun. We sleep late. You find another book project to work on and me…well, we'll see. But one more thing."

"What's that?" he asks.

"Never, ever do anything like this again, Tom Cornwall," I say. "Or I'll kill you and make it look like an accident."

A hesitant smile comes across my beloved's face.

"That's one heck of a threat," he says.

I kiss his forehead.

"Tom, you know me by now," I say. "I don't make threats. I make promises."

CHAPTER 94

THE LEARJET slowly taxis into a large and nearly empty hangar, and Pelayo glances out, sees a line of his men out there, waiting for him. The engines whine down and a stairway is wheeled up. A member of the flight crew unlatches the door, and Pelayo nearly prances down the stairs.

Home. Safe. And ready to go back to work.

Casper is behind him, and he strolls to his men, looks around for one of his armored Ford Expedition SUVs to take him to one of his expensive ranches.

There are no vehicles in the hangar.

Just his men and Casper, and the jet.

He turns to Casper.

"What's going on?"

"A readjustment," comes a voice, and Pelayo turns as a man emerges through the line of those he has paid, has trained, and once trusted.

The slim man wears cowboy boots, blue jeans, and a plain white shirt. The man's skin is the same color as his own, his hair is black, but unlike Pelayo, this man has a closely trimmed beard.

"Hello, cousin," the man says.

Pelayo feels like one of those carnival balloons, the helium emptying out, making the firm shape collapse upon itself, dying and never to recover.

"Miguel," he says.

"Pelayo," his cousin nods.

Once more, back to Casper. "Why?" he asks.

Casper spits on the concrete floor. "I have done so much for you, bloody year after bloody year. Always at your side. But...you became crazed, looking to kill your father. Crazed with your plans to go to Afghanistan. Afghanistan! And then you asked me to shoot a little girl. A little girl, as young as my own!" He steps forward, spits again, close to Pelayo's boots.

"I'm done with you, Abboud. And so is everyone else."

Pelayo slowly turns back to his smiling cousin.

"Please," Pelayo says. "Make it quick."

At some point Pelayo regains consciousness. His life now is nothing but pain, pain, and more pain. He is naked, secured in a heavy metal chair, and his chest is one burning mass where one by one, Miguel invited Pelayo's lieutenants to come up with a knife and carve their initials into his chest. All he knows is that he's in a small basement below the aircraft hangar's floor.

He moans, looks down to his bound wrists.

There are only seven fingers left.

His right eye blinks away a blood stream.

His left eye...

He moans again, and sees the little metal table next to him, with various tools, instruments, and razor-sharp knives. Resting in a bloody patch of gauze is his left eye.

Miguel comes into view, smiling, wiping his hands dry with a cloth. A chest-high leather apron covers most of his clothing. He steps forward, caresses Pelayo's cheek.

"Please...," Pelayo begs, whispering around his broken teeth and sliced tongue. "Please...make it quick..."

Miguel says, "I will, I will, cousin. But you know how religious I am, don't you?"

Pelayo says nothing and then screams as Miguel slaps the bloody stumps on his left hand. "Yes, yes, yes, I know you are a religious man! Please, Miguel, please...end it..."

Miguel leans down. "I will. But I believe in my Lord God. I believe He was the creator of all things. And I believe He created this world in six days."

He steps out of view and comes back with a large propane blowtorch, which he lights and starts to lower to Pelayo's waist.

"Which is why I'm going to take six days to end your world, cousin."

CHAPTER 95

ON A sunny, breezy day in this part of Virginia my family and I follow the directions given to us earlier. It's a breathtaking and melancholy sight, all the rows of simple tombstones, stretching out beyond us at every view, scattered here and there among trees whose branches look like they wish they were larger, to provide shade and comfort to all who rest here.

I'm in the middle, Tom holding my left hand, Denise holding my right, and during our long walk along a paved lane, Tom gives my hand a squeeze and I turn and see a horse-drawn carriage with slowly walking soldiers flanking it, a flag-draped coffin being drawn to its final resting place, the collection of grieving family members barely visible in the distance.

"Here we go," I say, as we leave the narrow road and pass through another lane of gravestones, to one that's fairly new. We pause there for a moment, looking down at the stone and the carved cross, her name, ROSARIO VASQUEZ, and under that, CW2, followed by US ARMY, and below that the short range of dates that marked her brief life.

I stand with my husband and daughter for a few minutes more, my eyes blurry, and then I reach down and caress the smooth top of the stone.

"Rosaria," I whisper. "Thank you, sister. Welcome to my family."

ACKNOWLEDGMENTS

Brendan DuBois thanks the following for their assistance: US Army Lieutenant Colonel Brian Thiem (Ret.), Former Deputy Commander, 3rd MP Group (Criminal Investigation Command); Captain Vincent O'Neil, former Company Commander, 1st Battalion (Airborne), 508th Infantry Regiment; and for information on weapons' tactics and self-defense, Stephen DuBois.

ABOUT THE AUTHORS

James Patterson is the world's bestselling author and most trusted storyteller. He has created many enduring fictional characters and series, including Alex Cross, the Women's Murder Club, Michael Bennett, Maximum Ride, Middle School, and I Funny. Among his notable literary collaborations are *The President Is Missing,* with President Bill Clinton, and the Max Einstein series, produced in partnership with the Albert Einstein Estate. Patterson's writing career is characterized by a single mission: to prove that there is no such thing as a person who "doesn't like to read," only people who haven't found the right book. He's given over three million books to schoolkids and the military, donated more than seventy million dollars to support education, and endowed over five thousand college scholarships for teachers. For his prodigious imagination and championship of literacy in America, Patterson was awarded the 2019 National Humanities Medal. The National Book Foundation recently presented him with the Literarian Award for Outstanding Service to the American Literary Community, and he is also the recipient of an Edgar Award and nine Emmy Awards. He lives in Florida with his family.

*   *   *

Brendan DuBois is the award-winning author of 29 novels and more than 160 short stories, garnering him three Shamus Awards from the Private Eye Writers of America. He is also a *Jeopardy!* game show champion.

JAMES
PATTERSON
RECOMMENDS

JAMES PATTERSON

THE BLACK BOOK

& DAVID ELLIS

THE BLACK BOOK

I have favorites among the novels I've written. *Kiss the Girls*, *Invisible*, *1st to Die*, and *Honeymoon* are top of the list. With each, I had a good feeling when the writing was finished. I believe this book — *The Black Book* — is the best work I've done in twenty-five years.

Meet Billy Harney. The son of Chicago's chief of detectives, he was born to be a cop. There's nothing he wouldn't sacrifice for his job. Enter Amy Lentini, an assistant state's attorney hell-bent on making a name for herself—by proving Billy isn't the cop he claims to be.

A horrifying murder leads investigators to a brothel that caters to Chicago's most powerful citizens. There's plenty of evidence on the scene, but what matters most is what's missing: the madam's black book.

JAMES
PATTERSON

THE FIRST
LADY

BRENDAN DUBOIS

THE FIRST LADY

The US government is at the forefront of everyone's mind these days and I've become incredibly fascinated by the idea that one secret can bring it all down. What if that secret is a US President's affair that results in a nightmarish outcome?

Sally Grissom, leader of the Presidential Protection Division, is summoned to a private meeting with the President and his chief of staff to discuss the disappearance of the First Lady. What at first seemed an escape to a safe haven turns into a kidnapping when a ransom note arrives along with what could be the First Lady's finger.

It's a race against the clock to collect the evidence that all leads to one troubling question: Could the kidnappers be from inside the White House?

JAMES
PATTERSON

TEXAS
RANGER

& ANDREW BOURELLE

TEXAS RANGER

So many of my detectives are dark and gritty and deal with crimes in some of our grimmest cities. That's why I'm thrilled to bring you Detective Rory Yates, my most honorable detective yet.

As a Texas Ranger, he has a code that he lives and works by. But when he comes home for a much-needed break, he walks into a crime scene where the victim is none other than his ex-wife—*and* he's the prime suspect. Yates has to risk everything in order to clear his name, and he dives into the inferno of the most twisted mind I've ever created. Can his code bring him back out alive?

JAMES
PATTERSON
THE HOUSE
NEXT DOOR
THE
WORLD'S
#1
BEST-
SELLING
WRITER
BIG
THRILLS.
SUSPENSE
THAT
KILLS.

THE HOUSE NEXT DOOR

The most terrifying danger is the one that lurks in plain sight; the one that is always there, but you don't notice it until it's too late. Here are three bone-chilling stories about exactly that.

In "The House Next Door," Laura Sherman is thrilled to have a new neighbor take an interest in her, but what happens when things go too far and things aren't really as they seem? In "The Killer's Wife," when six girls have gone missing, Detective McGrath will do anything to find them, even if that means getting too close with the suspect's wife. And finally, "We. Are. Not. Alone." proves that we aren't the only life in the universe, but what we didn't know is that they've been watching us...

For a complete list of books by
JAMES PATTERSON

VISIT
JamesPatterson.com